C000314417

A ROYAL
MURDER

BOOKS BY VERITY BRIGHT

THE LADY ELEANOR SWIFT MYSTERY SERIES

A ROYAL
MURDER

VERITY BRIGHT

bookouture

Published by Bookouture in 2022

An imprint of Storyfire Ltd.
Carmelite House
50 Victoria Embankment
London EC4Y 0DZ

www.bookouture.com

Copyright © Verity Bright, 2022

Verity Bright have asserted their right to be identified as the author of this work.

All rights reserved. No part of this publication may be reproduced, stored in any retrieval system, or transmitted, in any form or by any means, electronic, mechanical, photocopying, recording or otherwise, without the prior written permission of the publishers.

ISBN: 978-180019-569-1
eBook ISBN: 978-1-80019-568-4

This book is a work of fiction. Names, characters, businesses, organizations, places and events other than those clearly in the public domain, are either the product of the author's imagination or are used fictitiously. Any resemblance to actual persons, living or dead, events or locales is entirely coincidental.

To anyone who's ever kissed a prince, only to have him turn into a frog.

There is a charm about the forbidden that makes it unspeakably desirable.

Mark Twain

1

_____

'You simply have to trust me.'

Lady Eleanor Swift sighed. 'We've been over this. I don't need—'

'Nonsense!' Her companion's honeyed voice oozed concern. 'You know it's for your own good.'

Eleanor tugged on her fiery-red curls in frustration. Gladstone, her bulldog, had long tired of it all, and had lumbered huffily off to his bed by the kitchen range. Her butler silently materialised with more champagne.

She shook her head. 'Actually, Clifford, since it is, in fact, only breakfast and' – she glanced at the mantelpiece clock – 'a horribly early one at that, I think we'll pass on more—'

'Oh no, this definitely calls for more fizz!' Eleanor's self-appointed new best friend indicated for Clifford to refill their glasses. Her big brown eyes widened. 'That's not why everyone calls me Tipsy though.' She giggled, swinging her glossy dark mane over her shoulder, emphasising the sweetheart neckline of her sapphire silk dress. 'I mean, what did my parents expect, calling me Tiffany Persephone Fitzroy! Of course everyone was going to nickname me Tipsy!'

Eleanor had met the irrepressible Tipsy at a society do a few weeks back. And, despite their very different characters and backgrounds, they'd become firm friends – at least, that's what Tipsy repeatedly told Eleanor – after Tipsy had rescued her from the lecherous advances of an unbearably conceited count. And, in truth, Eleanor found something irresistible about her rather garrulous friend who was, once more, in full flow.

'But now, back to the important matters. Number one, you simply have to practise being better at drinking champers, especially in the morning, Eleanor. Honestly, four glasses and you go decidedly glassy-eyed. And you weren't given those incredible flame-red curls and mesmerising cat-green eyes to waste them skulking about here at Henley Hall. Certainly not waiting for the day you wake to find a' – Tipsy fanned her face in horror – 'a wrinkle on your forehead! I mean, that's game over! All hope gone of enticing a gorgeous man to skip you down the aisle after that! I won't have you sliding any further towards Dickens' Miss Havisham. Just look what happened to her!'

Eleanor decided to raid Clifford's infallible store of knowledge later about what exactly did happen to Miss Havisham.

'Look, Tipsy. We've been over this. I'm not in a hurry to scurry down the marriage route. Again.' *Definitely not, Ellie. Once bitten and all that!* Her previous marriage had ended in disaster. After a whirlwind affair in South Africa, she'd married her dashing officer, only to find he was anything but. Hastily forcing all memories of that chapter back into their tightly lidded box, she held up a hand to stop Tipsy's unceasing flow. 'And anyway, I've got a decent, and rather gorgeous man. Sort of.'

Tipsy let out an exasperated sigh. 'Sort of, won't do! You confessed you haven't seen this mysterious Mr Wonderful for over two weeks. Two weeks! Sweetie, you're only an inch away from cresting the well-known hill, if you get my drift.'

'Hugh is just very conscientious about his work, that's all.

He's a detective chief inspector and has to go wherever he's needed. And he's always needed... somewhere else.' Eleanor tried to cover up the quiet sigh that escaped by taking a sip of champagne. 'But anyway, what hill?'

This drew another round of giggles. 'Oh, you're so funny. I do love spending time with you. But I'm not at all fooled. You're honestly telling me you're content waiting around for this invisible beau who is too busy to make time for you? Tsh! Seriously, you're the most impatient person I have ever met. Don't let him change you.'

'Change me?' Eleanor mumbled. *Is that what Hugh is trying to do, Ellie?* She smoothed the frown from her face. 'Why don't you tell me more about the rowing races we'll watch later?'

Tipsy dabbed at her long-lashed eyes and cackled once more. 'You are too hilarious for words. As if we'll even see those stupid floating lumps of wood, or' – she whirled her hand in the air – 'or whatever they're made of. We'll be watching the crowd, silly. Because every eligible titled dish attends Henley Regatta. Mind you, I've noticed each year the rowers do get more dishy. And, lucky for you, I'm going to introduce you to the best of the best! You simply *have* to get to know the right people, Eleanor.' She hugged her arms. 'Oh, did I tell you that Xander Taylor-Howard will be there? He's the king's first cousin, once removed!'

Eleanor smiled at her friend's awe. Personally, the only thing that impressed her about anyone was their personality and generosity of attitude towards others.

'Isn't he like eighteenth or something in line to the throne?'

'A royal is a royal, sweetie. And, besides, who knows when there might be another of those monstrous influenza outbreaks? And then Xander might be king!'

Eleanor gasped. 'That's dreadful!'

Tipsy giggled. 'I can't help how my mind works. Now, we have an inordinate amount of work to do in getting you ready.

You need to be at your fabulous best. And' – she gestured over Eleanor's long, slender frame, wrapped in sage-green cashmere and matching twill trousers – 'frankly, that's hiding out in another country right at this moment.'

Eleanor fought another frown, knowing this was all said with the best of intentions. 'Um, Tipsy, thank you, but—'

'But nothing! Darling, I don't mean to be harsh, but we simply have to get down to business. So, I've made a list.'

Eleanor watched in horror as Tipsy opened her exquisite kid-leather handbag and extracted a gold pocketbook. She flipped to the first page with an immaculately painted nail.

'Number one, we've touched on.' She eyed Eleanor's still-full second glass and then added a neat cross to the first line. 'Failing badly, however. And also failing at number two, which is at least pretending you have a ladylike appetite.' She looked pointedly at Eleanor's sausage-and-egg-filled plate. In contrast, Tipsy's breakfast had so far consisted entirely of champagne. 'Number three, hair and make-up.' She shook her head. 'We'll get back to that. Number four, memorising who's who. Ditto. Number five, conversation dos and absolutely do nots...'

Eleanor tuned out and let her thoughts return to the man she wished was less in demand and had more time for her. But thinking like that made her feel bad. He wasn't the home counties' most sought after detective chief inspector without good reason. A vision of his chestnut curls and deep-brown eyes gazing down at her swam into her mind, making her smile.

'Good!' Tipsy said. 'I'm glad you're not going to make a fuss about number eleven.'

Eleanor wrenched herself back to the conversation, horrified that Tipsy had somehow managed to conjure up eleven points already.

'Hang on! Eleven is?'

'Fabulous, I agree. Now, number twelve is last because it's possibly the biggest hurdle. Heels, Eleanor. You have to be seen in heels.' She glanced at Eleanor's practical Oxford lace-ups and shuddered. 'And floating elegantly too, not falling off them every few minutes. Which brings us full circle to mastering champers.'

'Wonderful, I'm sure. Oh, but that reminds me. Wait right there. I... um, I want to show you something.'

Out in the oak-panelled corridor, she almost collided with her butler.

'What have I done to deserve this, Clifford?' she groaned.

His expression remained impassive. 'A great many things, my lady. Do you wish me to start with the most recent or the most distant? Or, perhaps, the vaguely disreputable before the vastly reprehensible?'

She couldn't help smiling at his teasing. He'd been her uncle's batman, butler and friend for more years than she'd been alive. And since her uncle's death, he had become more of a surrogate uncle than butler to her.

'Not now, Clifford. I've let myself in for a day of unimaginable hideousness. In fact, you've let me let myself in for it. What were you thinking of in encouraging me to agree? There's nothing on Tipsy's agenda except getting me to dress up like a giddy debutante and hobnob with a bunch of sniffy titles.'

He looked at her as if she had been hit on the head. And with a particularly blunt spade. 'My lady, you are about to attend the prestigious Henley Regatta. That is singularly the entire reason for going for the majority of attendees.'

'Well, it sounds horribly more like formality than fun.'

Her butler arched a brow. 'If you say so, my lady. However, it is too late now.'

'Yes, I'm aware of that, thank you very much.' She sighed. 'I know Tipsy means well, but surely she must need to take on air once in a while and stop talking? I mean, she's entertaining and dashedly good fun to be with. Really good fun, actually. Irresistibly so. But somehow it feels rather like being back at school with one's naughtiest chum.'

'Heartening news.'

'What! Clifford, you're always telling me off for being a disgrace to decorum.'

His brow suggested it might almost entertain the idea of creasing. 'Not words I remember expressing.'

She folded her arms. 'That's because you don't need words to tell me off and you know it. Even though you're always utterly respectful, somehow when you put on your disapproving face, you still make me feel like the irritating nine-year-old that plagued your summers.'

His inscrutable expression didn't flinch.

'That's the one.'

His features softened. 'My lady, forgive my overstepping, but you have now resided at Henley Hall since his lordship, your late uncle, passed away over two years ago.' His lips pursed. 'And yet the Windsor tea set has been called into service but three times.'

She bit back a smile. 'Is that really how you mark time?'

He sniffed. 'Time, my lady, no. But the woeful advancement in mastering social etiquette by a certain lady of the house, yes.'

She pulled a mock face. 'Mrs Trotman making you blush again, is she?'

Her attempt at humour was met with a withering look. 'I was not, as you are well aware, referring to your cook. The ballroom is still wearing its dust covers and the main dining room has taken on the distinct air of a forlorn mausoleum. Not to mention the suites in the west wing which have seen more dust motes than guests, since the number you have invited totals precisely...?'

'None,' she said quietly. 'But you know how free-spirited my parents were and how... carefree they brought me up abroad. I'm just not used to this suffocating life which revolves around etiquette and rules. I sincerely wish I could set fire to society's rulebook and delight in fanning the flames with unladylike gusto.'

He stiffened in horror. 'If we did not have rules, where would we be?'

She shrugged. 'Heaven?' At his pointed silence, she added. 'France?'

That made his lips quirk. 'Touché, my lady. But I fear the time for worming out of your promise is past.'

'Who's worming!?'

'I really couldn't say. But if I might interrupt your slithering off on a fictional ruse of obtaining a non-existent item to show Lady Fitzroy, perhaps you would be kind enough to assist Mrs Butters with a quick fitting?'

'A what?'

He tilted his head towards her housekeeper, hurrying down the corridor. Mrs Butters was trying to tame the sea of ivory silk frills billowing out below a clothes hanger, her diminutive frame struggling to hold the material off the floor. A matching hat with a flamboyantly wide brim, trimmed with ostrich feathers, was balanced across her other forearm. She bobbed a curtsey.

'I've done all the pinning, m'lady. Won't take long to run along the seams once we've checked that I know my mistress as well as I hope I do. A complete princess you'll look, and no mistake.'

Eleanor stared at her in horror, and then at the dress.

'Clifford, no, no, no! Tell me this isn't—'

He nodded. 'Number eleven, my lady. Lady Fitzroy was most explicit in her instructions, which I dutifully passed to Mrs Butters.'

'Without warning me! Have you lost your bearings? I'm going to resemble a... a walking wedding cake.'

'Most assuredly.' He waved the housekeeper on with a flick of a white-gloved finger.

Eleanor raised her hands. 'Look here, I am only thirty-one, yet everyone seems determined to see me married off. Tell me, just how many meddling maiden aunts are you secretly harbouring, Clifford?'

He patted his jacket down. 'Maiden aunt free, my lady. But would that were not the case. However, regrettably the Henley and Swift families are significantly depleted of relatives and I am merely endeavouring to fulfil my promise to his lordship.'

'You mean the unenviable task of saving me from my hopeless affairs of the heart, amongst a raft of other things, I know. And I am very grateful. But Hugh is in charge of security at the regatta. How is his seeing me in that frilled abomination of a dress supposed to help move things on between us in any way?'

'I seem to remember that the aforementioned detective chief inspector is an ardent fan of layered cake, my lady.' He winked. 'So you should be fine.'

'Fine! Why does everyone keep thinking I'm not fine as I am? And why, now I remember, does Tipsy refer to me as Miss Havisham?'

Clifford tried to hide his amusement from showing. 'Miss Havisham is a character from Mr Dickens' novel *Great Expectations*, my lady. She shuts herself away in her house and becomes an embittered recluse after she is jilted at the altar. She stops all the clocks, refuses to wear anything but her wedding dress, and leaves the wedding feast to rot in one of the rooms.' He momentarily closed his eyes and shuddered at the image this evidently brought to mind.

Eleanor laughed triumphantly. 'Ha! You see, I'm nothing like Miss Havisham. I'd never let the food go to waste! In fact, I'd eat it all just to show whoever jilted me that I didn't give a damn!'

'Eleanor, there you are!' Tipsy's voice called out from the

doorway. 'Champers and delicious titled dishes wait for no woman. Come along, sweetie. We only got as far as number twelve. There's six more yet!'

'Clifford,' Eleanor whispered, 'please instruct Mrs Trotman to never cook lamb again. Now I know precisely how being led to the slaughter feels! And, by the way, what does happen to Miss Havisham?'

'The lady unfortunately dies after her wedding dress catches fire.'

'Well, at least that won't happen to me. I burned mine myself about a month after I was married. And not while wearing it!' She slapped on a smile and called down the corridor. 'Coming, Tipsy. I'm all yours!'

2

The few previous trips she had taken to the River Thames had left Eleanor thinking it was pretty enough in parts. But now, there was no denying the breathtaking scene of sophisticated elegance before her. A sea of enormous striped marquees filled one bank like a veritable Arabian village of crimson and ivory silk. In front of them strolled an endless kaleidoscope of fashionable ladies swathed in feathers, silks, ruffs and ruches, arms draped over gentlemen in tailored suits. Topping off the lavish pageant, an incredible flotilla of close to two hundred flat-bottomed skiffs decked with bunting and paper rosettes hugged the banks of the river. She marvelled that each was thronged with men and women raising myriad champagne toasts, all standing in their rocking crafts, despite their exquisite finery.

Down the narrow centre channel a line of sleek rowing craft were each populated with eight singlet-clad young men, faces earnest, muscular arms eager to pull their team to victory.

With the air itself seemingly charged with electric expectancy, a childlike thrill surged through Eleanor. 'Too exquisite for words!' she breathed.

Tipsy looped her arm through Eleanor's as she swallowed a

large glug of champagne. 'Ooh, which treat for the eyes have you spotted? I'll tell you if he's one you should become acquainted with and then introduce you.'

'Huh? No, not a "he". I mean this incredible spectacle.'

Her companion groaned. 'It seems I omitted the most important thing of all from my list. But I thought that at least you would know.'

'Well, it appears I don't, whatever it is. I told you, I was brought up abroad by bohemian parents and I've spent three quarters of my life travelling.'

'A poor excuse, sweetie. I'm beginning to despair there is any hint of English aristocracy in you. Anyway, number thirteen. Act entirely as though you do this every day.'

Eleanor nudged her new friend in the ribs. 'But I'll be instantly rumbled, since the regatta is only on once a year, silly.'

The infectious giggles this drew turned heads in their direction. Clearly happy with the attention, Tipsy gave a raft of finger waves at various faces and then tugged on Eleanor's arm.

'What do you think of the pink blazer and top hat over there?'

Eleanor was surprised to see such an overt outfit among the swathes of conservative cream linen suits and navy blazers. 'Pink' was an understatement. The fellow holding court over a group of mid-twenties men lounging against an iron railing was decked head-to-toe in vibrant dahlia pink. A magenta band around his top hat matched the pinstripe of his blazer, while a carnation in his buttonhole completed the ensemble.

'Gracious! That is a bold statement.' She looked again and smiled. 'He looks like a fun chap, though. An evening spent with anyone willing to look that outrageous isn't going to consist of poetry readings or end with an invitation to view his stamp collection.'

Tipsy laughed. 'That's more like it. Although he always tries way too hard to be the centre of attention.'

'Oh, so you do know him then?'

'Sweetie, catch up! I know everyone. Well, everyone worth knowing. And Bartholomew Darnley, pink suit or otherwise, is definitely worth knowing.' She frowned and then quickly ran an anxious forefinger over her brow as if to ensure there could be no chance of a wrinkle remaining. 'But I need to get to know him a lot better since he runs with a slightly different set.'

Having concluded early on that Tipsy herself liked to be the centre of attention, Eleanor was surprised. 'Even though he tries too hard?'

Her companion nodded. 'Absolutely, his father's frightfully rich. And Barty is Xander Taylor-Howard's cousin and has royal blood himself.'

Eleanor groaned inwardly. *Meeting a raft of minor royals really won't be the highlight of your day, Ellie! You'll probably have nothing to say to them and they'll think you a complete waste of time.* She looked around. 'That reminds me, Tipsy. I must slip off in a minute and see if I can find Hugh.'

Her friend grabbed her arm. 'Oh, no you don't! Not for a long while yet. And certainly not until I've introduced you to Bartholomew.'

She dragged Eleanor over to the vision in pink, who tipped his champagne glass at her, took her hand and looked her over a little too salaciously for her liking.

'Well, I love the frill motif, new girl in our midst.' He laughed at her obvious disapproval. 'What's not to love about a pretty girl, fully iced with a spoonful of cherries on top.' He pointed at her shock of red curls.

She pulled her hand away. 'Like, what's not to love about a gentleman dressed up as a strawberry ice cream?'

He tried to look unconcerned at his entourage's laughter. Quickly recovering himself, he grinned cheekily at Tipsy. 'What ho, I remember you from the twins' bash in April. It's Toppy. Tiffy. No, Tipsy. Right?'

At her coquettish nod, he tapped his forehead. 'Not just a debonair rack for the old top hat, ha!' Pretending to whisper behind his hand, he gestured towards Eleanor. 'And you've remembered I like a lot of spirit in my girls, I see. Good show!'

'You are a dreadful man, Barty.' Tipsy giggled. 'Almost as dreadful as your cousin.'

'Oh, please.' He rolled his eyes. 'Don't. Wretched chap will be here all too soon. And then the rest of us might as well jump in the river. As usual!'

'Nonsense, darling,' Tipsy cooed. 'Xander's not so special. Besides' – Tipsy ran a polished nail down the arm of his blazer – 'some of us think strawberry is truly the only delicious flavour of ice cream there is. So, I'll be back later, Barty.'

'Bring a spoon,' Darnley chortled. Then, eyeing Eleanor sideways, he added, 'Actually, bring two.'

Giggling, Tipsy led Eleanor away, bumping her shapely hip against her side. 'Sashay, sweetie,' she whispered.

Eleanor frowned. 'I didn't come to be ogled.'

'Then you absolutely haven't got the point! You're making this very hard work, you know. Boys have very fragile egos. There's nothing wrong with stroking them a little to make them relax.'

'Even if that means putting one's back out trying to show off one's assets?' Eleanor stopped and turned to face her friend. 'Which is all you were doing, was it?'

'No, silly. I was making sure that when Xander appears we can both have Barty draped round our shoulders. Xander always takes what poor Barty's got. You know boys.'

Actually, Eleanor didn't know those kinds of boys, but she kept the information to herself, not wanting another lecture.

'Absolutely not going to happen. He's far too fresh.'

Tipsy dissolved into giggles. 'And you are too hilarious. You catch me every time with your Miss Havisham act. Come on, we've heaps more delectable eligible bachelors to meet.'

. . .

After almost two more hours of introductions to rafts of young men in tailored suits and blazers, Eleanor was as awash with champagne as she was with names she couldn't remember. Attractive aristocratic faces she could barely distinguish between, and rugby-honed forms had come and gone. Promises of a year's worth of invitations rang in her ears. And despite Tipsy's assertions she was actually beginning to look and sound the part, Eleanor was tiring of the merry-go-round.

'Oh, a food tent!' Eleanor pointed to one of the smaller marquees with a tempting sign listing all manner of delectable nibbles.

'Ladies worth marrying are not seen eating!' Tipsy hissed in horror. 'Remember rule number two! Have more champers instead. It will fill you up.' She whirled Eleanor round by the arm and then stamped her foot. 'No! The cat's got her claws in him first. What's she got that's so wonderful?' She flicked a thick glossy lock of hair over her shoulder and curled her lip. 'Certainly nothing I can see.'

Eleanor followed the direction of her friend's glare. She took in the tall, stunning blonde in an elegant cornflower-blue silk dress which hugged her enviable figure. Eleanor suddenly felt plain and all the more ridiculous in her white frilly creation.

'What rot. She's one of the most beautiful women I've ever seen. Who is she?'

Tipsy sniffed. 'Oh, some totty who's embarrassing herself by showing how desperate she is. And that unbelievably delicious dish she's pretending not to drool over is none other than Xander Taylor-Howard himself.'

'Ah, the minor royal finally makes his appearance.' Eleanor tried discreetly to see what all the fuss was about. To her mind, he was only a dash better looking than all the other athletic, dark-haired chaps she'd met, even with his chiselled jaw and perfect aquiline nose. Although there was *something* in his poise that definitely set him apart. The way he leaned jauntily on his cane showed confidence borne of impeccable breeding. That it was all packaged in an exquisitely tailored indigo and crimson blazer and form-fitting cream suit trousers, however, piqued her interest more than she'd care to admit.

Sneaking out the tiny folding field glasses Clifford had given her before leaving to park the Rolls, she peered through them at the much-touted Mr Taylor-Howard. Finally grateful for the flamboyantly large brim of her hat, she hummed with appreciation at the view.

'I've only seen blue that deep in the most heavenly exotic lagoons. Those eyes could melt a nun on an iceberg.'

'Don't let them see that we're looking!' Tipsy hissed, jerking Eleanor's arm down.

'But I thought you were about to introduce me to him?'

'Not with her around. Although...' Tipsy grabbed the glasses and took a short peep. 'Ha! I think he's going to... Yes, look, he's stepping back. Apologetic nod of the perfect gentleman, of course. Is he going to? Yes, yes! Hands behind his back now. Oh joy of joys.' She thrust the field glasses back at Eleanor. 'Quick, turn around.'

As the blonde woman stalked in their direction, Tipsy quickly turned away from her and made a great show of pointing something out to Eleanor. Checking the coast was clear a moment later, she turned back and let out a quiet whoop.

Eleanor frowned. 'What on earth are you so excited about?'

'Only the best news ever! I believe Xander's just thrown her over. Right, come on, let's meet him while he's free and then we need to go find the person who'll know for sure.'

'How am I supposed to address him?' Eleanor whispered as Tipsy hurried her over to the much-famed royal. But as she neared him, she felt a shove at her back and fell forward, knocking into him.

'Gracious, I'm so sorry.'

He turned and gave her a charming smile, his perfectly manicured hand reaching out to steady her arm. 'No harm done. I hope the same is true of you?'

'Oh absolutely. Yes, I'm not sure what happened though.' Eleanor turned to yank Tipsy forward to do the introductions, only to find no sign of her friend anywhere. It was then that she noticed the two men a few steps behind Lord Taylor-Howard. They were definitely shadowing him. Security she assumed. After all, he was a royal, however minor.

'Xander.' He shook her hand with gentlemanly firmness.

His magnetic smile felt as genuine as his effortless charm.

'Um, Eleanor.'

Dash it, Ellie! Stop blushing. Tipsy merely got you giddy by waffling on about him all day. You know you've only got eyes for Hugh. Go find him immediately after this, for heaven's sake.

'It's a pleasure.' He tilted his head as he took in the field glasses she still gripped. 'A genuine pleasure. It's refreshing to meet an interesting girl, one here for the sport, if you'll forgive me for saying so.' He grinned. 'And not only because sporty and naughty so often go together.' He bowed from the waist and shook her hand again. 'If you'll excuse me, I have to leave, but I hope to see you later, Eleanor. Truly.'

He strode away followed by the two men and was swallowed up by the crowd.

Tipsy reappeared from nowhere and grabbed Eleanor's wrist.

'Quick! We need to get him back before that odious totty returns. But first there's some people you absolutely have to meet.'

The 'people' Tipsy was referring to were, to Ellie's mind, a bunch of Hooray Henry's or 'Bright Young Things' as the press called them. One of them, a young man in yet another striped blazer and straw boater, grabbed a glass from the hamper at his feet and poured her a champagne. *Is that your fourth? Or fifth, Ellie? You really should keep count.* Unable to decide, she accepted it, anyway. The blazer raised his glass to her.

'You must be the long-awaited Lady Swift. Can't imagine how you managed that amazing cycling feat of circumnavigating the globe in that many frills.'

She giggled. 'But how did you know about my little trip?' *Oh, Lord, Ellie, you're turning into Tipsy! Maybe this is your fifth champers!*

'Hardly "little", old thing. My father knew your uncle. Members of the same club, don't you know? He heard all about your adventures.'

Tipsy manoeuvred Eleanor to one side so she could speak to the blazered young man. 'You can talk about that later. I'm worried about your sister. She looked really upset after talking to Xander.'

'No, she didn't,' a cool voice said behind them. The 'totty' Tipsy had pointed out to Eleanor walked round to the youth and extricated him from Tipsy's grip, snuggling into the arm he looped round her shoulder.

He scrutinised her face. 'Maybe just a little bit though, sis?'

She shook her head. 'Xander's overrated. I let him down gently, of course. But it had to be done. Poor chap hasn't got enough stamina for a girl like me.'

'Only because he's used it up everywhere else at the same time.' He winced at the slap his sister gave him. 'Oh, don't play the huffy card. You knew his reputation as well as the rest of us, sis.' He pulled her into a brotherly hug. 'I just hope you had fun.'

'Oh, yes.' She grinned evilly at Tipsy over his shoulder. 'Lots and lots of delicious fun.'

'Now that is the perfect shot.' A voice hailed their group. A hot and harried-looking man carrying a huge camera on an unwieldy tripod approached them hurriedly. 'Pose for the society pages, will you, elegant folks? Centre spread, I guarantee.'

'Not half!' the youth said. 'Chaps and chapesses gather round. Champers flutes to hand.' Dropping his arm from his sister's shoulder, he reached across and scooped up Eleanor's. Gently escorting her to his left side, he grinned. 'This will tickle Pater no end. Me and the illustrious lady adventurer, front and centre. Shame you didn't bring your bicycle.'

There was a quick shuffling into position, arms around waists, heads turned to show the best side which resulted in several straw boaters falling at even more jaunty angles. Amid the hilarity, Tipsy whispered to the youth, who nodded.

'Ready folks?' The photographer ducked down behind his camera. 'Then say cheese!'

But as she joined in the chorus, Eleanor realised the blazered young man was kissing her cheek. She stared at him in surprise as he winked, but then her gaze focused just over his shoulder. Standing at the front of the crowd, the only truly heart-stoppingly handsome man she'd seen all day was staring at her.

Hugh!

3

'Clifford!' Eleanor panted, rushing up to where her butler was standing near the officials' tent. 'Disaster. I can't find Hugh and I need your sage advice now!'

But she reeled as he shook his head. 'Unfortunately, my lady, I am devoid of an immediate answer to rectify such a significant calamity.'

'But you don't know what happ—' As he arched a brow, she groaned. 'You saw?'

'Regrettably, yes.'

She sank down onto a wooden crate and rubbed her forehead with her fingertips so hard it left a series of pink marks. 'But surely Hugh will understand? He'll realise that I wouldn't have encouraged that blazered oaf to kiss me?'

Clifford's silence was answer enough.

'But he can't really believe it was my fault, dash it.'

'Perhaps, my lady, if the chief inspector had witnessed you chastising the gentleman afterwards...'

'Slapped his face, you mean? But it was just a joke. His sort deliberately cause controversy.' She shrugged. 'They're "Bright Young Things".'

'Unlike the chief inspector, who is every inch the gentleman in that, and every other, regard. And who I suspect had gone to great lengths to busy his men elsewhere that he might exchange a few words with you.'

Her shoulders slumped. 'Then maybe I should leave him to his work today and telephone him this evening. Hugh can be rather... gruff sometimes, wouldn't you say?'

'It is far from my place to hold an opinion on the chief inspector's demeanour, my lady.'

'Balderdash, Clifford. You have a very firm opinion on everything.' She sighed. 'You've made it clear you approve of Hugh. On Uncle Byron's behalf, I know, since he is sadly not with us to give his blessing. And you're the ultimate master of smoothing every situation, no matter how difficult. Please come with me to help explain.'

'My lady, forgive my adding to Lady Fitzroy's unwelcome list of lessons, but no gentleman would countenance such a justification of events from another man. Most especially, not from the lady's butler.'

'But I'll probably make a hash of it on my own.'

'Most likely.' He gestured at Tipsy hurrying towards them. 'I will try to think of a solution to this conundrum while you continue your lessons on how to be a thoroughly modern young lady.'

'Well, there you are, sweetie.' Tipsy looped her arm through Eleanor's as Clifford melted away. 'I've been looking everywhere for you. Why on earth did you dash off like that?'

'Because I needed to find Hugh. And I still do.'

'Hugh who? Oh, you mean your invisible beau. Dear me, didn't you learn anything? Number five on my list? Never go chasing after a man, silly. You just look desperate. And there's nothing more likely to turn him off.'

Eleanor shook her head. 'I need to apologise. Hugh doesn't think like that.'

Tipsy patted Eleanor's cheek. 'Sweetie, you two are from such different worlds. How do you imagine you could ever be compatible?'

That drew a long confessional sigh from Eleanor. 'Honestly, I've no idea. We do seem to have more disagreements than otherwise, and a history of misunderstandings and—'

'And you spend more time pacing Henley Hall in the doldrums over him than out dancing or laughing with him.'

'I don't pace. Much.'

'Darling, when did he last invite you to his little pied-à-terre for an intimate dinner?'

'We haven't got that far.' She frowned. 'Actually, I still don't know where he lives.'

'Ooh, sweetie, that's not promising. Dancing?'

'Just once.' The beginnings of an inner glow suffused through her, bringing a smile that wouldn't budge. 'But it was honestly the most wonderful evening I've ever had. And he even conspired with Clifford to make it a surprise.'

Tipsy pulled a face. 'Plotting! With one of your servants! Eleanor, don't you see? This Hugh person sounds about as far from husband material as a man can get.' She tilted her head, scrutinising Eleanor's troubled expression. 'But, clearly there is something about him that makes you quite the giddy school-girl. So, we'll go and find him and sort out whatever his problem is.'

'Tipsy, I'm not sure. I mean, thank you, but—'

'But nothing, sweetie. This is the perfect opportunity for him to reveal if he is the Romeo to your Juliet that you think he is.'

Eleanor shook her head resolutely. 'On this occasion, I'm the only one who needs to account for themselves.'

'If you say so. Although surely a real man would take his girl being kissed by an impossibly handsome earl's son as a feather in his own cap?'

'Hugh doesn't wear a cap.' Eleanor sighed, more confused than ever about her feelings. 'He wears a bowler hat.'

Tipsy's shriek of laughter at her reply turned every head, including, Eleanor noted with horror, that of the very man she was looking for. Only she didn't want to meet him here. Not now. Not in front of everyone. And definitely not after what had just happened. As he came towards them, his chestnut curls and form-fitting charcoal suit set off all the usual butterflies in her stomach. He held her gaze for a moment before busying himself with his notebook.

She took a deep breath, wishing she was better with words, and stepped in front of him.

He looked up and acknowledged her arrival with a polite nod.

'Hugh! I—'

He interrupted her in a cool tone. 'Lady Swift. Good afternoon.' His deep-brown eyes flicked to the two suited men a step behind him, his firm inflection suggesting he was not in the mood for the knowing look that had passed between them. 'Watkins, Smith, round up the eight men I detailed earlier and go check the main stage area.'

'You not coming too, Chief?' the older man said nonchalantly.

'That was an order, Watkins. To the stage area. Now!'

He watched the men stride off and then turned back to Eleanor and Tipsy. 'I hope you continue to enjoy the regatta, ladies.' He sidestepped Eleanor and went to leave. There was something in his eyes that made Eleanor's stomach clench. A tinge of anger, but overlaid with a sadness that she had never seen in him before. She blocked his way.

'Hugh, I didn't mean to embarrass you in front of your men just then. I only came to apologise.'

He shook his head. 'No need to apologise, Eleanor.'

'I think there is.'

'As you wish. But there was no expectation.' A muscle twitched in his jaw. 'That would only have added to my long-standing foolhardiness. In fact, thank you for pointing it out to me.'

She opened her mouth, but no words would come. The awkward silence between them grew. Tipsy stepped forward.

'Well, do you know, I don't see how any policeman could ever be accused of being foolhardy. Especially such a senior officer.'

Seldon gave her a confused smile. 'An unusual observation, if you will forgive my saying so. I've never considered anyone to be above making a mistake.'

'Of course, but you see, that merely proves my point. I have no idea how you manage to keep such a clear and cool head in the dangerous situations you must find yourself in while on duty.' She stared at him, wide-eyed. 'Probably on a daily basis if you are stationed in London?'

'I am for the greater part, yes. With the rest of the week spent in Oxford.'

'Which is certainly no picnic either, I'll warrant. All those ancient buildings ringed by those narrow, dark alleys.' She threw her hands up, which made her shiny mane swing round her face. 'To say nothing of the river. I'll bet that crime, corruption and lawlessness have no reverence for tradition.'

Seldon surprised Eleanor by laughing. 'Indeed not. But how much easier a policeman's lot might be if they were. Securing a post in one of England's beautiful historic cities would guarantee a far more peaceful time of it.'

Grateful that her friend was trying so hard to diffuse Seldon's aggrieved mood, Eleanor still felt uncomfortably like a spare part as Tipsy laughed with him. 'Only that would make no difference to someone as dedicated as you, I'm sure. You can't earn the position of an inspector in chief if you always take the easy route.'

'It's chief inspector, actually.'

'Silly me. Honestly, Tipsy!' She slapped her forehead.

He nodded to her glass, which Eleanor noted with amazement had somehow appeared in her hand. 'Champagne can be tricky this early in the afternoon.'

'No, Hugh, Tipsy is her name,' Eleanor said.

'More and more unusual.' He held out his hand to Tipsy. 'We haven't been introduced, although it seems you know who I am. A pleasure to meet you, Lady...?'

'Fitzroy. Tiffany Fitzroy. It's Lady Fitzroy, but do call me "Tipsy", simply everyone does.' This was accompanied by an easy giggle. 'And an equal pleasure to meet you, Chief Inspector. You're not at all as I imagined from Eleanor's descriptions.'

Seldon's gruffness returned. 'Really? Now, forgive me, I must be going.' He gestured towards the stage, where a flurry of activity was beginning. Eleanor's heart constricted.

'Hugh, wait!'

'You know I can't, Eleanor.'

'Can't or won't?' she said quietly.

'I don't see that there is much of a difference.' He ran a hand through his hair. 'Good day.'

'Bye, Hugh!' Tipsy gave her signature finger wave. 'Do be careful.'

'I'll try.' The previously firm set line of his lips twitched upwards. 'Likewise, with the champagne.'

'Gracious, he's hard work, sweetie,' Tipsy said as she dragged Eleanor off towards the impressive three-storey viewing gallery.

Seldon's manner with Eleanor had left her smarting, but his manner with Tipsy had left her smarting even more.

'Actually, I'd say you seemed to make easy work of getting to know him!'

'Darling, it's simply practice. What have I been telling you? All men are the same. You just need to find their individual little button and figure out how hard they like it pressed. Anyway, you've absolutely no need to thank me. What are friends for, after all? Best friends, especially.'

'Um, thank you.'

'Oh, you are sweet,' Tipsy said, busily looking around the crowds. 'Honestly, though, I'm glad I managed to save you from a humiliating conversation.'

'You really think so?' Eleanor ran her hands over her still-scarlet cheeks.

'Of course! You would have wasted precious minutes apologising when the crest of that hill is galloping towards you. Hugh was enough of a gentleman to acknowledge that he's as relieved as you are that all your squabbles are over.'

'He did?' Eleanor's mind raced back over the conversation. Suddenly she stilled. 'You think he meant it's over?'

'And a good job, too. A neat parting of ways, leaving you free to find someone far more suitable and a great deal more delicious.'

'I think Hugh is delicious, actually, Tipsy,' Eleanor said with feeling.

But her friend wrinkled her nose. 'A long inch too tall. And a policeman, of all things. Sweetie, you need a man with enough money, standing and free time to forever treat you like you are his sun, moon and stars.' She leaned her head against Eleanor's shoulder. 'A husband can't do that if has a... *job,* can he?' She said the word with distaste. 'Especially one where any woman would obviously come second.'

As Tipsy led her through the crowd to meet even more eligible young men, Eleanor considered what her friend had said.

Maybe she's right, Ellie? A man can only have one wife, and Hugh's already married to his job. So where does that leave me?

4

Desperate to immerse herself in the distraction of the races she had finally cajoled Tipsy into watching, Eleanor joined in with the cheering crowds with extra gusto. So much so that several smart elderly couples either side of them moved away with disapproving head shaking and pointed comments about plummeting standards of decorum. Forty minutes later, having applauded every one of the rowing teams for fighting as fiercely for victory as a drowning man would for air, her hands were stinging.

Nevertheless, she felt a lump rise in her throat as the losing team in the last race shouldered their ridiculously long craft, slapped each other on the back in commiseration, and marched back to the boathouse. Something in their brotherly camaraderie made her feel even more alone, despite the crowds. *Years of solo travelling were all very well and exciting at times, Ellie, but it was dashedly lonely sometimes.*

Tipsy, having dragged her up to the top floor of the viewing gallery and into another group of friends, was busy occupying her favourite spot, that of centre stage. This left Eleanor rather too free to continue dwelling on whether a certain handsome chief inspector could ever be a permanent part of her life. At that moment she felt a welcome presence materialise behind her.

'What ho, Clifford. What a fabulous spectacle of sporting prowess, huh?'

'Indeed. And hopefully, the wherries and cutters have made rowing into a sufficiently distracting art form, my lady?'

'Wherries and cutters?'

'The official term for the racing craft. Both have pointed front ends, but only wherries have pointed sterns. Different classes yet both still built for speed.' He held up his leather pocketbook, lined with his meticulous handwriting, and then his pocket watch. 'Admirably, all the qualifying teams have maintained in excess of fourteen miles an hour for the length of the course.'

She couldn't hide her smile. 'It's a pity you aren't a betting man, Clifford. With that level of detail, you could have worked out the odds ahead of the selected teams being announced.'

'And the odds of Lady Fitzroy succumbing to the lure of the food marquee, perchance?'

She pulled a face. 'I think you'd have found them pretty low. Apparently, it isn't done for an eligible lady to be seen eating anything more than a single strawberry!'

His eyes flicked over to where Tipsy was basking in the attentions of two dapper-dressed young men. Eleanor tugged on his sleeve, ignoring the sharp tut he gave. Once at the furthest end of the balcony, away from the chance they could be overheard by anyone she'd met, she turned to him.

'Clifford, I don't want to be uncharitable. And maybe it's just the green-eyed monster raising its head, but—'

'But, regrettably, yes, I concur with your assessment of Lady Fitzroy's interactions with the chief inspector.' His hand strayed to his smart black tie. 'If you will forgive my happening to have witnessed the meeting.'

The concern in his expression and his thoughtfulness in having watched over her brought some much-needed comfort. 'You know I'm grateful as often as I am horrified that you can read my thoughts so readily. I did think I might have jumped to the conclusion that Tipsy was flirting with Hugh as a disgracefully selfish way to soothe my horribly bruised pride.'

'Not a characteristic I have ever observed in you, my lady. And you are right in that the lady was obviously flirting with the chief inspector. However, as you yourself remarked with the young gentleman who, ahem, kissed you, it is how Lady Fitzroy's "set" behave. I do not believe there is any malice or serious intent intended.'

He reached into his left pocket and produced a silver hip flask and a tiny sherry glass. 'His lordship's favoured prescription for bruised pride. Or indeed anything else bruised or otherwise.'

She took a sip and closed her eyes, savouring the Oloroso's perfectly blended flavour of figs, walnuts and warming tangy orange. 'I'm not really troubled by Tipsy's coquettish display back there, in truth. She has acted that way with all the chaps we've met today.'

'Perhaps more so by the chief inspector's... uncharacteristically animated response?'

Her shoulders sagged. 'Right, as always. It's not her fault. For now, I shall do my utmost to try and understand what our irrepressible Lady Fitzroy sees in all these ghastly superficial introductions, meaningless invitations and fickle flirtings.'

Clifford pinched the bridge of his nose. 'I believe, my lady, taken collectively, they are known as "Polite Society".'

'You can stop pretending now, Tipsy,' Eleanor said good-naturedly as they surged along with the crowd, linking arms to survive the perilously steep steps down from the viewing gallery in their high-heeled T-strap shoes. 'You didn't watch a single race so I fail to see why you are so keen to attend the awards ceremony.'

'And you can stop hiding behind the Happy Hermit of Henley Hall card, sweetie. Do try a little harder to follow my lead with all these delectable beaus. Many of whom are absolutely captivated by your fiery Titian curls and hypnotic green eyes.'

Eleanor stared at her friend's perfect feminine curves and then ran a hand down her own lack of them. 'I'm not at all sure that's the case.'

'Well, I am, which is why you need me. Now, we need to do a bit of ducking and weaving once we're on the ground to get nearer the front of this irritating wash of less-worthy spectators. Because You Know Who is the one making the presentations.'

Ah, Ellie! That's why Tipsy wants to attend the award ceremony. Xander.

There was no need to enquire of the many smart navy-blazered stewards which way the stage was. The ocean of frilled parasols, milliners' feathered masterpieces and jaunty straw boaters flowed on down the wide green swathe of immaculately cut grass towards one particular marquee.

Inside, sweeping garlands of red, white and blue looped along the front of the enthusiastically flower-decked stage, while tall, polished wooden scoreboards on either side listed the names of each team. Silver hooks protruded in a regimental line beside each scoreboard, ready to proudly display the number in which the team had been placed once announced.

'Bother!' Tipsy whispered to Eleanor. 'I've just been spotted by a friend of an aunt. I'd better exchange a few pleasantries.' She waved at a cluster of women on the other side of the tent and then glanced at the stage. 'Bother again. We'll never get a good spot now. Look, go and secure us a place as close to the front as you can while I fob off my aunt's friend as quickly as possible.' Without waiting for a reply, Tipsy sailed off to the other side of the marquee waving wildly.

Eleanor manfully edged her way as far forward as she could, but the marquee was so crowded that she had to give up still a way back from what she knew Tipsy would consider prime position.

A few minutes later, Tipsy reappeared looking flustered. 'Wretched aunts! And their even more wretched friends!'

Eleanor hid a smile. 'No worries. We're fairly near the front.' She looked around at the packed marquee. 'I say, the pull of a royal title really knows no bounds, does it?'

'Well, of course not, silly! Naturally, a girl is going to accept nothing short of the best titles on offer, and to bag a royal is the ultimate aim. But there simply aren't enough to go round. That's the attraction, you see!' She let out a huff of agitation. 'Now, we need to get nearer.'

'Why? We'll hear perfectly well. We're only six or so rows back.'

Tipsy stared at her and then let out a loud peal of giggles. 'Honestly, you're more hilarious by the minute. I thought you were being serious for a moment.'

It wasn't only the row of heads in front of them that glanced around to see what the amusement was all about. At the side of the stage, a group of men turned. Among them, a pair of broad, charcoal-suited shoulders and a head of chestnut curls. Eleanor groaned.

'Oh goody, it's Hugh.' Tipsy flicked her enviable dark mane. She caught his eye and then looked longingly at the stage.

'Tipsy, no! Please don't,' Eleanor hissed. Too late. Seldon had nodded to each of the men stationed at the marquee's entry points, then to each of the other seven lining the base of the stage. He stepped forward and addressed the crowd.

'Take a step to the right, everyone, please. Fire and medical access needed at all times.'

As the crowd shuffled back, Tipsy fluttered her lashes and whispered, 'Why, thank you, kind sir.' Gripping Eleanor's arm, she snuck them both past him to the front of the crowd.

He locked onto Eleanor's gaze as she turned back to smile at him, but then turned away, one hand running over his chest where he'd been shot. The very wound she had dressed herself.

Suddenly every head turned as Lord Taylor-Howard bounded up the rosette-and-flag-adorned steps to the stage, where he looked every inch the royal the crowd had come to see. Having recently given a speech at her old school, Eleanor well understood the fear of public speaking. But Xander displayed none of that. Captivated by his confidence, she watched him move along the line of officials, shaking hands, making them feel at ease.

In the centre, the most portly of the officials, whose blazer front was lost to a regiment of red and gold embroidered emblems, appeared to be waiting for a sign. When it was Xander himself who gave it, Eleanor couldn't help laughing. Particularly as he held his cane to his lips and gave a perfect rendition of a royal fanfare, drawing more laughter. As it died down, Xander caught Eleanor's eye and winked.

She blanched in surprise and stared at Tipsy, who had taken that moment to retrieve something from the bottom of her handbag.

'I'm sure I was seeing things,' Eleanor muttered.

'What's that, sweetie?' Tipsy looked up from under the brim of her hat.

'I... I was just saying that man makes putty of everyone he meets.'

'Darling,' Tipsy cooed in Eleanor's ear, 'those royal fingers could pat even you into submission.'

'You're terrible! That is not what I meant... exactly.'

'Fibber. But have it your way, whatever you meant. However,' – she cupped her hand round her mouth, making Eleanor lean in to hear – 'remember lesson nineteen. The trick is to make sure it's only us that he notices in the sea of faces.'

'Oh no!' Eleanor groaned, trying to pull out of Tipsy's grasp. 'Why do I have a sinking feeling about what you're planning?'

Tipsy's big brown eyes widened with glee as she held fast to Eleanor's arm. 'Because you're only just beginning to see how much fun all this really is, silly. But poor Hugh.' She gestured over to where Seldon was clearly on high alert, his eyes constantly darting from the royal visitor to his men. Eleanor caught several coded signals passing back and forth. Not that she had any clue what they meant.

'See?' Tipsy said. 'He and his men are having no fun at all. That's why you need to aim so much higher, sweetie.'

Eleanor shook her head and tore her eyes off Seldon, anxious that she didn't give his men any more ammunition to tease him with.

Tipsy tugged Eleanor's sleeve. 'Never mind, look, they're all about to toast with champers. We must go and get some more the moment this is over.'

'I thought you were waiting to work your irresistible charms on Xander?'

'Who will be escorted straight to the Stewards' Enclosure and... the what, Eleanor? Oh, keep up! The elite champagne reception. Which I can get us into no problem. Same as every year.'

Eleanor laughed. 'All this fuss over an oh-so-distant heir to the throne!'

Tipsy shrugged. 'Who cares if he isn't number one? I wouldn't want to be Queen, anyway. All that terribly boring nonsense of having to keep Parliament under control and granting royal pardons or whatever it is one has to do.' She gave a mock yawn. 'Quite happy with Princess, thank you. I look gorgeous in a tiara, don't you know?'

Eleanor nodded. 'Trust me, I can imagine.'

The portly official raised his champagne glass above his head. 'And with no further ado, ladies and gentlemen, please put your hands together for our most distinguished royal guest. Lord Taylor-Howard.'

The spectators watched in delighted silence as Xander let the entire contents of his champagne flute slide down his throat. He lowered the glass and bowed to applause and laughter.

'My favourite ceremony opener. And breakfast, dinner and supper, actually. In fact, that reminds me of the time...' He expertly took the crowd with him as he launched into a series of mock-scandalous tales.

Finally, he nodded to the head official who was discreetly pointing to his watch. Eleanor had no idea how long Lord Taylor-Howard had spoken for as she too had been captivated. He cleared his throat. 'But to business. Dear ladies, gents, good folks and everyone else.' He raised his voice as more laughter ripped through the rows. 'I am honoured to... to...' He paused, clearing his throat, seemingly distracted for a moment.

The smart lady who looked to be in her late sixties on Eleanor's right fanned her face with her programme. 'Such a charming humourist.'

'I know, dear,' her friend said. 'He's got us all totally spellbound. As usual.'

Her companion tittered. 'A royal rascal. What could be more tantalising?'

Eleanor would have found this amusing were she not still staring at Xander. His cheeks were flushed and his hand kept straying upwards, as if wanting to loosen his collar. He seemed breathless. Sympathy coursed through her. Those were all the hideous symptoms she had suffered on her one attempt at public speaking. But was he playing with the crowd, or had his apparently infallible confidence momentarily deserted him? Had he failed to prepare a speech and talked himself into a hole?

With a jerk, he seemed to recover. 'I... I am honoured to announce...' He looked around, his eyes moving over Eleanor, this time with no recognition. He clutched at his collar again. 'The winners—'

Seldon's jacket tails flew out behind him as he mounted the stage steps just in time to catch the eighteenth in line to the throne as he collapsed.

5

Horrified silence pervaded the marquee for one brief, stunned moment. Then a chorus of screams pierced the air. Women fainted into the hastily held out arms of gentlemen they probably hadn't even been introduced to. Stunned looks flashed through the crowd. Even the line of officials stood dumbstruck, staring in disbelief at their portly leader, whose jowls wobbled as his mouth opened and closed like a stranded cod.

Tipsy nudged Eleanor and huffed. 'Even for Xander, that's quite the stunt. I mean, really!'

'I don't think he's play-acting,' Eleanor said slowly.

'He did look a bit peaky.' Tipsy spotted someone she knew further into the crowd and waved. 'I'll be back in a mo, sweetie. Stay here so we can find each other again.'

Eleanor nodded but didn't take in her friend's words, distracted as she was by a fox-haired man sliding out of the marquee. She shook her head and looked back at the stage where Seldon was barking orders she couldn't hear above the pandemonium. Still kneeling at Xander's side and holding the royal's head, Seldon called through one cupped hand to the portly official. But on getting nothing more than wide-eyed head shaking in reply, he grabbed the arm of the nearest of the others and yanked him down to his level. After what looked like stern words, the messenger stood and stepped hesitantly to the front of the stage.

'Ladies and gentlemen, please remain calm and stay where you are for the moment. Thank you.'

Eleanor noticed a couple trying to leave were stopped by two of Seldon's officers. The man remonstrated with them, but soon gave up and returned to his place with his companion. Eleanor turned back to Seldon, realising in shock that he looked positively ashen. It took all her resolve and a great deal more she didn't know she could muster not to dash to his side. For a brief moment, he looked up and seemed to seek her out. Their eyes met. He shook his head.

Her butler reappeared at her side.

'Clifford,' she whispered. 'I have a horrible suspicion Xander is... you know. Reassure me I'm wrong, please.'

'Would that I could, my lady,' Clifford whispered back. 'Sadly, instead I must concur. From the inspector's bearing, it seems tragedy has claimed Lord Taylor-Howard for herself.'

Eleanor's breath caught in her throat. 'Maybe we're mistaken. Maybe he's just—' She broke off and willed herself to look at Xander's motionless form. 'Oh, Clifford, it doesn't make any sense! He was larger than life itself, delighting in playing to the gallery, only moments ago. Seriously, when I met him earlier, I couldn't help admiring how vibrant and vital he was.'

Clifford looked her face over anxiously. 'Though I sincerely hope to divert you from dwelling on the matter, my lady, one cannot pretend that even the most indomitable spirits must be called from this world, eventually.'

'But not usually at only late twenty-something, though. Poor Xander,' she muttered, her chest tightening as the reality sank in. She'd seen too many young men taken early in her years as a war nurse, but none just drop dead in front of her, seemingly without cause.

Clifford cleared his throat gently. 'My lady, please do not upset yourself too greatly. The gentleman did not appear to suffer.'

'True,' she managed with all the false brightness she could muster. 'What makes it even harder, though, is that poor Hugh looks like he is finding this particularly tough for some reason. I mean, he's used to, well, death. He does this kind of thing every day. Dealing with tragedy, that is.'

'Indeed. However, if I might suggest the chief inspector's uncharacteristic disquiet may be due to—'

'A royal dying on his watch?'

He nodded.

On stage, one of Seldon's men was directing the crowd to form a series of orderly groups by each of the marquee's six exits, all of which were now guarded. Despite the clear and urgent instructions, however, many people remained rooted to the spot, still gawping at the stage as if hypnotised. Seldon ran a frustrated hand through his hair, cast one last scrutinising look at the dead man and unfolded his long legs with a jerk. Standing up, he strode to the shaken officials. A moment later several of them screened off the area where the dead man lay with the tall wooden scoreboards.

'It won't be long now, folks,' the policeman at the front of her group called over the gaggle of heads. 'Thank you for your patience. We just need to take a few details.'

Take details? Why would they need to do that, Ellie, unless...

The sight of Seldon looking up from his notebook in her direction interrupted her thoughts. His long stride made short work of the stage and the steps.

'If I might start with you, Lady Swift.'

'Of course, Chief Inspector.' She was aware that several heads in front of her had turned at his approach. She tried to read his expression, but the familiar flutter she felt every time he was within touching distance dashed her concentration.

His pen hovered over his notebook. 'A few details from you, please, if I may. And then you will be free to return home.'

She was itching to whisper, 'But you know my details. You've visited and even stayed briefly when you were injured.' Instead she said, 'Of course. Though, I may choose not to return straight home.'

His eyes flicked up. 'Home would be an excellent choice.' He held up his pen to halt her next words. 'Shock is not to be trifled with.' Head down again, he muttered, 'No matter how many deceased one has unfortunately encountered. And all too recently.'

It dawned on her that perhaps he had started with her, so she might escape the tragic scene as quickly as possible. He knew she'd been witness to several deaths over the last year.

'Thank you.' She watched his pen move with the short efficient strokes she knew. 'I'm sure that's good and kindly intentioned advice.'

But his next words made her heart still. 'Where is your friend, please?'

So much for Hugh's concern for you, Ellie. He wants to speak to Tipsy. Dash her feminine curves and easy manner with all members of the opposite sex. Even ever-awkward Hugh has fallen for them!

With the perfunctory performance of Seldon taking her details over, she allowed herself to admit that home was indeed calling. With her warring emotions seesawing back and forth over the death of a man she had believed to be in the prime of his life and the bewildering actions of another she had only recently truly confessed to herself she cared deeply for, she felt totally wrung out.

She let out a long sigh and turned to Clifford. 'Let's go, please.'

'Unquestionably, my lady.' His brows flinched. 'However...'

'Oh dash it, you're right. We need to wait for Tipsy otherwise she'll be stuck without a car.' She shrugged. 'I'm not so petty as to leave her behind.'

'Eminently admirable, but if you will forgive my correction,' – he pointed to the other side of the marquee – 'I believe the lady has been trying to signal that she intends to depart with another party.'

'Well, there we are, then. I'm freer than I even imagined.' She frowned. 'Then what were you about to say?'

Clifford gestured discreetly to the stage where a line of officious men of military bearing were advancing towards the makeshift cubicle around the dead royal.

'My apologies. I was distracted by the regrettable knowledge that the chief inspector's difficulties are about to escalate most significantly.'

Despite her annoyance with Seldon, something in the way Clifford was staring at one of the men now mounting the stage made her hesitate to leave. A moment later, she led Clifford to the side rail of the steps under the pretext of needing somewhere to balance in order to adjust the straps of her shoes. Above her, the policeman assigned to watch the body whistled to Seldon, gesturing at the suited ranks closing in on him. In a trice, Seldon was back across the marquee, speeding past Eleanor to address the beakiest eagle nose she had ever seen.

'And just what do you think you're doing?'

'Aside from witnessing your personal ineptitude first-hand, you mean?'

'Ah, Sir Percival, it's you. Apologies. I believe that Lord Taylor-Howard was taken—'

'I'm sure you do,' the man barked. 'Which is precisely why you and your men are relieved of duty here. Lord Taylor-Howard was of the royal family and therefore his death will be investigated by the royal police. And as head of the royal police,

I order you to clear out of this marquee. I am personally taking charge here. With,' he continued, jabbing a finger into Seldon's chest, 'immediate effect.'

Eleanor silently cheered as Seldon removed the man's finger and stood his ground. But as she realised a moment later, wisely, only for a second.

'As you wish. But my men and I shall remain on site at the regatta, since Lord Taylor-Howard was not the only personage under my remit.'

'Then I suggest you scurry off before there are more bodies littering the grounds!'

Eleanor had heard enough, but at the tent's entrance she was brought up short.

'Lady Swift?'

She blinked at the young soldier blocking her path. 'Yes?'

'Please come this way, m'lady.'

Confused, and equally curious despite herself, she followed the soldier back into the tent, her butler bringing up the rear. At the side of the stage, the man who had berated Seldon was waiting, flanked by two aides. There was no sign, however, of Seldon.

He nodded curtly. 'Lady Swift.'

'Yes? I don't believe we've been introduced.'

He put his hands behind his back. 'Sir Percival Westlake, at your service. Although, actually, I am on His Majesty's.' He presented her with an ivory business card with silver scrolled lettering. 'Tomorrow at nine sharp. Here. Thank you. Now, you need to vacate the marquee.'

Leaving Eleanor open-mouthed, he spun on his heel, eyed her butler with poorly disguised contempt, and strode out followed by his aides.

6

The following morning, Eleanor was in no mood for the meeting that lay ahead. She stumbled down Henley Hall's sweeping staircase with bleary eyes, accompanied by an even blearier-eyed bulldog. Sleep never readily wrapped its arms around her when her thoughts were troubled. And last night they had kept her alternately pacing her room and sighing at the ceiling each time she'd flopped back onto her bed.

Having finally crept down to the kitchen at two in the morning to dognap Gladstone from his cosy spot by the range and take him back up to her bedroom for company, she had been comforted by a cup of hot Ovaltine. It had been magically waiting on the table, still hot, next to a penny dreadful novel, the perfect distraction. The note accompanying the book, written in Clifford's meticulous hand, had made her smile.

In extremis casibus! (*Only in extreme circumstances!*)

Now, however, the hours spent devouring the romantic exploits of a dashing highwayman instead of sleeping, even if fitfully, had left her little enough energy to dress. And certainly none for hurrying.

With a groan, she fumbled in her skirt pockets for her late uncle's pocket watch. She peered at the display disbelievingly.

'It can't be gone eight o'clock already! Say it isn't.'

'It isn't, my lady.'

Clifford appeared at her elbow, her new mint-green summer jacket over one arm, matching hat in hand.

She sighed in relief. 'Just as well because... wait a moment...' She checked the hall clock. 'It is, isn't it?'

'Most assuredly.' He bowed from the shoulders. 'However, I hate to be the bearer of bad news.'

'Dash it! That is positively the last time you catch me out like that.' Despite her morning grumpiness, she smiled and grabbed her hat. 'But it's hardly sporting of you when you know I haven't slept. And, rather dangerous, given that' – she pinned on her hat in the gold-framed mirror above the telephone table – 'I shall now have to stomach Sir Percival Westlake. And without so much as having swallowed a sip of coffee or nibbled the beginnings of breakfast.' She turned away from the mirror. 'I'd say as my butler, Clifford, your day is about to plunge into the first of Dante's Nine Circles of Hell.'

'Perhaps, my lady. Perhaps not.' He removed her jacket from his arm with a magician's flourish to reveal a neat wicker hamper in his hand.

'Thank heavens! How do you always know exactly what I need?'

'Because, I am, as you so shrewdly noted, your butler, my lady.'

She nodded. 'And I am grateful every day for that. So, breakfast on the move it is. Or' – she pulled an innocent face – 'should I say greasy sausage fingers and spilled coffee all over the inside of the Rolls?'

He shuddered. 'Perhaps I should phone Lady Fitzroy and

ask her to hasten round to reinforce rule number two – ladies should never be seen eating.'

'Oops! Too late!' She bit into a heavenly flaky pastry roll.

The beech-wood-lined lanes and sheep-dotted fields yielded to the picturesque town of Henley-on-Thames at exactly fifteen minutes to nine. Fuelled by a raft of sublime bite-sized creations, Eleanor stared appreciatively at the empty dishes in the hamper on her lap as Clifford eased the Rolls to a stop. Home-made sausage patties in freshly baked, generously buttered bread rolls dressed with her cook's famous paprika relish had been followed by delicate finger pastries of cherry and almond. All washed down with a Thermos flask of delectably roasted coffee. In her footwell, Gladstone licked his lips sorrowfully as he finished the last of the pastry crumbs.

'You totally missed out in not joining me, Clifford. That was just what I needed. I shall go straight to the kitchen to thank Mrs Trotman on our return.'

'Most kind, my lady. Might one surmise, therefore, that you feel sufficiently restored to meet Sir Percival in less than an, ahem, combative mode?'

'That depends.' She mimed rolling her sleeves up. 'On whether he starts it first. I mean, honestly, he just slapped that card in my hand and demanded that I be here at nine tomorrow. Well, today, now. The arrogant cheek!'

'My lady, Sir Percival is the head of the royal police. Even the chief inspector has no authority over him.'

'So? That doesn't mean he has any hold or jurisdiction over *me*.'

'Spoken precisely like your uncle, my lady.' He held up a finger. 'Hence my disquiet over his demand that you visit today.'

She turned to face him. 'I got the distinct impression

yesterday that you recognised Sir Percival. And that he recognised you. And that for neither of you was it a pleasant reunion?'

He hesitated, and then nodded. 'Without betraying his lordship's confidence, while your uncle was in India he had a dispute with Sir Percival, who was at the time his commanding officer. The dispute was over how orders needed to be followed. Your uncle was of the opinion that to carry out such orders in the manner Sir Percival wished would result in distressing consequences for the native population of the area, who, I must make clear, your uncle viewed as innocent parties.'

'Sufficiently understood, thank you. But then why has he summoned me, do you think?'

'I have an inkling he wishes to see you in regard to Lord Taylor-Howard's demise, but I cannot fathom why. My concern is that Sir Percival is not a person to forgive and forget, no matter how far back in his history something occurred. And, disconcertingly, he knew who I was on sight, as you say. But more concerningly, he is not the sort of man I would advise becoming involved with. He would, I think the colloquial expression is, shoot his own father if he thought it necessary to do his job. And without the least remorse.'

Eleanor considered this for a moment. 'Mmm, I can, however, see that you would need such a man under certain circumstances. And I suppose the country needs people who are willing to put their personal feelings second to the national good.' She shrugged. 'However, I trust you, and Uncle Byron, completely, and thus am here as you felt I should attend. I will make it clear, nonetheless, that I want nothing to do with whatever it is he wants to see me about. Now, let's get this over and done with.'

Henley Regatta was preparing for day two of the highly anticipated rowing events. And the even more highly anticipated social events. More bunting was being attached and marquee sides folded back while rowers herded back and forth, muttering tactics and taking on much-needed fluids against the unexpectedly fierce June sun. Further along the riverbank, more crates of champagne were being unloaded into the Stewards' Enclosure under the watchful eye of the portly official Eleanor recognised from the day before. She dragged her eyes away and willed her feet, and the happily sniffing Gladstone, to move faster as Clifford tapped his pocket watch.

'Sir Percival is not known for his patience, my lady.'

'Neither am I.'

An army of men in burgundy waistcoats carrying armfuls of folding chairs paused to let them pass.

'Oh gracious, thank you.' Once clear of the men and the chairs, she turned to Clifford. 'Surely an event this prestigious could run to some wheeled contraptions to help those poor chaps?'

'And leave indents in the grass of the main promenade with the subsequent risk of a lady in impractical but fashionable heels turning an ankle?' He shook his head.

The young soldier from the day before marched up. He gestured towards a medium-sized, dark-green marquee.

'Sir Percival is waiting for you in here, Lady Swift.'

As the soldier led them into the tent, she caught a flash of familiar chestnut curls at the far side of the meadow.

The scowl on Sir Percival's face that greeted her matched the heavy atmosphere of the dim interior of the tent.

'Lady Swift.' His eagle nose flared. 'I believe I said nine o'clock sharp. It is a full eleven minutes after the hour.' He was standing next to an astonishingly large and formal mahogany pedestal desk.

She pursed her lips. 'I don't believe I said I had actually

accepted your invitation yesterday. Yet, I have graciously rearranged my morning to be here.'

Behind her, she heard Clifford clear his throat.

Without unlocking his hard stare from hers, Sir Percival jutted his chin in her butler's direction. 'Your man can wait outside.'

She nodded. 'Yes, he can. But he shan't. Now, what is it you wanted to see me about?'

For a moment Sir Percival glowered at her, then grudgingly waved her towards eight high-backed oak chairs, set regimentally around a long map table. She strode over, taking in the two heavy bookcases against the far wall separated by a roll-top filing cabinet, all so incongruous with the canvas floor and flapping marquee roof.

She settled into the nearest chair and Gladstone lay against her leg, while Sir Percival lowered himself rigidly into the seat opposite her.

'Lady Swift. You are here for one reason. And one reason only. Lord Taylor-Howard was murdered. Poisoned, in fact.'

7

It took all her resolve not to let her horror at his words show in her expression. In her peripheral vision, she saw Clifford stiffen.

'Poor Xan— Lord Taylor-Howard,' she managed, scrabbling to gather her wits. 'However, since I am obviously not responsible, I am confused as to the reason for your summons. And surprised—'

'Surprised I did not dress up the details of Lord Taylor-Howard's death into some sugar-coated version suitable for the average lady to receive without fainting in a fit of hysterics? If so, then you disappoint me.'

'How fortunate I have disappointed you so early in our meeting.' She rose with a dignified smile. 'Since I have no wish to continue it.'

Sir Percival grunted. 'Perhaps not. But this meeting is not yet concluded. You are far too intrigued as to why one of His Majesty's most senior officials would ask you here and tell you something that is not in the public domain.'

She couldn't deny that was true, but certainly would not admit to it. 'And this terribly important senior person is?'

'My good self,' Sir Percival growled. 'As I believe, you are acutely aware. I have as little desire for this conversation as you evidently have, so shall we forgo any further time-wasting?'

She folded her arms. 'From your, I imagine, military background, surely you remember an armistice requires concessions on both sides?'

'Infernal creatures!' he muttered.

'Murderers?'

'Women. And murderers.' He narrowed his eyes as he watched her resume her seat. 'However, I accept that you are not the average histrionic female. Hence my succinct disclosure of the truth about Lord Taylor-Howard's death.'

'Fair enough. Let us jump then to why on earth you think I would have any interest—' Her words dried on her lips as she heard a familiar voice outside.

'Yes, he will. Stand aside, man!'

Seldon's long athletic frame ducked under the entrance to the tent.

'What are you doing here?' Sir Percival barked.

Seldon faltered on seeing Eleanor, then marched up to the table. 'I would like to ask Lady Swift the same question, actually.'

'Good morning, Chief Inspector.' Eleanor flashed him a polite smile, discreetly hanging onto Gladstone's collar to spare Seldon the inelegance of her bulldog's enthusiastic greetings. 'Sir Percival kindly summoned me to drop everything and appear at this unearthly hour so he could show me around his lavish field ops tent.'

Seldon's lips quirked upwards momentarily, softening his expression. But it hardened at her next words.

'And for reasons yet explained, to also tell me that Lord Taylor-Howard was murdered.'

Sir Percival rapped the table. 'I did not say, Lady Swift, that the news could be disseminated to any Tom, Dick and Harry!'

'Neither did you say it could not.' She sat back in her chair. 'May I suggest that you hurry to the point?'

Sir Percival's piercing stare remained on Seldon. 'Chief Inspector, I made it very clear yesterday that as Lord Taylor-Howard was of royal blood, any investigation into his death is a matter for the royal police alone and *not* the civilian police. If you do not leave, I will have you forcibly removed.'

'To be recalled later then, Sir Percival? Because I also came here to share my conclusion that Lord Taylor-Howard's death was not by natural causes.'

'I anticipated as much. And it is precisely because of that, as I just said, that this is not a case for the civilian police.'

Unable to stop herself, Eleanor let out a loud huff. 'Chief Inspector Seldon is the best detective in the entire South of England. If not the whole country. Which is precisely why you need him if Lord Taylor-Howard was murdered.'

Seldon ran a hand through his hair. 'Lady Swift, thank you, but this is perhaps not the time.'

'Well, I honestly can't see why not.' She turned to Sir Percival. 'It was the inspector who rushed to help Lord Taylor-Howard and who immediately had the tent exits blocked. What possible reason can you have for wishing to exclude him from this discussion?'

Sir Percival's nostrils flared as he snorted. 'This is a highly sensitive and delicate matter which only the royal police can handle.'

She threw her hands out. 'Then, dash it! Why have you got *me* involved? I'm neither sensitive nor delicate. A flat-footed rhinoceros is more diplomatic and circumspect than I am on an average day.'

This time Seldon's amusement got the better of him. He half-turned away but then caught Clifford's eye, which only seemed to make it worse.

Sir Percival was unamused. 'So you have amply demonstrated in the seven short minutes in my company. However, I have no choice. If I did, I would not countenance calling on your services, Lady Swift. To be clear, I trust no one. And that includes you.'

She frowned. 'I still don't understand—'

He slapped the desk. 'Because I have not yet had the chance to explain! Now, pay attention! Even if I relented in the case of the chief inspector and let him investigate Lord Taylor-Howard's death because he has already signed the Official Secrets Act, he could not operate without his men knowing he was working the case. I've done my homework on you, however, Lady Swift. You work alone and have proven your guile previously.' He waved a piece of paper. 'You will, of course, have to sign the Official Secrets Act as well.'

Seldon gaped at Sir Percival. 'You are asking Lady Swift to be embroiled in the investigation of Lord Taylor-Howard's murder! That is not only preposterous, it is irresponsible. Her answer is *no*.'

Despite appreciating Hugh's gallantry, Eeanor's natural stubbornness rose to the fore. 'Thank you, Chief Inspector, but I am able to decide for myself. However, Sir Percival, my response is indeed no.'

Sir Percival leaned back in his chair. 'Oh, really? Even though the royal family may very well be embroiled in a scandal that could damage their standing?'

'That sounded rather like a threat!'

'No, Lady Swift, it is merely the ugly truth. Something I spend every day wading through.' He nodded in her butler's direction. 'Now, your man will have to leave immediately, along with the chief inspector.'

'No. Clifford must have signed your dratted Official Secrets Act a long time ago when he was in the army under my late uncle, as I'm sure you're aware. If I were to become involved in whatever you are imagining I might, he will have to be a part of my undertaking. So he stays too. I'll sign your paper to hear what you have to say but promise nothing more at this stage.'

'Eleanor.' Seldon coughed as he cursed his tongue. 'Lady Swift, nothing good can come of this.' His pleading deep-brown eyes almost made her relent.

'What about justice for Lord Taylor-Howard?' she said softly, her heart aching at the memory of that awful scene. 'Despite doing your best to protect him, he still died in your arms.'

Sir Percival laughed cruelly. 'Perhaps *you* dreamed of being in Lord Taylor-Howard's arms, Lady Swift? I know you were seduced by his infallible charm, like all the ladies.'

Seldon let out a low gruff as he picked a piece of imaginary lint from his jacket sleeve. Eleanor threw him a look and shook her head. Unconvincingly, it seemed, as he pointedly avoided her eyes.

'Sir Percival,' she said firmly. 'I only met the deceased for a matter of moments and I do not appreciate your assumption, thank you.'

'It was no assumption, Lady Swift.' He leaned over the table. 'Your reaction was noted at the time. Did you really think my men were not watching his every move?' He shot Seldon a contemptuous look. 'Unlike certain others.'

'Actually,' Seldon said through a tight jaw, 'that is not the case. And if your men were watching his every move, he would be alive now!'

Eleanor's breath caught in horror. 'Hu— Chief Inspector, you were watching me?'

Seldon hesitated. 'I was watching Lord Taylor-Howard, as was my duty.'

Sir Percival laughed darkly. 'So, Lady Swift, we can safely return to the consensus. Our young lord had an uncanny charm. But not everyone appreciated it. But before we can go any further, the chief inspector needs to leave us. As I have repeatedly made clear.'

Seldon flapped a hand in surrender. 'If you need my assistance with any aspect of the investigation, Sir Percival, you know where to find me. Good day.' He strode from the tent.

'Finally,' Sir Percival grumbled. He passed Eleanor a copy of the Official Secrets Act and watched her sign the last page without having read a word of the narrow-lined, tightly spaced typescript. He folded the document and placed it in his inside jacket pocket. 'Now we are alone and you have signed, I can tell you more details. But they must not leave these four walls.' He waved a hand around the tent and scowled at her amused expression. 'You know perfectly well what I mean.'

'Do you have a theory on why anyone would want him dead?'

Sir Percival steepled his fingers over his impressive nose. 'A great many, Lady Swift. Any of which would result in a scandal if they came to light.' He strode to the roll-top filing cabinet and produced a key on a long chain from his waistcoat pocket. Returning, he slapped a slim manilla wallet on the table.

'Revenge. Jealousy. Greed. And more. Where would you like me to begin?'

8

Eleanor swallowed and peered sideways at Clifford, who arched an imperceptible brow. *You weren't expecting that, Ellie. But then again, what were you expecting?*

'So, Sir Percival, who exactly had such motives?'

He shrugged. 'Oh, only the husbands of the married women he engaged in liaisons with. Not to mention the women he had jilted. Oh, and the gambling bosses he reneged on paying his debts to.'

Her head was spinning. None of that sounded like the man she'd briefly met.

Well, maybe the illicit liaisons, Ellie.

Desperate to find a positive for the dead man, she said, 'At least, one can rule out the age-old motive of wanting to inherit his fortune then. If he was up to his cravat in debt, that is.'

Sir Percival shook his head. 'Not the case. Lord Taylor-Howard's funds were held in trust and released as a monthly allowance. A grossly generous one, but still it proved insufficient for his extravagant needs. There is still a significant fortune to be inherited.'

She studied him for a moment. 'It must have been hard for you.'

Sir Percival frowned. 'For me?'

'Trying to ensure the security of such a maverick member of the royal family. Especially when you obviously held him in contempt.'

'My job is to protect His Majesty and his family regardless,' he snapped. 'Personal feelings have no place in such a matter.'

'Well, mine do. And to save you any further trouble, I repeat that I am not interested in becoming involved in any investigation.'

Glancing at Clifford, she saw in surprise that his shoulders hadn't relaxed at all.

Sir Percival leaned back in his chair and lit a cigar.

'Lady Swift, England has recently been through a war and the British public need institutions they can cling to and believe in. A strong royal family is essential to the fabric of this nation.'

A puzzled look crossed her face. 'Lord Taylor-Howard was only a minor royal. If a few of his indiscretions come to light, it is hardly likely to rock the monarchy.'

'True, but I haven't told you all of his indiscretions. Not by a long way. You see, our young lord used his considerable charm to forge a relationship with a much more senior royal.' He glanced up. 'The details and identity of which you will never know.'

Eleanor shrugged. 'Alright, even I accept some things probably will have to remain secret. But you seem to be suggesting that Lord Taylor-Howard had an ulterior motive in forging this relationship?'

Sir Percival nodded. 'And one that, if it becomes general knowledge, would immerse the royal family in a true scandal. And, more seriously, possibly lose them much of the goodwill of the country. You see...'

Eleanor couldn't help leaning forward. Out of the corner of her eye, she noted Clifford remained seemingly unmoved.

Sir Percival took a couple of puffs on his cigar and then appeared to make up his mind.

'You see, our young lord was, we suspect, trying to find out certain... state secrets for the purpose of selling them to our enemies. Most notably, the Bolsheviks.'

Eleanor gasped. 'I can't believe Xand— I mean, Lord Taylor-Howard would do such a thing! Be a... a spy, I mean. And sell state secrets to... well, the enemy?' *But why not, Ellie? You only met him briefly. And you've been fooled before.* A brief image of her ex-husband flashed before her eyes.

Sir Percival was regarding her closely. 'Which is why, you'll now appreciate, I can't have the civilian police investigate. There is bound to be a leak somewhere. Despite his earlier incompetence, I am not suggesting the leak will come from the chief inspector. But further down the ranks someone won't be able to resist selling what they know to some newspaper hack. And then we'll have all of Fleet Street down on our backs. And I can't use my men because... because I believe there may be a similar problem.'

Eleanor bit back a laugh. *How ironic, Ellie, after his scathing attitude towards the civilian police.*

Sir Percival took a few more puffs of his cigar, the heavily scented smoke hanging in the air. 'We have had several leaks in the royal police recently. We're investigating, but haven't found the culprit yet. And we just can't take the risk with this matter. So we need an outsider. Someone like yourself, Lady Swift. Someone who works alone. Someone who no one would suspect of being involved in such an investigation. And, further-more, you will work directly through me so only you and I will know the truth as it is unearthed. And therefore only you, or I, could leak it. And if you do, Lady Swift, I will have you locked up in the Tower of London for longer than you can ever imagine.'

Eleanor went to reply, but Sir Percival held up a hand.

'Lady Swift, if you won't do it for King and Country alone, then do it for Lord Taylor-Howard at least.'

She stared at him. 'What do you mean?'

'Prove me wrong by finding who killed him and why. If it had nothing to do with his being a spy and selling state secrets, then you will have vindicated him in death, ignoring his few ill-advised liaisons and gambling debts. Prove me right, and you will have saved the royal family from a scandal that the country cannot afford at this crucial time.' He strode back to the desk and reached inside the manilla folder and pulled out a single sheet bearing a neatly written list. 'Unless I misjudged you, and the supposed Henley sense of justice died with your uncle, you'll start immediately, naturally.'

She sighed. 'Naturally.'

'Good. I have a list of names here of our most likely suspects.'

'Why most likely?'

'Lady Swift, Lord Taylor-Howard's wayward behaviour has naturally resulted in him having enemies, a number of whom could potentially embarrass the royal family. I created dossiers on each one in case I needed to intervene. I confess, however, I did not actually imagine one of them would go to the lengths of murdering Lord Taylor-Howard. Still, I have cross-referenced this list with the list of people present before, during and after Lord Taylor-Howard's death, given to me by the chief inspector. Any appearing on both lists who had the opportunity, means and, most importantly, motive, I have transferred to this list.' He tapped the paper in front of him. 'And not meaning to teach you to suck eggs, Lady Swift, but that makes them prime suspects.'

She nodded. 'No, you don't have to teach me to suck eggs

when it comes to murder, unfortunately. And, yes, I agree, that does indeed make them front runners.'

'Right.' Sir Percival skimmed the paper across the desk to her. 'There will doubtless be more names added as I unearth additional information my end, but for now first off is a certain Lady Montfort.'

She looked down at the name at the top and glanced at Clifford. He raised an eyebrow to show he had not heard of the lady in question. She noted that Sir Percival didn't miss the exchange. *We're not going to get much past him, Ellie.*

Sir Percival grunted. 'Lady Montfort is married to Lord Montfort, who holds the post in the cabinet of First Commissioner of Works. He is responsible for crown and government land and property, except the royal family's personal possessions. Anyway, Lord Taylor-Howard had an affair with Lady Montfort and then left her for another conquest. Not the only lady he did this to, for sure, but the only lady he did it to who was in the tent before his death.'

Eleanor nodded. 'So her motive would be one of revenge? Unless, of course, her husband—'

He shook his head. 'Her husband has been aware of the indiscretions for some time and never taken any action. He was also not at the regatta at the time of Lord Taylor-Howard's death, so the investigation is limited to Lady Montfort. Next up.' Much to her annoyance he rapped the next name on her list with the baton on the desk. 'Sir Roderick Rumbold. Lord Taylor-Howard openly slept with his wife and Sir Roderick is known to have a quick temper. Again, there are other cuckolded husbands, but none except him who were in the tent at the right time to have been able to poison Lord Taylor-Howard's champagne.'

'Understood.' She quickly glanced at the third name on the list and read it out before Sir Percival had a chance to take her eye out with his wretched baton. 'Bartholomew Darnley?'

'Ah! Mr Darnley. He is Lord Taylor-Howard's cousin. And now Lord Taylor-Howard is dead, Mr Darnley inherits Lord Taylor-Howard's money and estate. It's not much compared to some, but there is a generous monthly allowance, as I said, and somewhere more prestigious to live than where he currently resides. Also, Mr Darnley may have had another motive... but I have run out of time. Everything is detailed on the list you have. I assume you'll get started this afternoon and report back to me tomorrow or the day after at the latest? Speed is of the essence. As is discretion.' He rose. 'This meeting is now over.'

9

Right now, Eleanor yearned to be home with her soppy bulldog, her favourite house pyjamas, and nothing better to do than squabble with her butler over something inconsequential. Instead, she followed the head of the royal police towards the marquee where she had all too recently watched a man die.

At the entrance, Sir Percival stopped and swung around.

'Lady Swift, I fail to see why this is necessary. My men have already examined the tent for any evidence. This is merely a bootless drill.'

She looked to Clifford for a translation of what she assumed was a military term.

'A futile exercise, my lady.'

'Ah, thank you.' She gestured politely for Sir Percival to stand aside. 'Then to answer your question, in women's terms, visiting the crime scene separates the Mary Janes from the Oxford lace-ups.'

Sir Percival rolled his eyes and glanced grudgingly at her butler.

'Orders one's thoughts, Sir Percival,' Clifford translated.

Sir Percival snorted. 'Just get it over with. And be discreet.

Remember, my men are ignorant of this being a murder case. To their knowledge, I have merely granted you special permission to pay your respects at the scene of death to assist you in your grief.'

After nodding to the young soldier guarding the entrance, he turned and strode off.

Eleanor took a deep breath. Stepping back into the tent felt even eerier than she'd been dreading, even though she knew Lord Taylor-Howard's body had been removed.

Clifford distracted Gladstone with a handful of treats and stepped to her side.

'Are you alright, my lady?'

With an unconvincing nod, she walked up the steps onto the stage. She stopped and rubbed her hands over her cheeks.

'Right, Clifford, please can you scribble in my notebook?'

He produced it from his inside pocket and flipped it open to face her.

'If by "scribble" you mean emulate a three-legged spider crawling over the page after being dipped in ink, sincerely I am not sure I can.'

His mischievous humour went a long way to soothe her frayed nerves. 'Just write down what we both remember then.'

He drew a plan of the stage across two clean pages, making her smile as he added precisely paced out distances, the design of the table, and even the joins of the floor's wood-boarding.

She closed her eyes briefly and counted on her fingers. 'So, there were six officials.'

'I noted seven, if you will forgive the correction.'

'Actually, you're correct because the portly chap was in the middle with three others either side. Yet none of them are on Sir Percival's suspect list. Why not?'

'My lady, Sir Percival is His Majesty's right-hand man for security and, as such, was intimately acquainted with Lord Taylor-Howard's actions, habits and... ahem—'

'Proclivities.' She threw her arms out at his sharp tut. 'It was only to save you having to say it.'

'Thank you. Sir Percival's initial deductions, based on his knowledge of the ins and outs of Lord Taylor-Howard's life and who would profit most from his death, are a mystery to us. However, even though I may not admire Sir Percival on a personal level, he is known to be extremely thorough in his methods. Therefore, I imagine he found no evidence to suggest any of the officials on stage had a motive to murder Lord Taylor-Howard.' His brow wrinkled as he glanced from his hand-drawn map to the back of the tent. 'Unusually, there is no exit within the marquee's rear side at the back of the stage.'

'Why is that unusual?'

'Normally, there would be one for fire and medical access. I assume there was no rear exit to aid security.'

'So whoever poisoned Lord Taylor-Howard's champagne had to have entered the tent by the front. Which means they would have been seen by everyone, including security.'

'Which suggests, my lady, our poisoner has strong nerves.'

Eleanor's forehead furrowed. 'How do we know the poison wasn't administered prior to the champagne being brought into the marquee?'

'Champagne can be poured in advance, my lady. However, given the intense heat of the day, I am sure it would have been uncorked and poured only a few minutes at most before it was served.'

'Maybe it was just served warmer and flatter than normal, if they were pushed for time, say?'

Horror flicked across his face. 'My lady, a gentleman, royal or otherwise, who professed a love of champagne as proudly as Lord Taylor-Howard did, would not have accepted it if it had been' – he shuddered – 'warm or flat. And no regatta official would have dared present such to a distinguished guest of honour.'

She smiled. 'Fair point. And we can easily check if the bottles were opened before they reached the marquee. But assuming for the moment that they were not, that means our killer only had a short window to get the poison into Xander's glass.' She whistled softly. 'I think you're right, Clifford. I think we're dealing with someone with nerves of steel. I—'

The soldier on guard outside stuck his head in through the flap. 'Everything alright, miss?'

'Perfectly, thank you. A few more minutes alone and I shall feel a great deal better.'

'Right you are.' His head disappeared.

'Perhaps expediency needs be our modus, my lady?' Clifford whispered.

'Hmm.' She went to the back of the stage. 'The thing that's really bothering me, Clifford, is how on earth could our killer have been certain he had poisoned the correct glass?'

Clifford nodded appreciatively. 'How on earth indeed? From all the glasses on the tray, how could the murderer predict which glass the guest of honour would be given?'

She wrinkled her nose as her eyes strayed to the area behind the scoreboards. 'We'd best tackle...'

In truth, the bare stage floor where the dead man had lain was less upsetting than she had feared. As Lord Taylor-Howard had been poisoned, there was no bloodstain on the wooden boards or other ghastly reminder that a man had been murdered there. Clifford flipped up his jacket tails, dropped to his haunches, and began scouring the floor through his pince-nez, shining a pencil-thin torch back and forth. After a moment, he seemed satisfied enough to remove one glove and run the flat of his hand over the surface, still shining the torch.

She hunched down beside him. 'Wait! Do that again.'

He swept his hand back over the same spot. 'Nothing there, my lady.'

'No, look. There!' She held her hand out for the torch,

smiling as he cleaned the end with his handkerchief before handing it over.

'See! Along the edge of that scoreboard.'

He craned forward to peer more closely. 'Hmm, it looks like two fragments of glass. Possibly from Lord Taylor-Howard's champagne flute, which shattered when he fell. They were obviously caught under the scoreboards when Chief Inspector Seldon had them moved across the stage to shield Lord Taylor-Howard's body from the crowd.'

'Oh, dash it!' She sat back on her heels. 'I thought I'd found something useful.'

Clifford glanced sideways at her. 'Uncharacteristically defeatist, if I might suggest.'

'But Sir Percival told me that he has already sent some remains of the flute away to be analysed.'

'Indeed. However, with your permission, and your significantly smaller fingers, I believe we might at least collect the pieces as a souvenir.'

'A souvenir? Of what? Xander's passing? Because, honestly, that sounds rather macabre.'

'Nevertheless, my lady, if you would be so kind?' He braced a leg on either side of the scoreboard and rocked the weight back an inch.

She reached out. 'Got them!'

They stared at the two pieces of glass in her hand.

'That domed-shaped bit looks like part of the base of the champagne flute, Clifford, and that long sliver – which is perilously sharp by the way – looks like part of the middle crystal-cut section. I can't see that they reveal anything. Nor' – she looked at him quizzically – 'that they are much of a souvenir.'

He took the second piece at her nod and held it against the white of his gloved hand. 'I think you will find, if you shine the torch carefully, that there is in fact a scratch.' He pursed his lips.

'It is nothing tangible, regrettably. But I respectfully suggest we should take these and—'

'Lady Swift!' Sir Percival's bark echoed from the tent entrance. 'Have you finished' – he glanced behind him where the young soldier's outline could be seen outside – 'er, grieving?'

She quickly put the other piece of glass into the handkerchief Clifford held out, nodding that this would remain their secret. Sir Percival would probably only dismiss their find, as he had already sent pieces of the flute to be analysed. She stepped out from behind the screen.

'Thank you, Sir Percival. I have now!'

10

'What on earth?' Eleanor paused in ruffling her bulldog's heavy head in her lap and stared at the elaborately dressed shop window just ahead of where Clifford had parked the Rolls. 'This is not at all what I expected.'

'Really, my lady,' Clifford said impassively. 'Might one enquire what exactly you did expect to find at an establishment entitled Madame Vermeer's Gowns?'

'Given that we are here so I can grill the first suspect on Sir Percival's list, the evidently married fiftyish Lady Montfort, something far more... frumpy, I suppose.' She slapped her forehead. 'But that was rather blunt-witted of me, wasn't it? Sir Percival's information suggested that she and Xander are supposed to have been—'

'Well acquainted,' he said quickly.

She chuckled, still staring at the shop. '*Extremely* well acquainted. As in our naughty royal was precisely acquainted with what she's hiding under her Madame Vermeer gowns.' Catching how much her butler was repeatedly running a finger around his starched collar, she nudged his elbow. 'Sorry. But it stands to reason that she must be at least well-preserved enough for someone like Xander to be interested in her.'

Clifford reached behind his seat and retrieved *The Times* newspaper, meticulously folded open at the society page. He tapped a photograph with his leather-gloved forefinger.

Eleanor peered at it, wide-eyed. 'Oh, my! She's gorgeous. Dash it!'

He eyed her sideways. 'Problem, my lady?'

'Well, of course there's a problem, Clifford! Just look at her and then at those amazingly elegant gowns in the window. If she's the kind of clientele they're used to, I'll stick out like a stung nose.' She stared down at her sage jacket and unfussy skirt in panic. 'It's not my kind of style at all.'

'And how might your style be defined, my lady? Purely for future reference so one might source a more suitable establishment should you finally refresh your wardrobe, that is.'

His mischievousness got the better of her unease. 'Practical and comfortable, thank you! But, don't get excited. I shan't return with any bags of purchases, just artfully weeded-out information on our first suspect on Sir Percival's list – the jilted lover.'

'If you say so, my lady.'

The genteel ding of the shop's bell was as muted as the pastel pinks and blues of the luxurious decor. Dominating the marble-floored reception area was a deep-buttoned velvet-covered front desk with a gold telephone and appointment book. Two uphol-stered upright chairs sat on the clients' side along with the long-est, pale-rose chaise longue she'd ever seen, whispering of languid moneyed ladies who lunch lightly. A floor lamp in the shape of a Greek goddess swathed in the folds of a porcelain gown threw out a soft golden glow. Three red-carpeted steps with a single gold-painted swirling balustrade led up to a wall of thickly pleated ivory damask curtains.

She stepped around to the chaise longue to better admire the eye-catching backdrop of the silk wallpaper. Symmetrically dotted with fine ladies regaled in every conceivable elegant pose, she traced a mesmerised finger over the first few.

'May I help you, madam?' a soft voice said behind her. Eleanor spun round. The assistant blushed. 'Forgive me, I'm quite new to Madame Vermeer's so I haven't had the pleasure of serving you before.'

She tottered back behind the desk in her demure heels and smartly tailored suit and ran her finger down the open page of the appointment book. Something in the young woman's sweet demeanour allowed Eleanor's shoulders to relax.

'Well, it's my first visit so you wouldn't know who I am.'

The woman looked up. 'Oh, then you're Lady Swift! Goodness, welcome, welcome.'

Mystified why her name should be known, Eleanor took a seat as the assistant excused herself and disappeared through the curtains. Eleanor shook her head. She hadn't made an appointment. So how...? *Clifford! Of course! He's booked you in, Ellie. Ladies don't just wander in off the street into a boutique as chic as this.*

The young woman reappeared with a small gold-coloured tray bearing a tall glass of rose water and the tiniest coffee Eleanor had ever seen. At the sound of the shop bell, she bobbed another apology and hurried over to open the door.

'Lady Montfort, good morning.'

Eleanor hid a smile. She had to give Sir Percival credit. His information was accurate. His dossier on the suspects had included their daily movements and schedules, and here was the jilted lover right on cue.

Lady Montfort waggled a finger at the receptionist. 'Alice.

Try a subtle dash more rouge, dear. Remember boys love a woman to radiate health as well as confidence.'

'Good morning,' Eleanor said, trying not to stare at the new arrival. It seemed she failed.

Lady Montfort nodded to her. With effortless grace, she folded her Aphrodite-perfect silk-suited form onto the chaise longue and crossed one shapely ankle over the other. She looked Eleanor over, her dark eyes shining as brightly as the crown of her coiffured chocolate curls.

'And good morning to you, my dear. I haven't seen you in here before, but I can promise you we are going to have fun. Alice dear, please see that we are in adjoining booths. I think I shall have the added delight of shopping for two this morning.'

'Absolutely, Lady Montfort,' Alice said with evident glee. 'Lady Swift, what a lucky thing your appointments coincided.'

Eleanor smiled sweetly. 'So lucky, I'm sure.'

Just then, the curtains parted with a dramatic flourish. 'Ladies!'

Lady Montfort rose as if pulled on an invisible string. 'Ah, here is our couture master.'

Eleanor gawped at Madame Vermeer, whose neat black beard above a pastel-blue silk shirt and bold geometric-patterned cravat was not what she was expecting. She too stood up and tried to act as if she did this every day.

'Ladies,' their host cooed, 'come, come. My boudoir of treats awaits your hungry à la mode appetites.' Looping a manicured hand through each of their arms, he led them up the steps with all the reverence of a groom escorting two trembling brides.

A moment later Eleanor was staring at her reflection in confusion. The large private-curtained booth the so-called Madame Vermeer had left her in, was lit by vanilla-soft wall sconces, the light bouncing off the three walls of floor-to-ceiling mirrors. A silver-plated rail of silk, satin, ruffs, trains, tucks and pleats stared back at her; her clothes lay in a heap on the pink velvet chair. Her face fixed into a frown as she surveyed the scene around her. She'd planned on waylaying Lady Montfort with a few well-placed questions about her relationship with a certain minor royal, not ending up in nothing but her underthings.

It was, however, almost an hour and several glasses of champagne later that Eleanor remembered again that she was supposed to be grilling her companion. Despite her initial horror at being paraded around like an exhibit at a zoo – and a less than fashionable one at that – the luxurious fabrics that now hugged her slender frame made her feel like a princess. An à la mode princess, something she'd never felt before.

She sat back on a smaller blue chaise longue and shook her head at the next glass of champagne she was offered.

'Nonsense,' Lady Montfort said, with a wicked glint in her eye. 'Shopping is fabulous, but shopping with fizz is even better.'

She handed Eleanor a glass and took the other. Eleanor tutted to herself. It was like being back with Tipsy. *Perhaps when Tipsy gets older, Ellie, she'll turn into Lady Montfort?* The thought made her laugh.

Leaning on one elbow, Lady Montfort smiled, making her already beautiful face exude an extra vitality that a woman of her age really shouldn't have.

'What's your secret?' Eleanor said before she could stop her runaway tongue. 'I mean—'

'You mean' – her companion took a dainty sip of champagne – 'how do I manage to look years younger than I am?'

'Yes. Not that one is supposed to mention such things, I'm sure.'

'Nonsense! We women can't have secrets from each other. Hence my offering you a few fashion tips, dear. But to answer your question, I have fun. Lots of exquisite, delirious, delectable fun!'

Eleanor laughed again, feeling quite light-headed. 'Now that I like the sound of! So much more enticing than a bathroom filled with astringent ointments and a wardrobe bursting with corsets.'

'Instruments of torture.' Lady Montfort adjusted her position as if to better show off her model figure. 'Anyway, there are superior ways to keep one's curves in perfect order other than those old-fashioned things. So many women create their own curse of wrinkles, worrying over the passing of time rather than filling each moment of it with everything they desire. We none of us know how long we have' – she waved an airy hand – 'so make the most of every minute, I say.'

Eleanor seized the moment. 'Like Lord Taylor-Howard? Poor chap. Perhaps you heard the tragic news?'

Lady Montfort's eyes narrowed. 'Of course, I've heard.' She put down her glass and arranged the sweep of orange silk folds enveloping her legs. 'But Xander wouldn't want me to mourn. He was bursting with life.'

'Gracious, forgive me. You were well acquainted then?'

'You could say that.' She stared forward with a dreamy look. 'Now *he* was lots of delicious, delirious fun. And very good for the figure.'

Not expecting such candour, Eleanor blushed.

'Oh, never be bashful about such things, dear,' Lady Montfort said. 'There is no sense in you having been blessed by Titian's muse if you're going to be awkward about the realities of life.'

'I'm not awkward about them.'

Lady Montfort tapped Eleanor's empty ring finger with a perfect nail. 'Unmarried at your age. And unbetrothed too, I conjecture.' As Eleanor frowned, she continued, 'My dear girl, if only you'd accept it, you have the power to entrance all men, just as I have.'

'Surely not all men. What about if he's in a different class? Say a royal, like Lord Taylor-Howard?'

Lady Montfort tutted. 'There's no difference. It's no secret, for instance, that Xander adored me.' She picked up her glass and took a longer sip of champagne. 'For a while.'

'Oh? You must have been upset when he stopped feeling that way.'

Eleanor didn't miss the jerk of her companion's shoulders.

'Not a bit. Dalliances are only fun if they're spontaneous. Serendipitous.' Lady Montfort leaned in and whispered, 'And passionately stimulating. They are supposed to fizzle fast.' She laughed, but it sounded forced to Eleanor's ears. 'Between you and me, I was a little too... much for him. These younger men rarely have the stamina to keep up. I let him down gently, of course. Boys are so fragile in the ego stakes, even those who ooze self-possession like Xander.'

'I'm glad you had fun,' Eleanor said. 'I only met him briefly, but he struck me as a chap with a plan to take life on and win on his terms.' She paused. 'I did wonder if he knew something about his health though, since he seemed to be almost fighting to live every moment as if it was his last.'

'The very attitude he couldn't resist in me, dear. But as to the poor boy's health, I have no idea. We didn't talk about such things.' She smiled. 'We didn't talk much at all, but he certainly appeared to be in fine health!'

'So you've no regrets about him?'

Lady Montfort choked on her champagne. 'Why on earth, would I? We both knew what we were doing. And I'm sure when you're a little more advanced in years like I am, that you too will see the attentions of such a gorgeous specimen of honed youth as an extra feather in your cap. Or fascinator.'

'Well, it's good you've managed to move on so easily. For a moment, I thought I'd put my foot in it by mentioning him.'

Lady Montfort waved a dismissive hand. 'Not at all. Naturally, one has moved on. Men like Xander understand precisely how it works. As do I. You see an irresistible bauble and you play with it until you see the next. My ego is not so fragile as to need to pretend there weren't others among his conquests.'

'Ladies of more years than his, you mean?'

'Oh no!' Lady Montfort's voice held more than a hint of pride. 'That was my domain alone. But a fair few younger beauties, who are also married, fell to his charms.' She smirked. 'Some of them, I'm sure, were merely at it to ruffle the feathers of their husbands.'

So Xander liked to live dangerously, Ellie? Maybe it was a jealous husband rather than a jilted lover who poisoned him?

'Challenged to plenty of duels then, was he? Now I'm picturing Lord Taylor-Howard expertly battling off a raft of enraged spouses. Perhaps yours among them?'

Lady Montfort smiled like a cat with all the cream. 'My dear girl, what would be the point if one's husband *wasn't* consumed with jealousy? But in truth, Xander had more to fear from some of the young women he threw over. That's the problem. Their claws are desperate to have a ring slid onto that second-to-last knuckle.'

Ignoring that only a short while previously Lady Montfort had been criticising Eleanor's single status, she tried to sound casual. 'Anyone in particular?'

Lady Montfort leaned in conspiratorially. 'I was told the last one made a complete fool of herself, silly girl. Said the most unbecoming things about him. And with such vitriol, too.'

'Really? Who was it?'

Lady Montfort's expression turned to horror. 'My dear, tsk, one does not tattle the names of an old flame's subsequent mistakes. You've a lot to learn.'

. . .

'An exceptionally successful visit, I see, my lady,' Clifford said, having carefully loaded her numerous pink-and-blue-striped bags with satin ribbon handles into the boot of the Rolls. He eased the stately car into motion.

'No, it wasn't!' Eleanor groaned. 'I didn't get much at all of use.'

'Forgive my ignorance, but I rather thought the point of fashion is that it is entirely useless.' His lips quirked. 'Otherwise it would be designed for practicality and comfort.'

'Very funny! You know I mean I didn't get much out of Lady Montfort. Other than the most candid admission of an affair any married woman has surely ever given. She positively delighted in telling me a great many more details than I expected. Do you know, she even said—'

'More than it is appropriate for you to repeat to your butler? Yes, my lady,' – he gave her a firm look – 'I can imagine, but only with a shudder.'

'I'll have to tell you the salient points though.'

He swallowed hard. 'If we might at least refrain from such discussion until after luncheon.'

'As you wish. But even Mrs Trotman's delightful fayre won't make it any more savoury to your chivalrous ears.'

11

On the banks of the Thames, opposite a frothing weir, Eleanor stopped outside the simple, yet elegant entrance to the riverside restaurant. Through the glass in the door, she could see rich oak panelling and cosy alcoves.

'You've been dragging your feet all the way from the Rolls. What is it?'

'My lady, really, I must protest—'

She held up a hand. 'Not as much as I must protest at you setting me up to be paraded as the queen of the hopeless wardrobe at Madame Vermeer's. Enjoy a good chuckle while waiting for me, did you?'

Clifford's eyes twinkled. 'I couldn't say, my lady. But assuredly a worthy result if Mrs Butters' animation this afternoon over your purchases is anything to go by.'

'Mmm.' She held her arms out to emphasise the fact that she'd changed back into her old favourite sage-green jacket and matching blouse. 'Clifford, do make sure I'm present when you open the bill from Madame Vermeer's. Better yet, when you enter the numerous and outrageously expensive amounts into the household accounts, since I deliberately bought some extra gowns to teach you a lesson.'

'Touché.' He bowed from the shoulders. 'Artfully won, my lady. In fact, if I might be so bold as to borrow your favourite phrase... dash it!'

Eleanor hid a smile and took another peep through the glass partition at the heavy-set individual with florid jowls holding court on the riverside restaurant's outdoor terrace.

'Is that—?'

'Yes, my lady,' Clifford said, having evidently read her thoughts. He abandoned trying to get Gladstone to sit and stepped up beside her. 'That is the gentleman in question. The second suspect on Sir Percival's list. Sir Roderick Rumbold.'

'The cuckolded husband. The one Sir Percival reckons might have had a hand in poisoning our royal?'

'Ahem. Indeed.' He gestured to a waiter, who hurried over and then nodded at the detailed instructions Clifford delivered. Once she was seated outside in a tucked away corner, but still in good view of their quarry, she flapped her butler into the opposite seat.

'Stop sulking, Clifford. It doesn't suit you at all. Unlike your very smart togs, in which you look every inch the distinguished gentleman. It's a rare treat to see you out of your morning tails.' At his obvious discomfort, she smiled fondly. 'You're too much the gallant knight to ever countenance my reputation being tarnished by my sitting alone in a bar and then approaching a married man like Sir Roderick in public. Thus, there's no choice, since it was either snaring him here, at his regular post-golf reservation, or trying to find a plausible reason to visit him at his office. So, dispense with all butler-mistress formalities and sit, please. Besides, we pretended to be guardian and ward once before and it was good fun.'

'How fortuitous one of us found it so.'

With their drinks served, she plucked a strawberry slice

from the top of her tall glass of Pimm's and lemonade and looked about her. 'It's a good job you've got Gladstone tethered, Clifford, otherwise he'd be chasing those ducks. Wouldn't you, old thing?' She patted his head and then sat back up. 'You know, Clifford, this is absolutely delightful. The River Thames swishing along in front of us and those weeping willows cascading down to the water. Of course, we're not that far downstream from the regatta.'

She stole another glance at Sir Roderick, trying to gauge whether he really would have been capable of cold-bloodedly killing the man who had slept with his wife. *He doesn't look the jealous type, Ellie. But then again Sir Percival did say he's known for his temper.* She took in his green tweed golfing attire; his two younger companions being similarly dressed.

'I can imagine in his heyday, Clifford, he was quite the catch. Strong jaw, intelligent grey-blue eyes and likely a head of thick dark hair, before it started seriously receding as much as his waistline has expanded. Poor chap, time hasn't dealt him the kindest hand.'

'It is not easy for a gentleman in his sedentary business to maintain the healthiest lifestyle.'

'Not when he's also trying to maintain what I imagine is a trophy wife with expensive shopping habits, according to Sir Percival's notes.' She suddenly saw him with more sympathetic eyes. 'Hang on, though, what is his line of business?'

'In broad terms, one might say "communications". The gentleman has many investments in the manufacture of telephone and telegraph apparatuses. He has also recently become interested in wireless radio, particularly regarding its development for domestic usage.'

'Sir Percival didn't mention that, did he?' At his head shake, she stared at him in awe. 'Really, Clifford, you never cease to amaze me with your network of mostly dubious contacts. They seem to be able to inform you of just about everything.'

'Contacts, dubious or otherwise, notwithstanding, my lady, Sir Roderick himself was the one who informed me.'

'You said you've never met him.'

'Indeed not, but I do read the London newspapers. In particular *The Times*, to which Sir Roderick is an avid contributor.'

She frowned. 'So he's a journalist, too. Busy man.'

He sniffed. 'Forgive my contradiction, but Sir Roderick is *not* a wordsmith, which is distressingly evident in his many letters to the editor.'

She smiled at his horror over what he clearly saw as a mangling of the finer points of the English language he held so dear. 'But, Clifford, the editor still prints them.'

'Purely, I imagine, because their controversial tone sells more newspapers.'

'I see. And let me guess. Sir Roderick wrote a stinging letter on...' She paused, shooting the man in question another look. 'On how the wireless radio should be properly deployed to keep the nation correctly informed?'

'Warm.'

'More controversial, then? Oh, to keep the common man correctly informed?'

'Warmer. The common woman.'

She let out a long, low whistle. 'Well, that is a surprise. To my shame, I didn't have him pegged as a champion of women's equality.'

Clifford nodded. 'You are, in fact, correct, my lady. The entire point of Sir Roderick's lengthy letter was to recommend that husbands buy their wives a radio so that they stay in the house where they belong.'

'What!'

'He cited at length how the wireless already provides edifying content to occupy their minds while fulfilling their household duties. Something he believes the average housewife cannot obtain by perusing the society pages in magazines.'

Eleanor's eyes glinted. 'Where his wife is often featured parading about in the company of other men, it seems?'

'Quite.'

Their waiter reappeared with an impressive selection of finger nibbles and hurried away to answer a frantic waving from another customer.

Eleanor surveyed the spread. 'Top-notch ordering, Clifford. Thank you.'

He watched in dismay as she added one of each of the many savoury snacks to her plate.

'The food, my lady, was merely to add plausibility to our being here solely for refreshment. You have, if you remember, recently partaken of a hearty luncheon. If I might reiterate Lady Fitzroy's lesson number two, that an eligible lady is never seen—'

'No, you may not. Because I've decided the man who finally falls in love with me,' she said with a shrug, 'assuming one ever does, will have to delight in having a wife who eats like a horse, if that is the correct expression?'

He sighed. 'Not in polite society, no.'

She waved a cheese and mushroom palmier dusted with finely chopped chives in front of his nose. 'They're really good, you know. But since you've mentioned polite society, I was simply staggered this morning by the way Lady Montfort delighted in telling me, a perfect stranger, about her many... indecorous times with Xander. "Delicious" was the word she used. Quite scandalous.'

Clifford coughed. 'As you informed me before. That established, if we might hurry on to what you unearthed?'

'Well, as I said, she brazenly admitted to an affair with Xander, but was adamant that she wasn't at all devastated when they parted.'

'At the risk of prying, did the lady mention which party was responsible for calling a halt?'

'She suggested she had. She boasted that she'd been too much for him.'

'Plausibly delivered?'

Eleanor shook her head. 'She wasn't entirely convincing on that point, actually. When I dug deeper, she was quick to say that he'd dallied with other married ladies purely to anger their husbands.'

Clifford gave a sharp sniff. 'Disgraceful, if it is true.'

'Ah, that reminds me. The other interesting thing she said was that Xander's last unmarried conquest caused quite the spiteful scene when he threw her over. But she wouldn't give me the woman's name.'

He looked at her as if she were a small child. And one of markedly reduced intellect. 'Naturally, she wouldn't.'

'Hmm, so she admonished me, too. Anyway, she was definitely trying to hide how she really feels about her break-up with Xander. If you want my opinion, I'd say Xander broke it off with her. But whether afterwards she felt melancholic or murderous, I couldn't say at this juncture.'

'Ah!' Clifford gestured discreetly towards Sir Roderick's table, where the two younger men were making their escape. 'Ready?'

'Not a bit. But off you skip.'

'From whom?' Sir Roderick barked at the waiter as he placed a double brandy in front of him.

Eleanor watched the exchange closely.

'The gentleman over... oh!' The waiter looked around the terrace for the now vanished Clifford. 'He seems to have left momentarily, sir. He is with the lady in green. With red hair. His ward, I believe.'

'Oh, very well.'

Sir Roderick waited a few minutes, hoping the mysterious gentleman who had bought him a drink without including his business card would return. Having repeatedly checked his pocket watch, he gave a huff and strode over to her table.

'Good afternoon, miss. My apologies for approaching whilst you are alone.'

'Good afternoon. I'm not offended by your unorthodox approach. If it is well-intentioned, that is.' She smiled demurely.

'What! Well, of course it is. I came to meet the gentleman who sent me this brandy.' He waved the drink.

'Oh, yes. Then sit, please.' She pretended to scan the inside of the restaurant. 'He will be back in just a moment, I'm sure.'

As Sir Roderick reluctantly eased his straining-buttoned form into the third seat, she scanned his face up close. Beneath the deep lines of his hard expression, there was definitely a hint of youthful attractiveness.

'We haven't been introduced,' he said stiffly. 'Sir Roderick Rumbold.'

'Delighted.' She held her hand out, noting that he was displeased at the idea of having to shake it. 'Lady Swift. And this is Gladstone. My guardian sent you the brandy. I'm not sure why, but it may have been something to do with one of your estimable letters to the editor of *The Times*.'

'Oh yes?' His chest puffed. 'Which one particularly, if I might ask?'

'Um... the one on telephones? No, wait... wireless radios, perhaps?'

'Ah! Probably the latter. Obviously a very enlightened gentleman. I'm sure he takes his responsibilities as your guardian most seriously.'

'You have no idea how fiercely he fulfils his duties! Between you and me, I'm lucky if I get so much as a peep at the society pages of his newspapers.'

Sir Roderick grunted. 'If I were him, I would have them removed by the paperboy before delivery.'

'Oh, but they are such an important source of inspiration for us young ladies. And informative too.'

He looked at her with obvious disdain. 'Your guardian is there to pass on any appropriate and essential information.'

'Ah, but therein is my real problem, Sir Roderick. He's so over-protective. He won't tell me anything that might upset me.' The genuine truth of that made her smile as she caught sight of Clifford just along the riverbank, apparently engaged in deep conversation with the family of ducks. 'Like... what's a good example... let me see... oh, like the death of poor Lord Taylor-Howard only yesterday. He was a royal, you know.'

Sir Roderick looked at her sharply. 'Yes, I do.'

'Oh, my apologies. Perhaps you were closely acquainted?'

'No, I was not. I... I did happen to be at the regatta though. But I fail to understand why you feel that the news of his passing should have been imparted to you particularly?'

She tilted her head. 'Do you know, I heard the strangest thing about Lord Taylor-Howard.'

He shook his head. 'The thread of your conversation, young lady, is really quite hard to follow. Anyway, since the man is deceased, whatever it was can be of no import or interest.'

'Probably only to one gentleman in particular.' She held his stare. 'Jealousy is a hard pillow to lay one's head on every night, I imagine.'

Reaching for his glass, his fist balled momentarily. 'I wouldn't know.' He looked around as if tiring of their conversation, but he made no move to leave.

'Really? Because your wife is very beautiful.' It wasn't a lie. There'd been a picture of her in Sir Percival's dossier.

Sir Roderick glanced back at her. 'Wait, you know my wife?'

'I met her recently, actually.' *Okay, that was a lie, Ellie.* 'And as she's a very beautiful lady, it can't be easy watching her receive all manner of attentions from other gentlemen. Especially from notable figures. Someone mentioned even Lord Taylor-Howard himself might have... approached her.' She looked him over. 'You surprise me, Sir Roderick.'

He'd bristled at her open scrutiny. 'In what way?'

'No offence, but, personally, I shall choose a husband who would brook no such behaviour toward me from another gentleman, royal or not!' She lowered her voice. 'Be honest, Sir Roderick, you must be secretly delighted Lord Taylor-Howard is no longer with us.'

Sir Roderick's face turned purple. 'I... well, of all the...! I never said anything to suggest such a thing!'

She leaned back. 'You didn't need to. Your demeanour said it entirely for you.'

Sir Roderick's eyes glinted. 'I pity your guardian, since locking one's ward in the cellar is probably frowned upon in today's over-liberal times!'

'It doesn't stop him wishing it wasn't though,' she said genuinely. 'Honestly, if it wasn't frowned on, I'd be lucky to see the light of day most weeks.'

'I sympathise with the gentleman. Entirely.' He downed the last of his brandy. 'And I think you may be harbouring erroneous notions about life and marriage from those society pages you obviously devour. Marriage is a carriage of convenience in the majority of cases, including mine. I am not jealous about any of my wife's... indiscretions, especially if it was with a royal. Not that I am admitting she had any. But in my position, one's wife being courted by such a figure is nothing more than a feather in my cap. Something, indeed, to boast about down the club. You need to look for a more possessive and jealous man than I to tattle about.'

He rose. She rose too.

'Then why, Sir Roderick, were you in the marquee with Lord Taylor-Howard only moments before he died?'

He stared at her coldly. 'Your guardian, if he ever returns, needs to warn you about your dangerous fascination with other people's lives. I'll satisfy your curiosity this once. I was at the regatta, as I said before. As it happens, I was talking to one of the officials about an upgrade to their announcement system. It is most antiquated. My company is offering to replace it with an up-to-date system. However, I had no knowledge that Lord Taylor-Howard would be there. I did see the gentleman but left before he was announced. Good day.'

She watched him stride away.

Hmm, Ellie. I'd say despite his protestations he is the jealous type. Maybe he did leave before Xander was announced. But did he leave before he was poisoned?

12

'We'll be fine.'

'"We", my lady?' Clifford pursed his lips as he eased the Rolls around a tight bend. 'Please reassure me your next plan does not require my hurling all regard for my position as your butler to the wall again?'

'It doesn't.' She waited for his shoulders to relax. 'But only because I haven't made one yet.' She quickly turned away, hiding a smile. 'Oh, look! This is all rather pretty.' The sheep- and crow-filled fields, and beech- and birch-filled woods had given way to a small village. 'Just look at that half-timbered building there. So unusual.'

'That is a rare example in Beaconsfield village, which we have just entered, of a Wealden construction, my lady. It was built in 1524 for the princely sum of forty pounds at the bequest of the previous rector, Richard Capel. Over the centuries it has been the church house, meeting rooms and is currently used as stables to the rectory. As Hilaire Belloc remarked, "Unless a man understands the Weald, he cannot write about the beginnings of England."'

'Fascinating as ever, but' – she pointed down the tiny high

street – 'a bit rural for the likes of Bartholomew Darnley, isn't it? I would think his pink suit would stand out terribly. I know his address might change now, since Sir Percival said he is the main beneficiary of Xander's estate – which is why we are here – but, surely, he should live in the beating heart of fashionable London, anyway?'

'He would, if he could, I agree. However, it is not uncommon for concerned fathers to dispatch their errant sons to reside in more rural quarters to temper their wilder behaviours.'

Clifford slowed the car down once more. 'Though, the lesson has not yet been learned, it seems. Most especially as it is almost four in the afternoon.'

He waved a leather-gloved forefinger toward a dishevelled young man staggering along the road towards them. He was clad in what could only be the remains of the evening dress he had left the house in the night before. Shoeless, with his bow tie looped around his forehead, his bedraggled hair stuck out at all angles. And the hand he had clamped to his face left no doubt he was nursing a black eye.

'Well, at least it looks like he had a fun time.'

'Right up until he received a rather painful souvenir of the evening.' Clifford gave a sharp, disapproving sniff, but she could see he was concerned about the state of the pathetic figure now hunched over a low wall.

'Clifford, I heard you saying you only want to play the part of my butler. But any chance you might consider whipping your wizard's cape on and help stop our third suspect, Mr Bartholomew Darnley – or Barty to his friends – from expiring before our eyes?'

He tightened his leather driving gloves against his fingers. 'Luckily for Mr Darnley, I do happen to have a gentleman's rescue kit at my disposal.'

'Good. I say, Barty!' Eleanor jumped out of the car and

hurried over to the sprawled form of Darnley, now staring glassily at the sky. She recoiled at the sight of his near-closed left eye, an angry red-and-purple welt framing the socket.

Clifford, having followed her out of the car, slid his hands under the young man's arms, hauling him up. 'This way, sir.' Having heaved Darnley upright, he propelled him along the pavement towards the house at the end of the row. Sir Percival's information told them the young man lived on the top floor. Clifford trailed his stumbling charge along the side path to a tall iron gate. He propped Darnley against his shoulder, deftly picked the lock, and then slid both of them through. She followed, closing the gate behind her.

In front of them an ocean of immaculate green lawn stretched to a distant ornamental pond, the whole scene bordered by perfect flower beds. Against the side of the house, an iron staircase wound up to the top floor. Clifford paused at the bottom.

'Your key, sir?' Receiving only a grunt in reply, Clifford rolled his eyes and slid a hand inside the semi-conscious young man's jacket pockets, then the first of his trouser ones.

'Oi!' Darnley suddenly came to. 'What... what's your game? I'm not into that, *old* man!'

'As you wish, *sir.*' Clifford released his grip, letting Darnley crash to the ground. Seizing a watering can from the nearest flower bed, he sprinkled a generous amount over the dazed young man's head.

Eleanor couldn't help smiling, despite her concern at Darnley's condition. 'You really need to be more polite to my butler, Barty. He's only trying to help you.'

'Bleugh!' he spluttered, shaking his head. 'Who are you?' He squinted at her. 'Oh, white frills filly from the re... regatta. You're the strawberry dessert I never got. And this... this lunatic?' He tried to dodge the shower.

She forced herself to sound uncaring. After all, they were

here to find out if Darnley had murdered his cousin in order to inherit his estate. 'That lunatic, as you call him, is my butler. Now, I believe our work here is done. Good luck with convincing your aunt not to telephone your father.' She turned on her heel.

'Wait!' Darnley looked round in horror. 'No. Mustn't happen. My... my allowance!' He rolled out of the way of the fountain of water and scrambled to his knees. 'How... how d'you know this is my aunt's house?'

Eleanor pointed to the garden. 'Tended begonias, upright chair, Bible on the seat in the wooden pergola.' Actually, Sir Percival's information had told her, but she saw no point in letting on. 'Now,' – she leaned down, her hand held out – 'your key.'

Upstairs in the very bachelor sitting room, Eleanor admired the garden view while Clifford was busy running a bath. Once Darnley was safely sobering up in the water, Clifford applied himself to the mess of clothes, books and unwashed crockery littering the place. A short while later the quiet clink of coffee things behind her made her turn with a smile.

'That was masterful, Clifford, I don't think Barty needs to live with a maiden aunt. I think he just needs a butler like you.'

On cue, the coffee ready, a miraculously clean-shaven and rejuvenated Darnley stood in the doorway, a bag of ice held carefully to his face. Dressed in newly pressed navy trousers and a pristine shirt under a matching waistcoat, he looked first at Clifford, then at Eleanor. 'That green concoction your man gave me is rather—' He swallowed hard.

Eleanor nodded. 'Disgusting. But amazingly effective. I know.'

He stared back at her. 'You're not much like the lady I expected.' He started as Clifford took a step forward. 'No offence intended! I just meant, well, none of the other girls in my set would have given me a hand.' He gestured to his swollen eye. 'Nor the time of day with a shiner like this.'

Clifford opened the double glass doors through to the sparsely equipped kitchen area, allowing him to keep both Eleanor and the man she'd come to question in full view. Muted sounds of cooking soon filtered out to them.

She sat on the leather settee while Darnley hovered on the edge of a dining chair. For a moment he said nothing, then looked up. 'Did you just happen to pass through here, then?'

'Not a bit. I came to talk to you.'

'Oh, I like that.' Too much of the overeager chap she'd met at Henley Regatta instantly resurfaced.

'About Xander, your cousin,' she said firmly.

He folded his arms and stared at the floor. 'Of course. It's always about him. Even when he's dead!' He ran his slippered foot across the rug. 'Poor stupid blighter.'

'Why did you dislike him so much?'

He looked up. 'I didn't dislike him. Not really.' He shrugged. 'It's just that everyone says, well *said*, that I was just a hanger-on. A nobody cousin.' He scowled. 'It's been that way since we were kids. "Here comes Puppy Darnley." Well, maybe that will die as well now.'

'Who started that nickname?'

He laughed bitterly. 'Who do you think? Xander, of course. At boarding school.' He clutched at the plate of bacon sandwiches and hard-boiled eggs Clifford held out. Falling on the food like a starving man, between mouthfuls he said to Eleanor, 'I didn't actually see you as being one to tumble for Xander's charms. You seem more... intelligent.'

That made her laugh. 'I appreciate the compliment, but why would intelligence make one immune to charm?'

'Because I'd have thought a bright girl like you would know when it's fake. When it's honed and practised to nauseating perfection.'

'And why would Xander have gone to so much trouble?' She watched his reaction carefully. 'Wasn't being a royal enough to open every door?'

'And every boudoir he fancied slithering into, yes. This is awfully tricky to talk about appropriately with a girl.' He looked warily at Clifford. 'I mean, a lady, since Xander was the biggest scoundrel on earth.'

Eleanor glanced at her butler. 'Just keep it as decent as you can and I'll restrain my butler from manhandling you again.'

Darnley groaned. 'Xander had the world grovelling at his feet. All the ladies, partying, seats on all the right boards lined up. It got really tiring watching him take it all for granted.'

'I can imagine. But do you think that meant he deserved to die?'

He stared at her, a second sandwich halfway to his mouth. Putting it back down on the plate, he grabbed the glass of water Clifford held out to him. 'Strange question. Do *you* think he did?'

'No. Something took him, though, didn't it, Barty?'

'Now hold up! That makes a fellow feel as if he's under scrutiny.'

'It did seem odd the way poor Xander just collapsed. Had he been ill?'

'Only like I would have been without this hangover cure. He regularly got even more out of his box than I did last night.' He avoided her gaze. 'Maybe the drinking caught up with him.'

'Only you don't believe that any more than I do, do you? Did something else catch up with you last night though, Barty? Or rather someone who's had enough of your... habit?'

He dropped the glass with a shaky hand. 'It's not one I can't stop. Eventually. If they'd only let me be. But wait, how do you know about that?'

She stood up and went to the window. 'That's not really the important question, I'd say.'

'Then what is?'

'Who I'll be forced to tell.' She turned back to him. 'And I don't mean your aunt or your father.'

'Wh— what is all this?'

'Barty, be honest with us. You stand to inherit Xander's wealth now he's dead.'

'Pah! Is that it? Someone has set you up to find out how much I'm worth now. Seriously! Well, not much, I can tell you.' He shuffled forward in his seat. 'Xander's money was all tied up in a trust and it still is.'

'I know. But you still stand to inherit a generous allowance.'

He frowned. 'How did you know?' He shook his head. 'This is all really odd. But alright then, you probably also know that his so-called properties are as good as worthless.'

'Because?'

'Because almost all of them are in hock to some very bad people.'

'Did that have something to do with you getting that black eye?'

'No comment. I... I just got into a stupid fight. Can't actually remember what about. Or who with.' He cast his eyes down, but not before she noticed the look of panic – *no terror, Ellie* – in them.

She shook her head, trying to keep her natural sympathy out of her voice. 'Fights are best picked carefully, wouldn't you say?'

'And what if it isn't your choice to fight at all?' He raised his head, his eyes flashing. 'What if the whole stupid, sordid mess wasn't of one's own making? What if one's blo— wretched royal cousin made life impossible even in death!' Eleanor was amazed to see his eyes fill. 'I... I still didn't want him to die, though.'

'What do you suppose killed him?' she said quietly.

Darnley wiped his sleeve across his good eye with a sniff. 'I... I don't know. But if you really are as clever as you seem, do yourself a favour and stay out of anything to do with Xander. It can't end well.' He put his hand on his stomach. 'Just like I don't feel well, actually.'

'Grief? Or a bad conscience?'

'You decide,' he said, suddenly defiant. 'I'm not Xander's puppy any more. And I'm tired of being yours.' He tapped his head gingerly. 'But my brain isn't so addled from the gin and whisky and' – he waved a shaky hand – 'other things, to see that you're wondering if someone hastened the demise of the glorious Xander Taylor-Howard. But you've called at the wrong place to ask that. The paltry amount I'll gain from his death is nothing but his last laugh at my public expense. You need to find someone who stands to gain a great deal more than me.'

Eleanor nodded to Clifford and rose. 'Look after yourself, Barty. I may be back to ask you a few more questions.' She dropped a card on the table. 'Or you might want to give me a call if you get another black eye. Or worse. Maybe I'll be able to help.'

His nervous chuckle gurgled into his glass of water. 'Maybe.' He gestured to Clifford, who was holding open the door down to the outside staircase for her. 'And next time you come, you can leave him at home.'

Eleanor shook her head. 'No point. He knows where you live. And he can pick your locks.'

13

Back at Henley Regatta, Eleanor was struggling. Sir Percival's temporary headquarters felt stiflingly oppressive in the early evening heat and, in addition, Seldon was seated beside her. And near enough for her to catch tantalising hints of cedar, citrus and fresh soap. She groaned inwardly, wishing her feelings about him weren't so confused. He, on the other hand, seemed oblivious to her presence, his focus being on Sir Percival, who was holding forth.

'We in the royal police have our unique methods and resources.' His beak of a nose flared. 'Which is just one more reason this is not a task the ordinary police shall be involved in, as I've made abundantly clear to you on previous occasions.'

Seldon leaned forward. 'I am in charge of the safety of those who attend the regatta. There is a murderer loose and possibly still on site, which means it *is* my business.'

Sir Percival laughed curtly. 'Only if he kills again and it isn't another member of the royal family, God forbid. And, may I ask, just whom do you suggest he might be lining up as his next target anyway?'

Seldon threw up his hands. 'How am I supposed to deduce that when you are withholding information?'

Sir Percival snapped so sharply Gladstone jumped out from under the table with a growl. 'The reason you don't know is because there *isn't another target*. Lord Taylor-Howard was obviously the one and only, Inspector.'

Eleanor had had enough. 'Perhaps you meant to say "Chief Inspector", actually, Sir Percival?' Ignoring the grumbled response from him and the disconcerted glance from Seldon, she continued. 'It is a good point, though. Suppose Lord Taylor-Howard was just the first. It would make keeping things under wraps so much harder, wouldn't it?'

'Scandal is not an option,' Sir Percival said sharply.

She leaned forward. 'Either way, I'm questioning why I'm sitting here feeling like I'm stuck as the unwilling ball in a grudge match, thinly disguised as a gentlemanly round of tennis. I thought I had been seconded to help find out who killed Lord Taylor-Howard. If that is still the case, please continue. Otherwise, I shall leave you to carry on with whatever juvenile and inappropriate game is being played at his post-humous expense.'

In her peripheral vision, she caught Clifford's appreciative tilt of his head. But Seldon shuffled in his chair, looking more admonished than she had intended since he wasn't to blame. Sir Percival glared at her, but didn't argue.

She nodded. 'Good. Shall we get back to business then? I believe you were about to tell us the results of the post-mortem.'

From the same manilla file he had waved at her last time, Sir Percival slid out two sheets of paper. It was covered in a scrawl so indecipherable it could only have been by the hand of a medical man.

'I was about to tell you, Lady Swift.' Sir Percival shot Seldon a frosty look. 'We've a top-class pathologist chap, not just some seconded police surgeon who—' At Eleanor's look, he cleared his throat. 'Well, anyway, Bromley's had his experienced fingers in every notable corpse.'

'Lucky him,' she said. 'And are we allowed to know the full details of what he found?'

'You are, Lady Swift, but the inspector... the chief inspector will have to leave. I—'

'Potassium cyanide,' Seldon said, almost to himself.

Eleanor bit back a smile at Sir Percival's obvious annoyance. Evidently, he didn't appreciate his thunder being stolen. 'Is that correct?'

Sir Percival harrumphed. 'Yes. Alright, it was potassium cyanide. How did you know, Insp—' He glanced at Eleanor. 'Chief Inspector?'

Seldon's expression held that haunted tinge she'd noticed as he'd cradled the collapsed royal on stage.

'Two reasons. There are not many poisons which have such an immediate and yet masked effect on the body.' His tone softened as he stared at Eleanor. 'There is no need for you to be exposed to any more unpleasantness than is absolutely necessary, Lady Swift.'

Sir Percival waved his hand impatiently. 'Oh, do step down from your chivalrous charger and get to the point, man!'

Seldon eyed him coolly and pointedly turned away to address Eleanor.

'Lord Taylor-Howard initially appeared to have suffered a heart attack, but I noted the flushed colour to his face. His skin seemed quite pink. Not something associated with natural cardiac failure.'

She nodded. 'And just before you caught him, he seemed to be breathing rather hard and swaying like he was dizzy.' She hung her head in sadness. 'I thought the poor chap was struggling with stage fright. That was exactly how I felt the one time I was asked to give a speech. If only we'd realised, perhaps we might have been able to...'

She tailed off as Seldon shook his head gently. 'By the onset of the first symptoms, it was already too late for him.'

She sighed sadly. Gladstone let out a soft whine and laid his head in her lap.

'Then no one should feel bad that they couldn't save him,' she said quietly. 'Especially the only person who rushed to help.'

His deep-brown eyes locked onto hers. 'A kind thought, I'm sure.'

'Um, you said there were two reasons,' she stumbled, trying to hide that she was blushing.

Seldon hesitated. 'With apologies for not finding ready words to soften the image, as I laid his body down, a trickle of bloodied froth dribbled from his mouth.'

Eleanor turned to Sir Percival. 'Why precisely would that particular poison create such an emanation in the victim?'

He waved a dismissive hand. 'Because it does.'

She shared a look with Seldon. Clearly, their pompous would-be puppeteer was not as clever as he wished to appear.

Unable to stop herself from scoring a point for Seldon, she turned to her butler. 'Clifford?'

'My lady, cyanide salts are corrosive, extremely so in a potent dose. Given that the amount administered was significant enough to cause a fatal response in such a short space of time, regrettably, the salts would have—'

Sir Percival slapped the file on the table. 'The only pertinent fact, Lady Swift, is that it is a readily available substance. Anyone present in the tent could have gotten hold of it.'

Seldon flipped open his notebook. 'Then we have a window for the murder to have been committed. Since the poison would have begun its fatal effects within two to ten minutes—'

'Yes, and killed him within fifteen,' Sir Percival said. 'If you will refrain from spouting unnecessary details which our medical expert has already determined.'

Eleanor frowned. 'But that means anyone with a cool head could have spiked his champagne and then easily had time to leave the marquee.'

Seldon nodded. 'Although, I suspect they might have lingered.'

'To watch him die.' She swallowed hard. 'That's so macabre.'

Sir Percival laughed derisively. 'But then murder so often is, don't you find?'

Seldon glared at him. 'I imagine the murderer may have stayed to make sure of the result.' He turned back a few pages in his notebook. 'Whether they left or not before Lord Taylor-Howard died, we do not know at this point. However, we do know the murderer must have been in the tent just before the champagne was served. Now, I already have a list of all those present after Lord Taylor-Howard collapsed and—'

'Then you will surrender it to me forthwith,' Sir Percival barked.

Seldon's frown deepened. 'I will share it with you.'

'Surrender, I said.'

'On what authority? And for what purpose? It is police property, although I repeat, I am more than willing to share the contents with you.'

Sir Percival sat back in his chair and smugly tapped the row of medals on his jacket. 'On the king's authority, of course.'

Seldon opened his mouth and then closed it and shook his head as if to himself. 'Of course. But I might have additional information on your suspects.' He gave Eleanor a pointed sideways glance. 'If I were privy to who they are.'

Sir Percival snorted. 'Like you were privy to the one simple instruction to make sure nothing happened to Lord Taylor-Howard?'

'That was not the brief I received, as well you know. I was given no reason to suspect anything more than a routine police guard was required in case of any unexpected unpleasantness or embarrassment for Lord Taylor-Howard. Had I known that he was involved in nefarious activities—'

'You would have what? Blathered the information to any and everyone?'

Seldon rose to his full impressive height. 'Rank notwithstanding, I will not accept such a slur. Even from you.'

Their host's hawkish eyes narrowed. 'Your presence is no longer required, *Inspector*.'

'I am merely suggesting we cooperate, Sir Percival, in the interest of catching a murderer.'

'I repeat, your presence is not required! I will also be having words with your superior. Now,' –he waved towards the flap that served as the door – 'Lady Swift and I have some additional matters to discuss. And they do not concern *you*.'

Seldon nodded curtly and cleared the expanse of the tent in four exasperated strides. Her sharp ears heard him gruff a few short words to Clifford, who opened the flap and retied it once Seldon had passed through.

Eleanor bit her tongue, wishing it was Sir Percival's arrogant head between her teeth. *Remember, Ellie, you're doing this for King and Country.*

Sir Percival reached into the manilla folder for another, smaller piece of paper, which he skimmed across the table to her. 'The next, and, hopefully, last two suspects.'

'Marvellous.' She looked at the names and accompanying notes. Her eyebrows rose. 'So what motive do they both have for wanting Lord Taylor-Howard dead?'

Sir Percival leaned back in his chair. 'I very much look forward to you letting me know that, Lady Swift. The first, Sergei Orlov, is a Russian spy. He is considered relatively harmless and we let him operate in this country in exchange for one of our own men operating in Russia.'

She opened her mouth, and then closed it. She really didn't

want to prolong the meeting any longer than was necessary and doubtless Clifford would explain the oddities of international spying to her later.

'And why is he a suspect?'

'Apart from the fact that he was spotted in the marquee Lord Taylor-Howard was killed in, he has also been spotted having clandestine meet-ups with him. And, as you will recall, we suspected Lord Taylor-Howard of ingratiating himself with a certain royal in order to obtain titbits he could then sell to the Bolsheviks.'

'Ah! And you think Mr Orlov might have been his point of contact, as it were?'

'Exactly.'

She frowned. 'But what would induce Lord Taylor-Howard to do such a thing?'

She bit her lip as Sir Percival's baton rapped the second name on the list in front of her.

'Mr Treacher, Lady Swift. Our young royal owed him a considerable amount in late payments for gambling debts. You see, Mr Treacher not only runs gambling houses, he also lends money to foolish individuals like Lord Taylor-Howard and then recovers that money along with some hefty interest.'

'And if they don't pay up?'

'Then they are "encouraged" to do so by various methods we don't need to go in to right now. It's all in the accompanying notes. Now, this meeting—'

'Is over.'

It was childish, but she couldn't help herself.

Outside, she took a deep breath, mulling over the new information she'd been given. 'What's your estimation then, Clifford?'

She watched in confusion as he counted on his fingers. 'I should have to say that the score stands at six all, my lady.'

'Dash it! I didn't mean to get caught up in Sir Pompous Percy's relentless combativeness, but he was so awful to poor Hugh.'

'Who demonstrated he is eminently capable of standing up for himself, if you will forgive my articulating the observation.'

'With your unspoken addition that he didn't appreciate me wading in on his behalf, you mean?'

'A gentleman's bruised pride rarely feels soothed at being rescued by the fairer, ahem, gender. And never in public. Especially not in front of a man who is vastly his superior in rank.'

She groaned. 'Noted. Oh, what a rotten mess, Clifford. All my attempts to make things better with Hugh seem to go about as well as a train that's plunged off a cliff.'

'And then managed to defy physics and caught fire in the sea.' He nodded, but his eyes twinkled. 'Chin up, my lady.' He held up her bulldog's lead. 'I'm sure Master Gladstone will help you lick your wounds.'

That made her smile and wince at the same time. 'Quite literally, too. Might my favourite sounding board and distracting chess teacher also be available for a while?'

'I would look for both on our return, but,' – he whipped his leather pocket book from inside his jacket and flicked it open – 'it seems he was planning on working at winning tomorrow's squabbles with his mistress. But perhaps he can squeeze in a game or two in between.'

She smiled. 'Thank you. I'll beat you one day.'

Clifford looked at her in concern as her hand flew to her mouth. 'My lady, are you—?' He broke off as he followed her gaze.

On the other side of the field, among the crowd, Seldon could clearly be seen walking along.

Arm in arm with Tipsy, Ellie!

14

Saturday morning elbowed its way into Eleanor's bedroom at precisely eleven minutes to five. It was at that moment, with the sun rising on the promise of a perfect English summer's day, the dawn chorus so often lauded by romantic poets reached its crescendo. And with her windows left open overnight to capture the little breeze there had been, the birds' carefree tapestry of sound had her hurling a pillow at the fluttering curtains.

She clamped the remaining pillow over her head and groaned. 'Please shut up! It's too early!'

'But not for a soothing headache powder, perhaps?' Clifford's measured tone filtered through her closed door as a neatly folded paper sachet slid underneath.

Scrambling out of bed, she grabbed her robe and wrapped it over her nightdress as she wrenched open the door, only to see his suit tails disappear around the corner. On the marble-topped console table, a silver tray awaited bearing a glass of water, a cup of steaming tea and two ice-cold cucumber slices.

'GAH!'

There was no doubt about it. Unless she gave herself a good

talking to, she was going to find even her ever-thoughtful butler irritating in the extreme today. The problem was that despite Clifford's best efforts to distract her with a series of fiendishly fought draughts matches the evening before, the minute he'd finally bid her goodnight she'd felt desperately alone. Her bedroom had seemed a vast space cruelly designed to increase her loneliness. Her wardrobe a mausoleum of unnecessary frivolities she was sure a certain chief inspector wouldn't even notice her in had she paraded up and down on his desk. He'd likely just reach distractedly round her for his next, more pressing, case file. *Or for Tipsy, Ellie!*

Eventually having flopped onto her bed, her hand had run back and forth over the empty place beside her, unleashing an uncharacteristic river of tears as she'd mourned the impossible. That one day she would fall asleep cradled in his arms.

But this morning, the headache remedy, tea and her own resolve to pull herself together eased her mood soon enough. Even the cucumber slices had worked their magic in reducing her red-rimmed and puffy eyes, topped off with the barest brush of kohl. Or so she thought.

'All good, Clifford?' she said with forced brightness on entering the morning room.

'In truth, only if one were particularly myopic, my lady.'

'Huh?'

She followed his gaze as it slid to her waiting sunglasses, lined up as if part of her breakfast cutlery.

'Oh botheration. I can't get away with anything, can I?' She tried to peer at her reflection in her highly polished knife. 'I guess whoever it was who said that thing about "eyes being the windows of the soul" was as horribly perceptive as you are.'

'Shakespeare, my lady. Although the Roman philosopher Cicero and Sallustre Du Bartas, the sixteenth century French poet, are also often credited with the phrase. Did you enjoy our draughts tournament?'

'Enormously, thank you, although I lost as usual. And I thought we were going to pick up on our running chess battle. Ah! You'd sensed I would be too witless to be an even half-worthy opponent last night, hadn't you?'

'Not exactly, my lady. It merely struck me that a different white knight than that on the chessboard would have been uppermost in your thoughts, thus distracting you from your usual incisive game.'

'Only all night,' she groaned. Then, with a chiding slap of her own hand, she attacked the cheese and bacon soufflés accompanied by generous slices of black pudding. 'However, none of that today. No dwelling at all on the fact that I seem to be the only person I know incapable of getting their life together. I have an interview at noon.'

She glanced at the mantlepiece clock and then set to work clearing her breakfast plate.

As the Rolls drew to a stately halt, Eleanor turned to Clifford.

'Is nothing going to be as I expect on this investigation?'

'One can only conclude that depends on your expectations, my lady.' He tapped his leather-gloved finger on the paper she held, scrawled in Sir Percival's hand. 'Was the clue in the name insufficient?'

'Obviously, since I naturally assumed The Bolshevik Club was some kind of underground society inhabited by those living off backhanders or the intelligence gathered by moles of the infiltrating variety.'

His lips twitched. 'I think you may need to remove your sunglasses, my lady. This is, in fact, the Bowls Hevrick Club, not the Bolshevik Club, since we are in the village of Hevrick. However, you are, for the most part, correct. The Hevrick lawn bowls club is indeed home to backhanders, as that is a technical term for a bowl curved from left to right towards its target by a right-handed player. But moles are most definitely banned, since their burrowing habits play havoc with the bowling green's surface.'

'Alright, clever clogs!'

He shook his head. 'They too are banned, my lady. Only bowling shoes are allowed on the green.'

She gave him a withering look. 'I'm here to interview a possible murderer, not to learn about lawn bowls. Now, get out and help me find our man, you terror!'

'Oh, good shot!' Eleanor cheered from the smart white-painted bench seat on the edge of the green.

The owner of the winning throw turned with a knowing smile. 'Dat vos actually an excellent shot.'

Taken back by his unabashed self-congratulations, she tried to think of a more flattering description for him rather than "the perfect mix of everything average", but failed. He strode over to her, his white flannel trousers and matching blazer accentuating his medium-built frame. He offered her his hand.

'A pleasure, Lady Swift.'

He knows who you are, Ellie? How is that? Given the man's strong Russian accent, she was in little doubt he was the person they'd come to see. She shook his hand.

'Vill you indulge me in taking tea?' He gestured towards a table set apart from the others outside the neat wooden clubhouse.

'A charming invitation, thank you.'

Once they'd sat, she got straight down to business.

'It seems you were expecting me.' She pointed to the card on the table. 'Reserved for Mr Sergei Orlov and guest.'

'Ov course. It iz my buziness to know.'

A smart older lady, dressed head-to-toe in white cotton, set down a tray of tea things with a smile at her host and bustled away.

'And what exactly is your business, Mr Orlov?'

She started as he replied in a flawless aristocratic accent, worthy of King George himself. 'Oh come, come, dear lady. No need for coy games with a man of my venerated calibre. You know as well as I do.' He leaned in and tapped his nose. 'I'm a spy.'

Despite her surprise at his candour, she couldn't help smiling at the cheeky glint in his black eyes.

'Your ability to mimic, Mr Orlov, must be a distinct advantage if you want to play at being someone else.'

He rapped the table with his teaspoon. 'Oh, I never play at anything. I only take part to win.'

'Don't we all.' She stalled, trying to size up the real man behind the many evidently practised layers sitting in front of her.

Leaning back in his chair, he feigned a series of photographic poses. 'I shouldn't bother, my dear. I'm whoever I need to be.'

Something clicked in her memory. 'Like at Henley Regatta! You were a fox-haired gentleman of middling standing who slid out of the marquee after Lord Taylor-Howard collapsed. Conveniently just before we'd all been asked to remain by the police.' *Suspicious or what, Ellie!*

Orlov regarded her with evident amusement. 'Bright-eyed and sharp-witted. He chose well.'

'He who?'

'Sir Percival.'

'How—'

He held up a hand. 'All in good time, my dear. First, let us enjoy the fine English tradition of sipping insipid brown liquid and pretending not to wish it was stiff black coffee, swimming in vodka.'

She laughed. 'Agreed. Well, minus the vodka for me.'

He eyed her shrewdly as they sipped their tea. 'So you are interested in knowing what I know about a certain no-longer-with-us royal person? And perhaps, more pointedly, about his... suspicious death?'

She choked on her tea, and then tried to discreetly fan her scalded tongue with her napkin, hoping Clifford hadn't noticed. In her peripheral vision she saw him at the corner of the club-house, seemingly deep in conversation with one member over the science of throwing a lawn bowl. He caught her eye, his imperceptible nod letting her know he too was surprised by the unexpected demeanour of their quarry, but equally appalled by her lack of ladylike behaviour.

She turned back to the table. 'You really are all kinds of surprising, Mr Orlov.'

'Likewise. As I said, I see now why Sir Percival sought you out for being his backscratcher.'

'His what?'

'Oh, it is just a little one of your English phrases that makes me smile, about men like him. He's too important to do such things for himself.' He sat rigidly upright and flared his nostrils, a beady stare boring into her skull. Again, he had switched persona seamlessly. 'Nonsense! You will do it and my row of medals won't hear of anything less!'

'That's Sir Percival to a tee. You really are an uncanny mimic.'

He bowed. 'I can be booked for parties, weddings and birthdays.'

'I think you missed a vocation on the stage, actually. But how did you know Sir Percival had cantered unwelcomely over my horizon recently?'

He laughed at her description. 'Because like so many other things and events chugging along in your pleasant...' – he tapped his forehead – 'no, *green* and pleasant isle, it is the only reason I am here.' His eyes seemed focused elsewhere as he whispered to himself. 'Except you, *moya dorogaya devochka*.' Snapping to, he shook his head. 'However, Sir Percival is not a man I choose to displease.'

'Any particular reason?'

'He knows too many people who know other people. Dangerous people for me. But how rude of me. One moment.' He gave Clifford a cheery wave. 'Do join us, my friend.'

'Alright, so you've done your homework on me,' Eleanor said as her butler stepped over and stood respectfully to one side.

'Of course. So what would you like to know?'

'What your connection was with Lord Taylor-Howard.'

He tutted. 'Try again. We have no need for foxtrotting around the bushes.'

She laughed. 'For a man who has mastered so many nuances of various English accents, you need to work on your grasp of our idioms.'

'Not a bit. I just enjoy the image.'

'Are you ever serious?'

'Oh, deadly serious when the situation calls for it.'

Clifford stiffened at this, even though Orlov's tone hadn't changed from the jocular one he'd maintained since she'd first sat down.

'Then tell me seriously. Was Lord Taylor-Howard somehow feeding your professional habit, as it were?'

'My professional habit is obtaining secrets, my dear. So, no, he wasn't.'

'Peculiar. Because something our eagle-nosed friend said made me think that is precisely what was going on.'

He laughed. 'I agree, Sir Percival's nose is a nasal protrusion worthy of winning prizes. But, seriously, any such "secrets" Taylor-Howard might have wished to trade to me would have been worthless. He was not a trustworthy gentleman. Besides, it is not the done thing.' He gestured to Clifford, topping up both their teas. 'And I know how important the niceties of behaviour are to members of your hospitable nation.'

She frowned. 'But obtaining secrets is surely the very backbone of being a spy? And why would you find our powers-that-be hospitable? Or are they stupid questions?'

'Not at all, my dear. Because like this supposed haven of sporting prowess here,' – he waved his hand around the bowling green – 'only the actual players in the game are privy to the truth.' He lowered his voice. 'To everyone else, it seems so much more than simply lobbing a wooden ball at a patch of neatly mown grass. But only devotees know the reality.' He looked over both shoulders and then whispered, 'It is a game for people who need nothing more than arms and legs, a set of perfectly ironed white flannels, and the oh-so special softly shoes.'

This time, she roared with laughter. Even Clifford's inscrutable expression flickered momentarily.

'Then how does the game of spying really work?'

He held out his hands. 'Exactly the same. By gentlemanly rules, of course. Your fancy-suited men in authority don't deport me because I stick to the rules, just as my British counterpart does in my beloved motherland of Russia. As with all agreements, there is a code.'

She shook her head. 'It's not like that in spy novels, you know.'

'I certainly do! Aren't they simply captivating all the same? Joseph Conrad. John Buchan. Rudyard Kipling.' He spread his hands. 'I do love that man's name. Rudyard, so unusual. Now, next question, since your man has kindly furnished our cups with more of this watery brown piffle.'

'Why were you in the marquee when Lord Taylor-Howard died?'

'Because I adore rowing, unlike all you English who simply

attend the Henley Royal Regatta to be seen. In Russia, I rowed a lot.'

She wrinkled her nose. 'Sir Percival's men also saw you with him before that, however.'

'Tut, tut, did they indeed?' He shrugged, but his eyes narrowed briefly.

'Yes, several times, in fact.'

'Then they mistook me for someone else.'

'But you knew Lord Taylor-Howard to speak to?'

'Oh, we met at the occasional drinks do or other and shared a polite chuckle over the odd thing, I seem to remember.'

Eleanor folded her arms and shook her head. 'Hmm, definitely wouldn't book you for a party now. Your act falls down quicker than the stage curtain.'

Orlov laughed, a little uneasily this time to Eleanor's ears. 'How you crush me, my dear. Are we done?'

'Not quite. Tell me one honest thing. Did Lord Taylor-Howard seem his usual self when you last met?'

Her companion seemed to genuinely think about this. 'Do you know, it would be impossible to say with any accuracy. He played more parts than I ever do.'

She rose. 'Thank you, Mr Orlov. That's all for now. We may be crossing paths again. Soon.'

As she turned to leave, he called her back. 'Lady Swift, I won't let on that you are investigating on His Majesty's behalf. Your secret is safe with me, I assure you.' He nodded to Clifford. 'And with you, my friend.'

Clifford bowed. '*Dobriy den*, Mr Orlov.'

'Please assure me,' Eleanor said as they walked away, 'that you'll at least consider doing a double act with Orlov. If he turns out not to be the murderer, of course.'

Clifford seemed to consider this for a moment. 'If I get top billing, maybe, my lady.'

15

Back in the Rolls, Eleanor sat staring blankly at the second name and address Sir Percival had given her, balanced as it was on Gladstone's head, who was sprawled on her lap. A long sigh escaped her.

Clifford paused in easing the Rolls out of the bowls club car park. 'My lady, an uncharacteristically swift decline in mood for you, if I might be forgiven the observation.'

'Sorry, I don't mean to be the wet blanket. I just seem to keep falling into the doldrums lately. Tipsy was right, dash her!' She ran her finger down the wider of the sage stripes on her tweed skirt. 'Even the clearly untrustworthy Sergei Orlov has managed what I'm incapable of.'

Clifford arched a questioning brow.

She sighed again. 'I dared not ask because I think I know the answer, but it will only eat me up if I don't.'

'Ask what, my lady?'

'What Orlov said was the reason that keeps him here in England.'

'Forgive me, I was not within hearing distance at that juncture in the conversation.'

'Since you have amazed me yet again by casually revealing a mastery over foreign languages, I hoped you could translate it. He said he was here, apart from the spying, because of... something like *mya doroga devoka*.'

'Ah, yes.' Clifford coughed. '*Moya dorogaya devochka*, my lady, means... my darling girl.'

Gladstone let out a quiet whine and shuffled further up into her lap, as if sensing the ache in her heart.

At her silence, Clifford gently coughed again. 'If I might be so bold? As our next appointment is at no particular time...'

They had just turned into Henley High Street after crossing the bridge over the Thames. Clifford brought the Rolls to a stop a hundred yards further on. Eleanor glanced out the window in confusion.

'What? Ah! Perfect!'

The tantalising aroma of cocoa, nuts and caramel mingling with richly roasted coffee made her feel brighter before she had even crossed the threshold. At the long, polished glass counter, she stared at the chocolates displayed as carefully as art treasures.

'Oh, just look at all those beautiful handmade creations!'

'A pot of coffee for two, please,' Clifford said to the hovering waitress, who was beaming with pride at Eleanor's praise. 'And to accompany your beverage, my lady?'

'The larger of the two chocolate policemen,' she said with a glint in her eye.

'That's the spirit,' he whispered, gesturing her towards an out of the way table, behind a pretty rose-print wallpapered pillar.

Having agreed to take a break from discussing anything to do with murder and matters of the heart, Eleanor was grateful to relax. She sipped her coffee while Clifford related a potted history of how the English had fallen head-over-heels in love with chocolate.

'The offerings of the cocoa plant have been revered since approximately three thousand years before Christ in South America, most notably in Ecuador. It is said that Christopher Columbus introduced it to Europe in 1502, albeit only in his native Spain, after stumbling upon it amongst other commodities his crew had, ahem, sequestered. In 1729, the enterprising Mr Walter Churchman of Bristol petitioned King George the Second for a sole patent covering his water-powered cocoa grinder, which led to England's love of chocolate. And, less than one generation later' – his lips quirked as she bit off one of her policeman's legs with obvious relish – 'galvanised the Royal College of Surgeons to dedicate a branch to studying dentistry as a result.'

'Well, I'm eternally thankful to everyone who had any hand in creating this over the centuries, whatever the ruinous effect on one's teeth. It is beyond sublime.' She smiled at his untouched treat and ruffled her bulldog's ears under the table. 'You softie, Clifford! You can't bring yourself to snap the limbs off the miniature Gladstone you chose, can you?'

Before he could answer, the ding of the doorbell made her look up. Peering around the pillar, she hastily hunched back behind it, gesturing for Clifford to do the same as she pointed at the remains of her chocolate figure. He clamped his hands over Gladstone's ears without a word.

'Ah, yes, please, some help would be greatly appreciated. Thank you.' Seldon's deep voice resounded around the shop.

'No problem. And what is sir looking for?' the waitress asked from behind the counter.

'Um, I don't really know.'

With only a small crane of her neck, Eleanor could see his suited elbow bend to run an uncertain hand through his chestnut curls.

'It's a gift.'

'How perfect,' the sales assistant said. 'I can prepare a personal box for you. What does the lucky lady favour? Caramel? Nuts? Liqueurs?'

'Blast it, I wish I knew.'

Eleanor's heart skipped as she snuck a sideways glance at Clifford, but his expression gave nothing away. Then her stomach rolled over at Seldon's next words.

'But it is for a lady. A *proper* lady.'

As the doorbell dinged once more a few minutes later after Seldon's striding form, Eleanor slapped the table, her cheeks flushed with a mixture of anger and disappointment. 'Is there no end to that man's impossibly irritating and confusing behaviour? Chocolates for Tipsy now!'

Clifford raised an eyebrow. 'My lady, that is possibly quite an Olympian leap in assumptions?'

'No, it isn't and you know it. I saw them arm in arm, giggling away like a couple of schoolchildren. And Hugh is always saying I'm not a "proper" lady because I'm too unorthodox, so it can't be for me.' She held a hand up as he went to reply. Emphatically biting the head off her chocolate policeman, she rose. 'At least I can stop moping over him once and for all. Now, let's go solve the murder he can't!'

The journey to their appointment was a near silent seventeen-mile trip, Clifford only daring to raise his head above the parapet in the last two miles.

'Dare one suggest that our next quarry probably has a signif-icantly less... sympathetic nature than anyone you have yet questioned, my lady?'

'Without getting their head bitten off too, you mean?'

'Perhaps.'

She sighed. 'Sorry, Clifford, you don't need a rollercoaster of histrionics to sour your day. Rest assured, I'm back on track. At least for now.'

'Heartening news, my lady, for this is not a character to be trifled with. I respectfully suggest I accompany you.'

'Naturally. Ah! But this' – she gestured to the Velvet Saloon nightclub on the corner just ahead of them – 'is finally what I was expecting.'

The plain two-storey brick building had no windows, with classical sculptures running the full length of each side of the building. The entrance, also windowless, was flanked by two oversized, matt-black painted columns.

'Mr Treacher, please,' she said genially to the doorman, a lanky chap with a face more gnarled than the thirty years she thought he'd probably seen of life.

He squinted at her calling card, holding it upside down. With a grunt, he slid it into his double-breasted waistcoat. 'Doubt it, but I'll ask the boss if he's here or not.'

'Wouldn't he need to be here for him to answer that either way?'

'Dunno. I'll ask him that too.' He waved them into the club. 'Grab a perch if ya like.'

As he disappeared, Clifford went to dust off one of the black velvet chairs with his handkerchief, but then gave an appreciative nod and indicated to Eleanor that it was, in fact, suitably spotless.

In fairness, she admitted to herself, the club's decor was a notch up from what she'd imagined from the outside. Black-leather upholstered booths occupied two walls, while a line of high-backed stools ran round the central mirror-fronted bar. Through a large archway was a myriad of smart baize-topped gaming tables, the green matching that of the walls. Chandeliers, modernised with electric bulbs, hung low over the tables.

'Lady Swift.'

She spun around, but stilled in surprise at the well-turned-out man making no bones about the fact he was sizing her up. Dressed head-to-toe in an exquisitely tailored green wool suit, he sported not only a smart gold watch chain but also, unusually, a monocle. She found his flawless complexion, fine features and piercing green-blue eyes mesmerising.

'Mr Treacher?'

'The same. But I go by "Fingers" as a rule.' This time she caught the distinct Irish lilt of his accent, underlaid with a toughness that didn't match his expensive suit.

'Ah, so he is here,' she said to the lanky chap who had returned with Treacher.

He shrugged. 'Depends whose asking, dunnit.'

She nodded. 'Of course, it does.' She turned back to Treacher and pointed to her red curls, and then his. 'We with Irish roots are rarely blessed with a great deal of patience, are we, Fingers? Especially when we've been dragged into something we wish we hadn't.'

He grunted. 'So, Taylor-Howard did cop for his sins.' He ran his tongue down the inside of his cheek. 'That'll have whipped the wind up at Buck House.'

She glanced at Clifford in confusion.

'A term favoured in certain circles for Buckingham Palace, my lady.'

She nodded, gathering her wits. *It seems 'Fingers' is as well versed as Orlov, Ellie. He also knows or suspects Xander's death was, in fact, murder.*

'Ah! I see you are well informed. Then, yes, Fingers, Lord Taylor-Howard's demise has, as you say, whipped the wind up at the palace. But elsewhere too, I've heard. One place in particular.'

'No breezes have blown through my house.' He gestured around him. 'Nor past my ears.'

'Of course not.'

'And as I wasn't even at the event in question' – *that was a mighty quick denial, Ellie* – 'I've no idea why you're here asking me questions about it.' Treacher held her gaze, his tone steely. 'So tell your beaky-nosed boss, I didn't kill Taylor-Howard.'

So, he knows about Sir Percival, as well, Ellie. It seems Sir Percival might have been right about leaks in the royal police.

'I know you didn't kill him,' she said sincerely.

He cocked his head. 'And how's it you're so sure then?'

She was sure because Sir Percival's notes had made it clear that Treacher had been the only suspect on that list who hadn't been spotted in the marquee where Lord Taylor-Howard died.

She nodded at the lanky lackey leaning against the wall, rolling a cigarette. 'Because if you had wanted Lord Taylor-Howard dead, you have enough people willing to carry out the murderous deed, without you needing to personally get your fingers dirty.'

He shrugged. 'Maybe. But why would I want the idiot dead, anyway?'

'Oh, because you'd grown tired of him owing you money, perhaps?'

He nodded. 'I had. But he didn't owe enough for me to kill him. Besides, if I'd done for him then he'd never have been able to pay. It's bad for business, killing off the bread and butter. Better to send the boys round to frighten them into paying.'

'Can't hurt to make an example out of a non-paying customer every now and again, though? Especially a high-profile one?'

Something flashed in those piercing blue-green eyes. 'If I had arranged for him to meet an untimely end, it wouldn't have been with poison. That's a woman's weapon. No offence.'

She didn't need to glance at Clifford to know he would have registered that no one had mentioned Lord Taylor-Howard had been poisoned.

'That's where you should be sniffing about,' Treacher added sharply.

'Hmm, sorry, I think I tuned out. But blarney does that to me.'

'It isn't blarney, my girl. His nibs had more than an eye for the ladies and wasn't fussy if they were married or not, either. I reckon you'd better get off and go looking for a husband who didn't appreciate his wife being courted between the sheets by young Lord Taylor-Howard. Or, if you've the time, go ask all the women he dumped. Take you longer than walking the road to hell though, seeing as the list must be mighty long.'

'Oh, Fingers, you're very disappointing. You don't seriously think that isn't the oldest news ever. If that's the best you've got, I'll leave you in peace. But I'm not sure Sir Percival will.'

Her reluctant informant glanced over his shoulder at the lackey and jerked his head. The lad made himself scarce. Once alone, Treacher turned back to her.

'I see you like skating, Lady Swift.'

She wrinkled her nose. 'Haven't tried it much.'

'Then I suggest you take your muscle and go practice because you are on very thin ice, right now.'

'Thanks for the advice.' She pulled out her trump card courtesy of Sir Percival's accompanying notes about each suspect. 'But I know Lord Taylor-Howard came to you the day before he died. Was it to beg for more time to pay you what he owed?'

'You don't give up, do you?' At her head shake, he half-smiled. 'Kind of. He said he'd have plenty of money soon.'

'And you actually believed him?'

'For once, yes, I did. He'd said he'd got into something he could finally make pay. But before you waste your breath, no I don't know what it was.'

She held out her hand. 'We really should do this again. It's been both delightful and enlightening.'

His handsome face broke into a crocodile grin. 'I could put what you've got to very good use, you know.'

She smiled. 'I'll think about it. Good day, Fingers.'

'Lady Swift?' She turned back to him. 'Don't grieve for men like Taylor-Howard. He's not worth it. Men like him, they come and go.'

'And what about men like you?'

He smirked and pulled out an engraved silver cigarette case. 'Men like me, we're immortal.'

16

'Luncheon at four o'clock, Clifford! Tsk, tsk, surely one should forgo such a transgression and settle for afternoon tea, instead?'

'My thoughts entirely, my lady.' He bowed. 'Thank you for ceding to propriety.'

She stared in horror at her butler's retreating back. They'd returned from their trip to the Velvet Saloon only fifteen minutes earlier. She had hastily changed into her favourite wide-legged linen trousers and matching sea-green silk blouse and sprinted down the central staircase with her stomach rumbling. It seemed, however, that her 'joke' had misfired!

Dash it, Ellie! You'll just have to raid the biscuit barrel and the cake tin later.

She sighed and wandered out to Henley Hall's secret, Italian-inspired garden. The weather was glorious enough to dine al fresco.

Hidden on all sides by high box hedging, the many teardrop-shaped flower beds were bursting with exotic palms, lavish ferns, striped bamboo and clusters of dwarf rubber trees. A small bubbling stream flowed down the centre, feeding the fountain at the bottom where Gladstone was drinking noisily. In the middle of the garden was a circular terrace where she was now sitting. The stream ran underneath the terrace, visible through an ornate glass panel thick enough to withstand the weight of the scrollwork table and any associated guests. Although, as Clifford constantly reminded her, there had been precious few guests in the garden or anywhere else at Henley Hall.

As she sat there fanning herself – it was the hottest part of the day with no breeze to alleviate the heat – she ran over her recent meetings with Sergei Orlov and Fingers Treacher. Before she could come to any significant conclusions, she was interrupted by the arrival of her always cheerful, no-nonsense cook with a most unusual accompaniment.

'Mrs Trotman! I've never before had an afternoon tea that requires a silver trolley to wheel it out!' She stared at the row of lidded salvers as Clifford appeared and helped her cook navigate the winding Cotswold-stone staircase down to the terrace. Eleanor shook her head. 'You're an absolute treasure, but I would have happily come inside.'

Mrs Trotman tutted. 'It's a pleasure, m'lady. Nothing brightens the day more than a satisfied customer.' She bobbed a curtsey before bustling back towards the house, humming cheerfully.

Eleanor turned to her butler with an inquiring look.

'I am sorry, my lady. It appears Mrs Trotman misunderstood my instructions.'

He removed the lids of the salvers to reveal beef, venison and field mushroom Wellington, accompanied by roasted button potatoes and chestnuts with flaked almonds and runner beans sautéed in butter.

She tried to hide her smile of delight, but failed. 'Dash it! You got me completely this time.'

He bowed. 'Mrs Trotters and I both feared the biscuit barrel and cake tin might otherwise never recover from the inevitable onslaught were you to bypass luncheon, my lady.'

'Well, for once, Clifford,' she said, tucking into her meal with gusto, 'I don't mind being fooled. And on an unrelated note,' – she nodded as he offered her a serving of her cook's sublime port and plum preserve sauce – 'do you know the question that's running around my head most about Lord Taylor-Howard's murder?'

'Why kill him at Henley Regatta?'

'Exactly!'

'Perhaps because it was easy to blend in among the crowds, creating opportunity and anonymity? And because the killer would have known that Lord Taylor-Howard was going to be the guest of honour for the race results?'

'Both good points. But how did the killer know which glass was Xander's?' She speared a forkful of the runner beans, relishing the saltiness of the butter against their natural summer sweetness.

Clifford thought for a moment. 'Well remembered, my lady. Without that knowledge, it would have been extremely risky for the killer to have been sure to poison the correct glass.'

'And, even if the killer was so cold-blooded as to care little about whether another was poisoned by mistake, he would have cared if Xander wasn't.'

'Actually, my lady, we know the killer wasn't so callous. More Wellington?'

'Absolutely! But how can we be certain of that?'

'If our killer had been that merciless, he would simply have put poison in all the glasses at the table – or at least several – to make sure he got his man.'

Eleanor waved her fork at him. 'And even though I have met such creatures in my travels, as I'm sure you have, Clifford?' He nodded. 'I think you will agree with me that they are thankfully few and far between.'

For the next few minutes, Eleanor concentrated on finishing her meal while it was still hot.

After clearing her plate away, Clifford picked up the conversation. 'The thought has just struck me, my lady, that perhaps it wasn't the event, but the timing that was crucial?'

'An excellent point we haven't yet considered. Let's see if any of our suspects fit that idea better than the last. Well, to start, why would Lady Montfort want to kill Xander at that precise time? I suppose, having bagged a royal—'

'"Bagged", my lady? I did not realise one purchased a royal like an item of shopping?'

She waggled a finger at him. 'Yes, Clifford. "Bagging" a royal is apparently every society girl's ultimate aim, as Tipsy put it. Do try and stay up to date like me!' She avoided his eye. 'And women like Lady Montfort would do anything for the kudos of being the victress who bagged a royal.'

'And, having "bagged" a royal, my lady, might she equally do anything to avenge herself at him "dumping" her as I believe the up-to-date lingo is?'

'If she really loved him, maybe.'

'"What anger worse or slower to abate, than lovers love when it turns to hate,"' as the ancient Greek tragedian, Euripides, put it.'

'I agree with the chap, but why exact her revenge at that precise time?'

They both thought for a moment. Clifford broke the silence. 'Perhaps Lord Taylor-Howard was going to reveal their affair to her husband that evening?'

'Possible. But she gave me the impression her husband would react much the same way as Sir Roderick. He told me he knew his wife had an affair and rather considered it a feather in his cap. Mind you, I didn't believe him.'

He raised an eyebrow. 'Perhaps we need to ask the chief

inspector to investigate our jilted lover and cuckolded husband further before drawing any more conclusions?'

Her brow furrowed. 'Don't mention that man to me after seeing him with Tipsy! Or after that chocolate-shop incident! For the moment, let's move on.'

They paused while Clifford served her a large slice of Mrs Trotman's strawberry and raspberry meringue with lashings of fresh cream. She turned her spoon, staring at the bright-pink fruit juice. 'Heavenly! This reminds me of Barty in his suit at the regatta. I hate to say it, but Tipsy was right again. He seems to try way too hard to be noticed.'

Clifford cleared her dessert plate and offered her a steaming coffee.

'Thank you. Now, we come to Mr Sergei Orlov.' She considered for a moment. 'Perhaps Xander threatened to expose Orlov at the regatta? No, wait. That doesn't work. Xander was supposed to be passing secrets to Orlov, according to Sir Percival's notes, so what would he have to gain by exposing Orlov?'

Clifford nodded. 'And, confusingly, Mr Orlov appears not to be operating in secret.'

She sighed. 'Dash it! I was hoping to rule someone out quickly. Anyway, on to Fingers then. I bet you had the same thought that he, or one of his thugs, gave Barty that souvenir black eye?'

'I did, my lady. With Lord Taylor-Howard dead, Mr Treacher's only means of obtaining payment for what he was apparently owed, was to pass the debt on to Lord Taylor-Howard's successor. And Mr Darnley, I'd wager, is a significantly easier character to get to buckle and pay up under a certain form of persuasion.'

She tapped the table. 'Maybe, but like our other suspects, it still doesn't quite add up, though. If Fingers had killed Xander, then he also killed any chance he had of getting his money directly, which seems—'

'My lady, please excuse my interruption.' Clifford gestured to where Mrs Butters, the housekeeper, was semaphoring from the top step with a duster. 'I believe you have a telephone call.'

'Hello?' she said a little breathlessly into the mouthpiece, having hurried back to the house.

'Eleanor!' Seldon's deep voice barked into her ear. 'Finally.'

She stiffened. 'Good afternoon to you too. You're in a fearful rush, I see.'

There was a pause at the other end. 'Yes, actually. I need to tell you something, but not on this blasted apparatus, since... well, it's something you probably won't want to hear.'

Her heart sank. 'Well, you're lucky I can hear you on this "blasted apparatus" as you put it. It keeps cutting out when I'm on a call. The telephone engineer is apparently coming to correct it. In the meantime, don't waste your time driving all the way out here. If it's something I don't want to hear, just get it over with now.' She looked in the reflection of the hallway mirror at Clifford, who was hovering discreetly. Seldon's next words, however, drew a gasp that had him striding over to her in concern. 'Say that again?'

'Eleanor, for Pete's sake, listen. I think you're in serious danger!'

17

It seemed like an absolute eternity before the rumble of tyres on gravel finally heralded Seldon's arrival. Determined not to seem keen to see him, she stepped away from the drawing-room window. A few minutes later she heard Clifford answer the ring of the doorbell, then a long silence which had her cocking her ear in confusion.

'My lady?'

'Agh!' She jumped away from where she'd been trying to eavesdrop. 'Yes, Clifford?'

'Chief Inspector Seldon is here.'

'Is he?' she said airily. 'Very well. Please show him in.'

He nodded. 'Yes, of course, my lady.'

'Hello, Eleanor.' Seldon stepped into the doorway, his broad shoulders filling the space.

However confused her feelings were about him at the moment, there was no lessening in the way he made her stomach somersault. That he wore his charcoal-grey suit, which set off his athletic frame far too well, was equally unfair. This was going to prove even more difficult than she'd feared.

His awkward smile faded, his overworked face making it

hard to read what he was thinking. Behind him, a very excited Gladstone was eagerly trying to nose him into the room.

'Someone at least wants me to come in.'

'Oh gracious, sorry. My brain is rather full. Please, do come in.'

He waited for her to sit. She perched herself on the edge of one of the long Wedgewood-blue settees designed to fit the curve of the tower. Mirroring her position, he took the opposite one. Gladstone lumbered up to Seldon and flapped a soggy leather slipper in his favourite guest's face.

'You're not helping, old friend,' he whispered in the bull-dog's ear but accepted the gift anyway, holding it away from his suit trousers. 'Eleanor, I'm... I'm here in two respects. Primarily, however, with my policeman's hat on.'

'As always,' she muttered. Not wanting to be churlish or childish though, she quipped, 'I thought policemen wore helmets, not hats.'

His lips twitched into almost a smile. Then he caught sight of his smart bowler hat crushed under the bulldog's heavy head. 'If I was wearing one, it might have fared better.'

'Master Gladstone.' Clifford's measured tone made them both spin round to where he stood with a large silver tray of coffee and warmed fruit cake. 'Stand! Down!' As the bulldog grumpily retreated to the furthest end of the settee with an injured sigh, Clifford gestured to the bowler hat. 'My apologies, I will attend to this.'

Clifford's departure made Eleanor snap to attention.

'Ah, yes. You said you're here to talk about something in your official capacity? On the telephone, you mentioned I might be—'

'In serious danger.' He nodded, his deep-brown eyes looking genuinely troubled. 'But, honestly, I am beginning to wonder when you aren't.'

'A mere misunderstanding. Clifford knows I spend most of

my days engaged in quite deathly dull pursuits.' She shrugged at his disbelieving look. 'Alright, maybe some of them. Now look, what's this about me being in danger?'

Seldon took a sip of coffee and a bite of his cake. 'That feels better.'

'Fruit cake does that to me too.'

'I know.' His cheeks coloured. 'However, to business. Now, you'll roll your eyes and fob me off with your usual casually delivered justifications because you have the peculiar impression that you are invincible. But at least listen to what I have to say. This isn't a joking matter.'

'It never is. Not with you.' She bit her lip and waved a hand. 'Please explain and I'll keep quiet.'

He pulled his leather notebook from his inside pocket and balanced it on Gladstone's head, which had somehow crept back onto his lap unnoticed by either of them. He gave the bulldog's ears an absent-minded ruffle with one hand, flipping through the pages with the thumb of the other.

'Forgive my souring the flavour of our meeting, which would otherwise be set by this really very fine fruit cake, but a person died late yesterday afternoon or early evening.'

'Oh gracious! How sad. I hope they didn't suffer.' She scanned his face. 'Nor you, if it was difficult to—'

'Thank you. Actually, I was not present. The episode only came to my attention by chance when I overheard two of the officers at the station discussing the call. Evidently, a lady went to check if anything was amiss next door on hearing something unusual, only to have her nephew drop dead in front of her.'

'How awful. That poor woman.'

'It happens. Anyway, the aunt contacted the police who sent someone round, but he concluded all signs of death pointed to a heart attack.'

Eleanor caught her breath. 'And you didn't agree? Or rather your intuition didn't agree as you weren't at the scene?'

He nodded. 'It felt wrong. Honestly, I fear it might be a little too much mixing in the wrong company.' She shot him a look, and he coughed. 'But either way, something didn't sit right, so I sought out the officer. He related everything to me.' Seldon waved his pen at her, shuffling forward as far as Gladstone's bulky form would allow. 'As well as a few other observations, the officer said the person's face was unusually flushed. So, I asked him to check for poisoning.'

'I bet he was surprised?'

'More like miffed, actually. No one likes someone coming behind them, highlighting possible errors.'

'Is that so?'

'Yes. However, back to the point of my visit. The results came back positive. Potassium cyanide poisoning.'

She gasped. 'The same as Xander!' She thought for a moment. 'A coincidence, do you think? Sir Percival said it was a common substance. Is it a common murder weapon, though?'

'Not so common as to occur within forty-eight hours of another incident, committed only ten or so miles from the first.' A muscle in his jaw twitched. 'But since Sir Percival won't release his list of suspects to me, all I've got to go on is my list of people who were present in the marquee when Lord Taylor-Howard died.'

'And is the second murdered man on that list?'

'Yes. A Mr Bartholomew Darnley.'

'Barty!' she cried just as Clifford returned with more coffee and cake. 'Clifford! Barty's dead.'

'Tragic news, my lady. Sincerely.' Clifford was clearly more moved by the news than he would normally show. He scanned her face. 'May the young gentleman rest in peace. Safe at least in the knowledge he need no longer worry about receiving more vengeful black eyes.'

'Nor how to hang onto the last of his allowance.'

Seldon coughed. 'Hello?'

She turned back to him. 'Sorry.'

'No problem, Eleanor. But I gather from your reaction that this Darnley person was a suspect in Lord Taylor-Howard's murder, then?'

'Yes.' She reached across to the comfort of Gladstone's soft ears, still sprawled as he was along Seldon's lap. 'I... I'm shocked. And horrified that another man has died so young.'

'It doesn't get any easier. I wish it did.'

Suddenly aware of how close to his body she was, she blushed and sat upright.

'Clifford and I went to his lodgings. He is... was Lord Taylor-Howard's cousin.'

'And the main benefactor of said gentleman's will, Chief Inspector,' Clifford said. He looked down at the tray he was holding. 'One moment if you will, I shall find something more fitting.'

He returned with two glasses and a bottle of port.

Eleanor shook her head. 'One for all of us. You included. Despite you frightening the wits out of him, I think Barty really appreciated what you did for him.'

Seldon accepted his drink. 'What did you do for him?'

Clifford's usually inscrutable expression faltered. 'Her ladyship and I might have taught the gentleman a lesson, albeit distressingly too late.'

'Enough said. Now I pity the poor chap even more.' Seldon looked between Eleanor and her butler. 'But why do I wish I'd been there to see it?'

Clifford having returned with a third glass, a sombre toast to Darnley was made.

Seldon's brow furrowed as he regarded his notes. 'One moment. When were the two of you teaching a lesson to the now deceased Mr Darnley?'

'Yesterday afternoon. About... Clifford?'

'Five and ten past six, my lady.'

Seldon shook his head. 'Just as I feared. The murderer struck only an hour later. Don't you see? He may have seen you there. He might not know that you are investigating Lord Taylor-Howard's death, but nevertheless, I mean...' He threw his hands up and turned to Clifford. 'Blast it! Can't *you* do something to stop your mistress running headfirst into danger every day!'

'I try my best, but—'

'Yes. He does.' Putting her glass down, Eleanor took her notebook from Clifford. 'So, Chief Inspector, what was the other thing you came to tell me?'

Seldon looked confused and hurt. 'What happened to Hugh?'

She looked away quickly. 'I'm not sure.'

They both turned sharply as Clifford cleared his throat. 'If you will excuse me a moment.'

After his departure, there was an awkward silence, broken by Seldon.

'Eleanor, I'm sorry.' He shot a glance towards the open door and then lowered his voice. 'I genuinely don't know how to fix whatever is wrong between us. But one of us has to broach the subject, because this is exhausting.'

She couldn't bring herself to look at him.

'Oh, for Pete's sake, Eleanor, help a chap out here. You're confusing every day. But lately... I've been totally lost.'

She spun around. 'Me confusing!' Not trusting her tongue, she bit her bottom lip so hard it made her wince.

His face fell. 'Yes, you are confusing.' His tone was softer than she'd ever heard him use. 'Stand in my shoes a moment. Last time I was here, you moved heaven, earth and everything beyond to make sure I could stay here and convalesce over New Year, after you...' – his hand strayed to his chest as his face paled – 'you saved my life.'

That brought back that sickening feeling she'd had when she thought she'd lost him forever.

'It wasn't just me... Hugh. Clifford did just as much. And the others that were there.'

'But you were the only one that held my hand all that time in the hospital before I came to.'

'Actually,' – she wrinkled her nose – 'you were delirious. That was Clifford's hand.'

'What!'

'Joke.'

'With terrible timing.' He let out a long breath. 'You *are* impossible!'

'So you said then, too. Well, on coming round.'

'Well, it's my turn for terrible timing. Blast it! Why do I always end up talking about such indelicate matters as death, or near death, with you, Eleanor?' His hand shot out. 'Don't answer that.' He sighed. 'Look, I need to explain—'

'Ah! So you *have* come to tell me about what's been going on then!'

He stared at her as if they had just met. 'See, now I've fallen back down the blasted mineshaft! One sentence and I'm lost in the dark. Again.' He looked her in the eyes. 'Whatever I've done to upset you, Eleanor, I'm sorry. But truly, aside from having this excruciating conversation with you, I have never been in so much pain as when I was here last with a bullet wound in my chest.' His tone softened. 'But despite that, it was still the most wonderful New Year's. Ever. And the most special.'

She nodded. 'I thought so, too. But somehow, almost imme-diately, we went straight back to—'

'Floundering.'

'And fighting.'

Neither of them could find the next words. Finally, she decided it was now or never.

'Hugh? It's my turn to blather on.'

'Blather! Really, is that how you saw my best opening efforts just now?'

'No.' She see-sawed her head. 'Maybe a little. But you did better than I would have done. I'm even more hopeless at this kind of thing.'

'I know,' he said, then quickly followed up with a small smile. 'Joke!'

She took a deep breath. 'Look, Hugh. Please be honest with me. Why were you with Tipsy at the regatta?'

'Tipsy?' He looked genuinely confused. 'Oh, you mean your Lady Fitzroy? She came to report her handbag had been stolen.'

'To you? That was a job for a constable, not someone in your position.'

'Absolutely. But she asked for me personally, apparently.'

'She did?'

'Yes. I had no idea what it was about or who I was expecting to see. I just got a message to go urgently to the lost property tent!' He shook his head. 'What was the problem with that, though? She's your friend, I thought.'

'Me too. I mean, she is. But, you two were... *you were arm in arm*, Hugh!'

'Don't remind me!' He tugged uncomfortably on his jacket collar. 'My men have had endless mileage out of that. It's been a wretched nightmare. She grabbed my arm and failed to register everything I did to shake myself free.' Looking up at her, he paused. 'Oh, no! Tell me you didn't think...'

She nodded.

'Well, that's rich! After I saw you kissing that blasted chap at the very same regatta!'

She blushed. 'I... I tried to explain. He just leaned across and kissed *me*. He's a "Bright Young Thing" or whatever they're supposed to be called. He thought it was harmless fun.' She hesitated. 'I'm... I'm sorry, Hugh. I realise it probably looked bad.'

'Like me and Tipsy arm in arm?'

She nodded again. 'I imagined the worst. Why wouldn't I?'

Unexpectedly, he laughed. 'Why? Someone like her would never be interested in someone like me.'

'What! Someone incredibly courageous. Kind. An unbelievable gentleman and... and dashingly handsome.'

He looked stunned. 'That's honestly what you think? Of me?' His beaming smile faded. 'But then, why would you imagine I would... I mean, Eleanor, that's unthinkable. I would never...'

She stared at his deep-brown eyes, seeing only sincere anxiety.

'I realise that, Hugh. Now. I'm so sorry I distrusted you. It's... it's not you. Since my parents' disappearance and then my... my husband – well ex-husband now – lying to me about... well, everything, I...' She opened her eyes and looked up at him. 'I've been a fool. I should never have doubted you.'

He sighed with relief and reached under his coat and held out a beautiful rectangular box, a green velvet ribbon tied over the delicate mint-and-cream print of seashells. 'Likewise, Eleanor. A peace offering and sincere apology.'

'A gift?' she breathed.

His cheeks burned. 'Only chocolates. I couldn't work out what to buy a *proper* lady who has everything. But I asked for them to be picked out for you. The intention goes far deeper than the box.' He smiled. 'Although I did ask for a good few layers to be included.'

'Hugh, chocolates. Really?' Her heart pounded. 'From Henley High Street?'

'Ah, so you've seen the shop. They really are excellent.'

She smiled at him through the happy tears swimming behind her lashes. 'I know. I bit the head off their chocolate policeman recently.'

18

Eleanor tightened her grip on Gladstone's lead as she wafted the young guard to one side. 'Please don't add to the tiresomeness of all this. Sir Percival said he would only be free to see me at this hideous hour. And it might interest you to know that I have an excellent memory and I'm sure I haven't seen a clock this early on a Sunday for as long as I can remember!'

'Nor any other day, in fact,' Clifford muttered as the man hastily held the tent flap aside.

'Good morning, Sir P— oh, I do apologise!' She rubbed her forehead where it had collided with something firm but familiar. And tantalisingly arousing. 'Ah! Chief Inspector.'

Clifford quickly took Gladstone's lead from behind her back before her bulldog revealed she and Seldon were more than vague acquaintances by launching into the exuberant greeting he reserved for the policeman.

Eleanor meanwhile put on her best frown. 'Please excuse me. I have an appointment with Sir Percival. What are you doing here, by the way?'

'Aside from being given the usual runaround.' Seldon

pulled his eyes back from throwing Sir Percival a pointed look. 'I was, in fact, leaving.'

'I had no idea you were working on the investigation into Lord Taylor-Howard's murder now.'

'I am not. Nor will I be. That has been made abundantly clear. I was here regarding another matter. One which does not concern yourself, Lady Swift. Good day.'

Sir Percival snorted and turned his back as he bent over the drawers of his roll-top filing cabinet.

Seldon gave her a quick knowing smile, which she returned before he left the tent. She recalled their conversation from the night before. He'd looked pensive, but she'd been adamant...

'Hugh, we need to tackle this together. I know up to now we haven't due to Sir Percival and... and, well, our silly misunderstanding. But we're both on the same side, after all. We both want justice done.'

'That's part of the trouble, though, isn't it? You're working for Sir Percival, whose brief is to stop any scandal affecting the royal family. And I'm working for the police, whose job it is to bring the guilty to justice.'

'Surely they can be the same thing?'

'Not necessarily, Eleanor, as you know. Let's be honest here. Sir Percival is under orders to cover up any hint of scandal. Even if it means—'

'The killer not being brought to justice?'

'It wouldn't be the first time, I'm sure.'

'I know. I've just been trying to ignore it. But look, we know what has to be done.'

'Find Lord Taylor-Howard and Mr Darnley's murderer.'

'Exactly. And then, well, I suppose all we can do is leave it up to Sir Percival and the royal family to decide what's done with them.'

'It sticks in the throat, but yes. And, you never know, maybe they'll decide they can put the killer on trial without risking any scandal. So how do we proceed?'

'We work together and do whatever it takes to solve Xander and Barty's murders. You know we make an excellent team.'

'True, Eleanor, but I can't reconcile my conscience over you being—'

'Involved with anything even resembling death or murder? Me neither, trust me. But, Hugh, they were both younger than I am, yet someone took their lives. I'll never forgive myself if I don't try and get justice for them.'

He'd nodded resignedly. 'Though it doesn't sit easily, I do appreciate that, Eleanor. But Sir Percival mustn't get wind we are working together. I don't trust him. Not in regard to doing his job. In fact, the opposite. *Because* of him doing his job. And doing it religiously. The truth is, I fear he is quite willing to put your life in danger if he sees it necessary.'

She'd smiled reassuringly, but at the same time remembered Clifford's sombre words. 'From experience, I agree. Sir Percival was known during the war for his bravery and highly successful missions. They were, however, also highly costly in terms of lives!'

'Lady Swift! Are you paying attention? I don't intend to repeat myself.'

Pulling herself back to the present, she bit her lip, reminding herself that she was doing this for King and Country. 'Yes. I am. So, what news have you got for me?'

Sir Percival frowned. 'That is my question to you, Lady Swift.'

She smiled frostily at him. 'Well, Sir Percival, I do expect you to be doing your part too, you know. But I suppose I can go first.' She regarded her notebook. 'Let's see, Lady Montfort

confirmed her liaison with Lord Taylor-Howard and unconvincingly insisted she ended it. I believe she does hold a grudge
against Lord Taylor-Howard, but whether it is one strong
enough to lead her to have killed him, I can't say as yet.'

Sir Percival grunted. 'Fine. Next.'

'Sir Roderick also confirmed his wife's liaison with Lord
Taylor-Howard and, equally unconvincingly, tried to convince
me – as well as himself – that he was proud of it. Again, I got
the distinct impression that he was lying, but have no idea yet if
his pride was wounded deeply enough for him to have killed
Lord Taylor-Howard.' Before Sir Percival could ask her to go on
to the next suspect, she jumped in. She wanted to keep Darnley
to last. 'Sergei Orlov denied outright that he would ever have
accepted any secrets from Lord Taylor-Howard as he thought
him untrustworthy. Although he did not actually confirm they
had been offered in the first place. Orlov is definitely not telling
me everything about his relationship with Lord Taylor-Howard,
so I need to dig deeper. And Mr Treacher was happy to tell me
that Lord Taylor-Howard did owe him money, as we suspected.
According to Mr Treacher, however, it would have been poor
business practice to kill him. And if he was going to, he
wouldn't have used poison, which he pointedly insisted was a
woman's weapon!'

Sir Percival nodded curtly and wrote a few notes on the file
in front of him. 'And what did you learn from the Darnley
person?'

Her eyes narrowed. *Why didn't he mention Barty was dead,
Ellie? He must know.* She tried to keep the frown off her face. *It
seems Hugh is right. He isn't even going to warn you there's been
another death!*

'A sobering lesson,' she said genuinely. 'But for our
purposes, I learned that he had received a beating. Someone
doesn't like Mr Darnley. Or they were merely warning him of
the consequences if he didn't play ball. I need to investigate

further to find out which. What I really need to know for certain, however, is just how much Darnley stands to gain from his cousin's death.'

Sir Percival waved one hand as he wrote a few more lines. 'I shouldn't bother. Mr Darnley is off the suspect list.'

'Oh.' She feigned surprise. 'How so?'

He scrutinised her face before replying. 'Because he is dead, Lady Swift. However,' he continued as he rose, 'his death is of no interest to you. Focus on the remaining suspects.'

This time she couldn't help frowning. *So he did mention Barty was dead. But he failed to mention that it might have been murder. You need to force his hand, Ellie.*

'So it seems the chief inspector was correct about the murderer being likely to strike again.'

Sir Percival snorted. 'Lady Swift, I have no reason at this moment to believe Mr Darnley's death is related to Lord Taylor-Howard's. I will make sure, however, that this unexpected development does not reach the ears of the press. And I expect you to do the same. Our meeting is concluded.'

As they exited the tent, Eleanor turned to Clifford.

'I never mind a walk, but as we've a busy day, I really don't see why you had to park so far away from the main part of the regatta.'

Clifford said nothing until a few minutes later when she went to step into the Rolls. 'Perhaps, now, my rationale might be more evident, my lady?' He nodded towards the back seat.

'Hugh!'

Seldon smiled at her. 'Eleanor. I have to be quick. Sir Percival's men will be doing their rounds all too soon and we cannot be seen together, as you know. Now we're working together, I just wanted to keep you up to date and tell you what Sir Percival told me before you came in. Despite my sharing my findings on the poison being the same as the one that killed Lord Taylor-Howard, he insists there is no reason to suppose they are linked.'

She nodded. 'He basically said the same to me. But that's good news, isn't it? It means he can't object to you investigating Barty's death.'

Seldon shook his head. 'You'd think so, wouldn't you? But he says it's under his jurisdiction because Darnley still had connections to the royal family.'

Clifford started the Rolls. 'Why in reality, Chief Inspector, do you believe he is interested in investigating Mr Darnley's death?'

Seldon shrugged. 'I'm not sure, but I think he may be trying to control the investigation into Darnley's death to avert an even bigger scandal than he suggested to us previously.'

Eleanor threw up her hands. 'Which is exactly the same as admitting that the two deaths are linked!'

Seldon nodded. 'I agree, but in the end, though I dislike him personally – and his methods – Sir Percival is working to protect the king, as well as the rest of the royal family, and I have to respect that. But somehow I need to find a way around him regarding Darnley's murder. His methods are too slow. He's so fearful for the royal family's standing – which I fully understand – he's too focused on keeping everything completely under wraps and out of the eyes – and ears – of the papers.'

Eleanor nodded. 'I know. Every time I want to strangle him, I remind myself that he is doing vital work.'

'Most admirable, my lady,' Clifford said. 'And, Chief Inspector, have you any more news?'

'Absolutely. It's only been a short while since I learned of Darnley's death but with some careful probing, I have got as far as discovering none of the four names you gave me last night seem to have a cast-iron alibi for the time he was murdered.' He peered at his notebook. 'Lady Montfort, Sir Roderick Rumbold, Sergei Orlov and' – he shook his head – '"Fingers" Treacher.'

She tutted. 'Now, Hugh, you gave me the lecture last night about how every policeman in the area knows Fingers and how dangerous he is. Anyway, I'm off to see Lady Montfort again now. I'll see what I can winkle out about her movements around the time of Barty's death, as well as anything else incriminating. I just need a moment to change, since I can't just bump into her again at Madame Vermeer's Gowns.'

Seldon wiggled a finger in his ear as if he hadn't heard correctly. 'Gowns? For Lady Swift? The one sitting in front of me wearing the same green—?'

She held up her hand. 'Don't you start with the Miss Havisham stuff, or we might not be able to remain friends, Chief Inspector!'

Seldon's cheeks coloured. 'I liked the one you wore to the regatta. The white cake creation.'

She folded her arms. 'Clifford, did you pack a big enough spade to help the chief inspector extricate himself out of the very deep hole he's just dug himself?'

'Regrettably remiss of me, my lady.'

'A shame.' She tried not to smile. 'You do know Tipsy picked that one out for me?'

Seldon groaned. 'Don't mention that woman to me! In fact, keep her away from me at all times.'

Eleanor pouted. 'Don't be unfair. She means well. But I think it's best we do keep you away from her.'

Seldon nodded. 'Definitely! And now, I'd better go since Sir Percival delighted in telling me again he's going to be having words with my superior.'

'Oh, Hugh! Not to suggest promotion, I'm guessing?'

'Why, Lady Swift, your powers of deduction really are sharpening. But don't worry, my boss is no fan of Sir Percival either. But that won't stop the man for long. He'll simply go up the chain of command until he finds the ear he needs to keep me out of it all.' He stepped out of the car, looked around, and then ducked his head back in. 'Remember what I said about Sir Percival being more concerned about doing his job than your safety. Be careful, Eleanor. And for Pete's sake, heed Clifford's cautions for once. Please!'

19

'Yoo hoo, sweetie!' Tipsy waved both sets of fingers as Clifford eased the car to a stop at the exit gate. She sashayed over, ensuring the azure silk of her dress accentuated her enviable figure and leaned on the sill of Eleanor's now open Rolls' window. 'Where have you been? I know I said you needed to get out more but I didn't mean without me. Or at least, not without some handsome plaything on your arm.' As Eleanor went to reply, Tipsy sighed theatrically. 'Don't tell me you haven't snared one yet!'

Eleanor rolled her eyes. 'Hello, Tipsy. It's lovely to see you. But no, I haven't even tried to snare some poor unsuspecting chap. I've been back at the regatta to, er, enjoy a few hours watching the racing on the water. I'm just off home.'

This was met with a peal of giggles. 'Please don't get any less hilarious, Eleanor. You are simply too irresistible to be with. Now, who have you grasped recently, sweetie?'

Out of the corner of her eye, Eleanor caught Clifford's silent sniff. 'Um, no one. Why?'

Tipsy slapped her arm. 'Don't be mean. Best friends are

supposed to share. Why were you coming out of Sir Percival Westlake's tent a while ago then?'

'Oh, no particular... hang on, how did you know that is his tent?'

Tipsy's big brown eyes widened. 'Everyone knows Sir Percival, silly. He's the head of royal police. Apparently he's looking into Xander's death.' She leaned forward and lowered her voice. 'Something about it being suspicious. Can you believe it?'

Not wanting to lie to her friend, Eleanor merely shook her head.

'So?' Tipsy leaned in further and lowered her voice. 'Did you find out any gossip from Sir Percival?'

At least that was easier to answer. 'No. No gossip at all. He knew my late uncle, you see.'

Tipsy gave an exaggerated yawn. 'Just boring stuff then. Sweetie, thirty-one and unmarried is all too few sips of fizz away from the ghastly 'S' word.' She lowered her voice. 'Spinsterhood, darling!'

Eleanor thought back to the flutter Seldon's parting smile had given her only minutes ago. 'Tipsy, you need to accept I'm a little different and—'

'Your invisible beau? Is that it?' Scrutinising Eleanor's face, Tipsy waved a weary hand. 'Alright, alright. Then I shall call round later at three. Make sure there's plenty of champers, we have an absolute mountain of work to do.'

'By all means, come this afternoon. But to work on what?'

'*You,* silly! And I'm the girl to do it.' She swung her long glossy tresses over her shoulder. 'Tootle-ooh.' She turned and held her arm out to a dapper-blazered chap who had clearly been hovering a short distance off. 'Come on, Robbo, let's go get this party started.'

As they strolled away, arm in arm, Eleanor eyed her butler sideways. 'Tell me, how well are your plans for me joining polite society holding up, Clifford?'

'I really couldn't say, my lady.' He winked. 'But only because they are currently on fire in the litter bin over there. Shall we?'

Through the glass partition of the riverside restaurant, where she had observed Sir Roderick previously, Eleanor now watched Lady Montfort flip through a copy of *Vogue* magazine out on the terrace. A waiter passed with a tray filled with all manner of tantalising pastries, reminding her how hungry she was. Once again, she'd had nothing to eat but a picnic breakfast on the way to meet Sir Percival.

Behind her, she heard Clifford order a coffee and a small fruit salad.

'I can't work on an empty stomach,' she grumbled as he stepped up to her side.

'Nor convince Lady Montfort that you are genuinely seeking fashion advice whilst attacking a plate of pastries, perhaps?'

'Oh, stop it.' She tugged awkwardly on her neck scarf and then the silk frills of her Madame Vermeer mint-green tea dress. The skirt hung in soft folds, which highlighted her slender hips more than she was quite comfortable with.

'You look perfect, my lady. Good luck.' Slipping her a copy of *Vogue*, he melted away.

'A Parisian knot needs to hang precisely three fingers in front of your left shoulder, dear,' Lady Montfort called to Eleanor's back as she passed, apparently engrossed in *Vogue*'s fashionable must-haves.

'Sorry?' She spun round. 'Lady Montfort! What a surprise.'

'Oh, don't play coy, Lady Swift. It doesn't suit you.' Eleanor's quarry looked her over with the fiercely critical eye of a race-horse owner. 'Unlike the dress I picked out for you at

Madame Vermeer's. That suits you to perfection. Besides, it was inevitable.'

'What was?'

'That you would seek me out.' She ran an elegant hand along each of her perfect collarbones, framed by the ivory ermine trim of her chocolate silk suit, which matched her coiffured curls perfectly.

A waiter appeared bearing a ludicrously small coffee and an equally small bone china boat of artfully displayed fruit. He hovered uncertainly.

'Yes, Frederick, Lady Swift will join me. We need a fashion conference.'

For the next few minutes Eleanor sipped her coffee and tried hard to pretend she regularly ate fruit not in pastry. At the same time, she dipped back and forth through the magazine, pointing out various outfits she genuinely liked.

'No, dear. Really,' Lady Montfort said a moment later, brushing Eleanor's hand away again. 'Your tastes are...' She shook her head.

'Eclectic?'

'Misplaced. There's no other word for it. You're beyond striking and yet you're determined to smother all your best attributes in all the wrong fabrics, colours, and' – she tapped a manicured nail on the photograph Eleanor had turned to – 'designs. Men don't have much imagination, dear. Our job is to tantalise them with a sneak preview of our feminine blessings, whilst appearing decorously attired to the rest of the world. That's why it's such fun. Oh, and you simply have to look more irresistible than all the competition.' She tilted her chin. 'Like I do.'

Eleanor speared a sliver of strawberry, wishing it was a hearty slice of black pudding. 'For who? Men like Xander. Or Barty?' Over the rim of her coffee cup, Eleanor watched Lady

Montfort's face carefully. 'You must know, Barty. Xander's cousin. Bartholomew Darnley.'

This was met with a shrug, but only after the briefest of pauses. 'I know of him, but never met him. Obviously neither noteworthy nor dashingly edible.' Lady Montfort turned back to the magazine and became engrossed in the list of London fashion events.

Suffering a few forkfuls of apple, which she thought would have greatly benefitted from being cocooned in a moist sultana sponge or drenched in custard, Eleanor tried another tack.

'I must attend some of those wonderful shows. Have you been to any recently?'

'Dear girl, I am invited to them all.'

'Then you must have been at the' – Eleanor tried to read upside down – 'Savoy's Celebrating Eve in Silk last night. Was it too divine for words?'

'An invitation does not mean one chooses to attend.' The look accompanying this made it clear no further explanation would follow.

A while later, Eleanor had grown tired of trying to be subtle. It was almost as exhausting as the impossible-to-remember list of fashion tips Lady Montfort had moved on to regaling her with.

'And you epitomise that Parisian chic so perfectly. And effortlessly,' Eleanor said. 'Like in this photograph.' She delved into her handbag. 'I confess I cut it out as a reminder of what I'm striving for.' She placed the society-page cutting on the table.

Lady Montfort smiled. 'Ah! Royal Ascot horse races.'

'And that's Sir Roderick Rumbold beside you, isn't it? I bumped into him here, funnily enough. I didn't realise you were close.'

Lady Montfort's tone never faltered. 'We attend many of

the same functions, naturally. He's a great patron of all things that will enhance his communications business.'

'How would Ascot races have any bearing on the radio advancements he mentioned to me?' She already knew the answer, Sir Roderick having told her.

'Because potential investors haunt all the prestigious events. Honestly, dear, where have you been? Locked in a cave?'

Eleanor crossed her fingers behind her back. 'I liked Sir Roderick. He was, er, very honest and forgiving.'

'About what?'

'Oh gracious, I didn't mean to tattle. Perhaps you're not aware that Xander might have paid some attentions to Sir Roderick's wife?'

'Dear girl, it would be a shorter conversation to ask me who I know that did not succumb to Xander's attentions.' Lady Montfort's tone remained light, but the briefest hint of anger flashed in her eyes.

'Well, I for one dismissed the rumours the minute I'd met you at Madame Vermeer's.'

Lady Montfort frowned. 'Why?'

'Because you said the domain of Xander's dalliances with, er, ladies of more years than his, was yours alone.'

The cupid-bow lips in front of her pursed into a thin line. 'I might have forgotten about Sir Roderick's wife.'

'Easily done,' Eleanor said nonchalantly. 'But I'm learning from you. Now I see that it was entirely fair that you took up with Sir Roderick when Xander dumped... sorry, I mean left you.'

Lady Montfort regarded her with a guarded look. 'I never said I was... intimate with Sir Roderick. I did, however, say at Madame Vermeer's that *I* dropped Xander.'

Eleanor smiled. 'Of course, silly me. Anyway, when I met Sir Roderick, it struck me there was a very passionate man behind his intelligent green eyes.'

'Grey-blue,' Lady Montfort corrected. 'And yes, he's passionate, intense and adoring.' She sat back and regarded Eleanor shrewdly. 'It seems there is no point in my playing coy with you either. Sir Roderick and I are more than acquaintances. In fact, the reason I missed last night's fashion show was because I was delighting him with a private one of my own.'

20

'Don't you ever tire of being able to pick up anything new at the drop of a hat?' Eleanor hissed as she tried to balance her weight across the width of her shoulders, while trying to remember which was her leading hand and which her trailing one.

'Actually, my lady, I am not a stranger to the golf course.'

Eleanor looked around. The sea of gently undulating green all around her was broken only by the occasional patch of sand or "bunker" as Clifford informed her the correct name was. A long ribbon of water split the course in two, while on three sides distant beech woods lined the perimeter. The fourth was dominated by the club house, an imposing black-and-white Tudor mansion.

'Really? I thought you were more one for pitting your wits against a wily fish than a small hard ball that deserves every whack it gets.'

'You mean the disgracefully ill-mannered ball that has so far outwitted your every attempt at hitting it?' His eyes twinkled. 'Actually, some years ago, his lordship had a seasonal affection for the sport. Hence my familiarity with the correct technique.'

'A fair-weather golfer? Uncle Byron? Surely not after all his international adventures.'

'His lordship's seeming caprice was not due to the weather, my lady. More that he was an exceptional player and reduced his handicap so expeditiously, he soon ran out of worthy opponents each season.'

'Except you, I have no doubt.'

He shook his head. 'I learned the game to the point where I could caddy for his lordship, but rarely beat him.'

'Well, give me a moment and I'm sure I'll unearth my natural aptitude. I bet it runs in the family.'

She took another swipe at the ball, making Clifford tut as she showered him in muddy grass. Then he frowned in concern as the club slipped out of her hand and hit her ankle with a crack that made them both wince.

'Perhaps you would prefer me to teach you fishing, my lady?'

She rubbed her ankle vigorously. 'For the sake of my ankle and your very dapper and vividly patterned jumper, perhaps.'

He brushed the dirt off his front. 'Well, since you so kindly insisted on purchasing it for me from the clubhouse shop...' He left that hanging with a withering look.

She bit back a smile. 'I only made you wear it so you looked the part.'

'Bravo, my dear,' Clifford shouted across to her on the course some time later. 'A hole in twelve. Excellent progress.'

'Not to your four, it isn't. I don't think you're teaching me properly,' she called out loudly.

He strode over with the flag and lowered his voice. 'Sir Roderick is on the ninth tee just ahead, my lady. Might I respectfully request we hurry along this torturous charade of my being your guardian again?'

She pretended to hum and haw for a moment, and then, at his pained look, relented. 'Oh, alright. Let's bag our prey.' After Lady Montfort's admission of her affair with Sir Roderick, they'd agreed that the next step was to get Sir Roderick to confess to the liaison. And then to quiz him about his where-abouts at the time of Darnley's death, as well as anything else of use they could shoehorn out of him. The first essential, however, was to get him on his own.

'But why can't I play at the same time?' she whined loudly over her shoulder to Clifford. 'I'm sure this nice gentleman won't mind. Each of our balls is marked, after all. We can play around each other.'

'What on earth!' Sir Roderick jerked up from placing his ball on his tee to glare at Eleanor and then Clifford. 'Sir, what is the meaning of this?'

Clifford strode up behind Eleanor and held up a hand. 'My sincere apologies. We are engaged in a birthday treat for my ward who can, I confess, be a little headstrong on occasions.'

Sir Roderick threw his arms out. 'Headstrong be the devil, sir. For the sanctity of golf...' His words dried on his lips as he recognised Eleanor. 'You!'

'Ah! You!' She tapped her forehead. 'Sir Roderick, wasn't it? Well, how fortuitous. You wanted to meet my guardian.'

'I did?' He stared at Clifford. 'Ah, the brandy delivered without a calling card at the riverside restaurant. Good morning.'

The two men shook hands, only Eleanor able to detect the discomfort this caused her ever-respectful-of-his-station butler. She frowned, however, as Sir Roderick pulled Clifford in closer and lowered his voice.

'I believe you are due a medal, sir. Headstrong can so easily descend into wilfulness. And then!'

Clifford shrugged. 'Quite so. But such is the difficulty of taking on a ward when they have already been allowed to run wild in their early childhood. One's hand has already been set.'

As Sir Roderick turned to the three men of his party, all huffing impatiently, Clifford nodded to Eleanor.

'If I was to go really quickly, Sir Roderick, would you mind awfully if I jumped ahead?' she said demurely.

He shook his head. 'That is quite out of the question. It is against club etiquette.'

'But there are four of you and only two of us, so why can't I?'

'Because it simply isn't done.' He turned to Clifford. 'I believe you wished to make my acquaintance previously? Hence the brandy?'

'Indeed,' Clifford said. 'Your commendable and unwavering dedication to providing every household with access to wireless radio holds my sincere admiration. Keeping the nation informed ensures cohesion. It must also be an interesting investment opportunity.'

'Kind words. Good to meet such an intelligent fellow.' He licked his bottom lip and eyed Clifford up as if he were a roll of banknotes. 'And, yes, the epitome of secure investments.' He scrutinised Clifford's face, then waved to his fellow players.

'Chaps, we were going to break for coffee after the ninth. Let's do so now and we'll pick up back here in twenty minutes.'

'Break before clearing the halfway point, Rodders old man?' the shortest of the group spluttered. 'Unheard of!'

Sir Roderick glared at him, waving his scorecard. 'Since we are the losing pair this morning, I thought a break would be welcome, Grimsby, *old* man!'

'You're in charge,' his partner said begrudgingly.

With a lot of grumbling, the other three shouldered their golf bags and set off across the manicured course.

Good, Ellie, now we've got him on his own we can get some answers.

She hit her ball straight over the toe of Sir Roderick's shoe and into his shin.

'Oh, this is so much more fun than I imagined.' She ignored his irritated snorts.

'If only I could have got Barty to play with us, we'd have had such a hoot. Maybe he was a member all along and never said.' She skipped up close to Sir Roderick. 'Bartholomew Darnley. Perhaps his name is on the club list?'

'Not that I know of.'

'But your friend just said you're club captain, didn't he?'

'No, he did not. I am, however, the club committee secretary. An equally important role.'

'Oh, well done you. But even if Barty's name isn't there, you've probably heard of him, anyway?'

'No. I have not. Now, if you will excuse us. I wish to discuss a more pressing matter with your guardian.'

'Oh, go ahead. It was only an idle thought because of the photograph.' She turned her back and made a show of trying to master her golf swing.

'What photograph?' he said slowly.

'No, no. Keep your left arm straight and twist through the waist, my dear,' Clifford said to Eleanor. 'Excuse me one moment, Sir Roderick.'

'Oh, like that.' She cooed over Clifford's demonstration, then straightened up. 'Sorry, Sir Roderick, did you ask me something?'

'I did. I said, what photograph?'

'Oh, it's a very fine one of you both. In fact, I've got it in a pocket somewhere...'

'Is it this one, dear?' Clifford pulled out the first of the images Seldon had entrusted to her earlier. 'The one you dropped at the last hole?'

'Why yes!' She held it out to Sir Roderick. 'See, there's you.

And there's Barty with you. You can't tell how vibrant pink his suit was in that, of course.'

Sir Roderick shrugged. 'There were hundreds, if not thousands, attending the regatta that day. He must have been merely passing. That young man was not with me, then, or at any other time.'

'Now, that's really strange because I thought you were with him last night?'

Sir Roderick froze like a waxwork. After a beat, he seemed to gather his wits. 'I was not. How could I be since I did not know the man?'

At his use of the past tense, Clifford caught her eye momentarily.

'My mistake,' she said airily. 'Were you dining at your favourite restaurant, then? That one where we met on the river. I do like the delectable platters of finger nibbles, don't you?'

His glare bore into her skull. 'My whereabouts last night are of no one's concern. Now,' – he gestured at Clifford – 'please let the grown-ups talk.'

'As you wish, but I haven't recorded my last score and my guardian hasn't taken his shot yet.' She scribbled on her already illegible scorecard. 'Besides, I thought you might like to see the *other* photograph, Sir Roderick. You mentioned how much you appreciate the society pages.'

Sir Roderick snorted. 'I most certainly do not! I said quite the opposite.'

'Yes, you did, didn't you? Then I'll leave you in peace and let you and my guardian talk business. I just do hope the second photograph doesn't set tongues wagging. You know how gossipy people who read those over-romanticised fiction novels can be.'

'My card,' Sir Roderick said, holding one out to Clifford. To Eleanor, he said, 'I would like to see the second photograph.'

'I don't want to hold up your game any further.'

'I don't play games. Golf is a sport.'

'Yes, yes. But I'm really only interested in seeing how hard I can whack the ball.' As if to prove her point, she dropped her ball and hit it over a bank of trees.

Sir Roderick stared between her and Clifford. 'Uncanny power for a novice, sir.'

'My ward used to play elephant polo with the maharajas,' he said as if it was perfectly normal.

'A well-travelled, young lady.' Sir Roderick drew himself up. 'But, please excuse me one moment.' He turned back to Eleanor. 'Now, might I see the photograph? A gentleman in business can't be too careful with his reputation.'

'Of course,' Eleanor said. 'Another very good shot of you. The lady looks very distinguished as well.'

This time Sir Roderick paled. He turned the photograph in his hand. 'This is not from the society pages of the newspaper. Neither was the other, I realise now.'

'I know,' she said conspiratorially. 'Which is why I thought you might want to see them. Clearly, it isn't only journalists who wander about taking photographs willy-nilly. Do you know your apparent companion in this one?'

As he started to shake his head, she nodded slowly.

'Okay, yes, I might,' he said. 'That is Lady Montfort. We attend many of the same functions. I was merely stressing she is not "known" to me as a close acquaintance.'

'Really? Well then, I shan't repeat what Lady Montfort told me about your... relationship.'

'You are a...' Sir Roderick faltered as Clifford stepped towards him, his height towering over the other man. 'A busy socialite, I see. Busy... talking to so many people.'

She wrinkled her nose. 'Your companions are only five hundred yards away.'

'Four hundred and forty, my dear,' Clifford corrected her. 'Accurate estimation of distance is a critical part of golf.'

'Thank you. I really am learning lots today.' She looked

back at Sir Roderick. 'But maybe you might not wish them to learn about you and Lady Montfort.'

'What on earth is this?' Sir Roderick snapped. He swallowed hard, but then squared up to Clifford. 'Well?'

'I'd have to say headstrong has indeed descended into wilfulness. Perhaps it's safest to simply answer the question.'

'Alright, alright. Not that it is any of your business. But, yes, Lady Montfort and I are... closely acquainted.'

Eleanor gestured to his fast-approaching golf party. 'And last night, you weren't at the riverside restaurant or any other. Nor at home. Nor anywhere your wife would find you, were you?'

'No! I was with her from dinner until half an hour before my club closed at two this morning. Satisfied?'

'Almost. I think you fobbed me off at our first meeting about Lord Taylor-Howard.'

'That blighter. I suggest you leave well alone. He failed to heed all warnings and look where it got him. Dead. And all over a series of hopeless bets on the horses.'

So horses were Xander's weakness, Ellie? That's probably why he borrowed money from Treacher. To bet on the horses.

'So, you're a betting man too, Sir Roderick?'

'Yes, I am not ashamed to admit so. But where Lord Taylor-Howard was beyond hopeless at judging form, I am excellent.'

'So did you ever see or hear Mr Treacher or his men threaten Lord Taylor-Howard?'

Sir Roderick looked at Clifford with poorly disguised disgust. 'Guardianship responsibilities have failed you in their entirety, sir!'

Clifford shrugged. 'Indeed. I'd prefer to lock my ward in the cellar, but did you know, it's heavily frowned upon?'

'I'm waiting for an answer, Sir Roderick.' Eleanor cocked her thumb behind her at his three golfing companions who were now at the edge of the tee, all staring at him, arms folded.

Sir Roderick's face set in a triumphant leer. 'Very well. Yes. And Treacher promised Lord Taylor-Howard he would ensure more than his kneecaps were taken in recompense for the money he owed him. He promised to take his life!'

'He actually threatened to kill him?'

'In as many words, yes.'

'And you were there?'

'Oh, yes. Entitled young wastrels, royal or not, like Taylor-Howard think they are above the rest of us. Treacher taught him otherwise.' He picked up his club. 'Now, clear off our hole or I'll have the steward eject both of you!'

Once out of sight, Clifford stopped and fixed her with a haughty look. 'My lady, since my protest previously fell on deaf ears, please forgive the uncharacteristic vehemence of my tone. But that is positively the last time—'

'You wear that jumper. I couldn't agree more. We're supposed to be undercover.' She shook her head. 'Honestly, Clifford, a court jester would be less noticeable!'

21

Back at Henley Hall, Eleanor bounded into the snug with Gladstone hot on her heels. She threw herself onto her favourite chaise longue, looped her arm around Gladstone's neck and stared at the mantlepiece clock.

'Not long now, boy!'

Clifford materialised in the doorway. 'With apologies, my lady, luncheon will be delayed.'

She shared a look of horror with her bulldog as her stomach let out a loud gurgle.

'Oh gracious, I'm ravenous.'

He sniffed. 'So it would appear, my lady. However, while you were indisposed, there was a telephone call. From the chief inspector. I hope you will excuse my taking it on your behalf as he was in a great hurry.'

Secretly disappointed, she waved an airy hand instead. 'Of course. Did he have some news for us?'

'Yes. However, he requested that he impart the information in person. Again, I hope I did not overstep the mark, but I told him it would be fine to come straight over.'

Her heart gave a little skip. 'So lunch has been delayed until he arrives?'

'Indeed, my lady.' His eyes ran over her clothes. 'And until you have changed, naturally.'

A short while later, Eleanor smiled at the sound of a crash, followed by anxious mutterings outside her bedroom.

'Come in, Polly,' she called out.

As the door swung back, smacking into the wall, her young maid skipped in.

'Oh lawks, your ladyship!'

Eleanor hurried over. 'Whatever is it?'

''Pologies for saying' – Polly's voice fell to a whisper – 'but looks like an explosion.' Eyes wide, her maid pointed to the mounds of clothes on Eleanor's bed.

'Ah, yes. Well, the thing is, Polly...' Eleanor turned to look at her reflection again. She frowned. 'I seem to be a tad indecisive about what to wear to luncheon for... for some reason.'

'Oh, right, your ladyship. I comes with a message. Mr Clifford says he's here. The policeman. The one Mrs Trotman calls a long, thirst-quenching glass of tasty lemonade.' She clapped her hands over her mouth in horror. ''Pologies again, your ladyship. Never meant to say that out loud, like.'

Eleanor folded her arms. 'Does she now?'

The morning room had somehow been transformed into the perfect informal dining space. The table had been shortened by two leaves and was now dressed in a green-spotted linen tablecloth. Two places were set across from each other, rather than at opposite ends of the table. Matching napkins sat under the everyday silver cutlery Eleanor always preferred. The soft velvet occasional chairs, being the most comfortable of all those at Henley Hall, had replaced the usual straight-backed affairs. The full bank of windows had been folded open, letting in the cooling breeze and the sounds of an idyllic July day whispered outside. And to top it all off, the long run of salvers along the back wall normally reserved for breakfast let loose delectable-smelling wisps of her all-time favourite Sunday lunch.

'It's perfect. Thank you,' she mouthed to Clifford as he appeared at her elbow.

'The staff's collective pleasure, my lady.' He gestured to a jug of her cook's iced raspberry and elderflower cordial. 'The chief inspector is on duty. Hence no alcohol.'

'And in a frightful rush.' Seldon's voice echoed around the corridor outside. 'As always, I know.' He ducked his long frame into the room. 'I've time for a quick coff—' A look of confusion crossed his face. He looked at her emerald-green silk dress, then stepped back outside and glanced up and down as if trying to get his bearings. 'I thought this was—'

'Absolutely.' Eleanor pulled him back into the room. 'Now, no arguments that you haven't time for lunch. Sit. Talk. Eat lots. And you can leave as soon as you need to without anyone thinking it's impolite.'

'Well, it's been frustratingly slow trying to investigate without Sir Percival finding out,' Seldon said, a minute later, one hand hovering over his notebook, the other running his long fingers over the tablecloth. 'But I have managed to find something on the Darnley chap.' He looked up, his face alight with joy, as Clifford placed a generously filled plate in front of him.

'Slow-roasted beef in mustard, sir.'

'Thank you. Really. That's my absolute favourite.'

'Her ladyship's too, Chief Inspector. How odd. Served with crisp rosemary-roasted potatoes, Yorkshire puddings, courgette and carrot gratin, horseradish cauliflower mash, creamed leeks and red wine gravy.'

'Dig in,' Eleanor said, enthusiastically doing so herself.

Seldon, however, paused, staring at his food, then up at her. 'Blast it! Why do I keep ending up souring Mrs Trotman's amazing fare with talk of murder?' He dropped his voice. 'And ruining a rare minute with you, as well.'

She smiled. 'No idea. It's a terrible habit.' Spearing a potato, she added absentmindedly, 'But I'm resigned to the fact that it will likely be the same over breakfast, lunch and dinner one day.'

'Encouraging.' Seldon laughed with that deep rumble that she found irresistible. 'If dauntingly presumptuous, since that conversation was a horribly long way off to my bumbling thoughts.'

Her cheeks coloured.

He cleared his throat and held up his notebook. Accepting hers from Clifford, she waved it at him.

'Ladies first, then?'

Seldon nodded as he took a mouthful of roast beef, savouring it with a quiet moan of pleasure.

'Well, I managed to discover that Lady Montfort and Sir Roderick Rumbold – one an ex-lover and one a cuckold of Xander's – are, in fact, engaged in... their own illicit liaison! And all discovered, I might say, with only the minimal of under-hand tactics.'

She was surprised, and a little disappointed, when Seldon merely nodded. 'Stands to reason.'

'I expected you to be more shocked, Hugh, in truth. It's hardly the done thing.'

'It absolutely isn't to my mind. But in my line of work, I'm afraid I come across such occurrences all too regularly. And mostly not among the working classes.'

She threw Clifford a pointed look. 'So much for the polite society I'm supposed to be shoehorning myself into!'

'More gravy, Chief Inspector?' Clifford said hurriedly.

Seldon accepted it with alacrity. 'Having been wronged by the same party, it's not that uncommon that the two injured parties, so to speak, have an affair of their own.'

'Although,' Clifford said, 'a quite illogical liaison as it does not affect the gentleman they seem to be trying to get revenge on.'

Seldon shrugged. 'If people acted logically, I'd have half the cases to solve!'

'But most importantly,' Eleanor continued, 'they each confessed that they were together yesterday evening until disgraceful o'clock this morning.' She put a couple of roast potatoes and a spoonful of sublime creamed leeks onto her plate.

Seldon looked up from taking notes with his usual short, efficient strokes. 'Disgraceful o'clock? What on earth time is that?' He eyed the recent additions to her plate and helped himself to the same.

'High time they should both have stopped rolling around under a sheet that wasn't theirs, I imagine.' She hid a smile as Seldon and Clifford both ran a finger along their collars in unison.

'Could be a story planned together, however,' Seldon said. 'If they are in cahoots over one or both murders, that is.' He frowned. 'Dare I ask, Eleanor, the less than "underhand tactics" you mentioned? Were they such that the two of them were caught off guard by your questions?'

'Hmm. What would you say, Clifford?'

'Regarding Lady Montfort, Chief Inspector, from my discreet vantage point, I would say that the lady was convinced her ladyship had sought her out only for some much-needed fashion advice.'

Seldon's lips gave away his evident amusement at the thought of this.

'And,' Eleanor said, giving him a haughty look, 'Sir Roderick seemed genuinely put out when he fumed his answer in my face.'

'Not because you had elbowed him out of his turn on the ninth hole, perhaps, my lady?'

Seldon looked between them, shaking his head slowly. 'You pretended you were playing golf?'

'Oh no, we really did play, with Clifford as my guardian and me as his ward.' She laughed. 'Oh stop sulking, Clifford. It was good fun and you know it. So, Hugh, if they were telling the truth, that means that neither of them had time to rush over to Beaconsfield to finish off poor old Barty.'

'Although,' Clifford said, 'your questioning was discreet enough not to enquire from either suspect the exact time they had got together and where their... ahem, late evening meeting had taken place.'

'Dash it! I didn't ask that, did I?'

'I might have taken a liberty in that regard, subsequently, my lady.'

'Good work, Clifford,' Seldon said. 'I hope?'

'As do I, Chief Inspector. I happened to discover from a member of each suspect's staff where their respective mistress and master had travelled to. And when.'

Seldon looked uncomfortable. 'No disrespect at all to you, Clifford, but mightn't staff pass on a gross mistruth if instructed by their employers for fear of losing their jobs?'

'That can be regretfully true.'

'But,' Eleanor said, silently thanking her late uncle for bequeathing her staff who would never pass on any truths, or mistruths, about her to anyone, 'you can easily check whether they were where they said they were, now Clifford has the address, I mean.'

'Agreed,' Seldon said. 'Thank you for taking the initiative on that, Clifford. It's a shame you never wanted a career in the police, you know.'

Eleanor laughed. 'No, it isn't! Aside from the fact that he is far too precious as my butler-cum-bodyguard, his methods are so dubious and his skills so questionable you'd spend half the time arresting *him*.'

Clifford tutted. 'Her ladyship sorely maligns me, Chief Inspector.'

Seldon laughed. 'I sincerely doubt that, actually. But I'm particularly grateful, since your dubious and questionable skills have helped me out on several occasions. And' – his tone turned to one of concern as he glanced at Eleanor – 'especially for your skills as a bodyguard since I fear they may be called upon again.'

Eleanor clapped her hands. 'Well, let's at least lighten the news with pudding, shall we?'

'I really haven't time, Eleanor, sorry.'

She glanced at the clock. 'Yes, you have. You've exactly twenty minutes as Tipsy is due here in ten, but will be fashionably late as always.'

A look of panic crossed Seldon's face. He gestured at Clifford. 'Come on, man, you can bring the pudding in while we finish the main course! Protocol can go hang!'

Over his second bowl of rhubarb and apple crumble, Seldon sighed. 'Do you really have to visit Treacher again, Eleanor?'

'Clifford will be with me. And you know what a Jack Russell he is if he thinks I'm in the slightest hint of danger.'

Seldon relaxed as Clifford reappeared with a loaded silver tray. 'A Jack Russell with dubious skills. You've quite the reputation, Clifford.'

He bowed. 'With questionable methods, do not forget, Chief Inspector. Although I do prefer the assumed image of the

Fox Terrier. Equally fast and impossible to shake off, but considerably less yappy.' He set about serving coffee.

Eleanor took a sip. 'Come on then, Hugh. You've got another ten minutes before the force of nature that is Tipsy arrives. Now you're as comfortable as you'll ever be that I'm in the best hands, next to yours, of course,' – she blushed and hurried on – 'and as I'm going to visit Mr Treacher anyway, do you need me to ask anything for you while I'm there?'

He hesitated and then gave in. 'I need to find out if a rumour I extracted from a contact has any merit. I was told that Mr Darnley owed money to Treacher. Which would explain the black eye and beating.'

She frowned. 'Hang on, though. I thought Barty was only a target for Fingers because he owed him money by proxy, as it were? He was a substitute for Xander?'

Seldon shrugged. 'My information is that Darnley owed Treacher money independently of anyone else.' He glanced at the clock. 'I really have to go now. And not just because your rather scary friend is arriving.'

With Clifford bringing up the rear, Eleanor followed Seldon out into the corridor.

'Does it feel a little like we're making progress, Hugh? In our individual investigations, of course.'

'Yes. And no. Honestly, Eleanor, something doesn't feel right about it all, but blast it, I can't put my finger on it.'

'More feelings? You need to start keeping different company.'

'I might have to.' He smiled, lightening up his already far too handsome face. 'Although, anyone who knows someone who can create a roast beef dinner that impossibly superb is worth associating with. Can I ask for my compliments to be passed to Mrs Trotman?'

'Actually,' Eleanor said casually, 'if Clifford can bear the rules being broken just this once, you'd make her day if we could pop along to the kitchen quickly and you told her yourself.'

Seldon nodded. They both looked at Clifford.

'As you wish, my lady, if you are happy that very few further duties will subsequently be completed satisfactorily for the remainder of the afternoon.'

'Why wouldn't they be?' Seldon said.

'Unimportant,' Eleanor said as she tugged Hugh off down the corridor. 'But if you could just ask Mrs Trotman while you're there for a long, thirst-quenching glass of tasty lemonade...'

22

Clifford slowed the Rolls to a stop outside Fingers' nightclub and turned to Eleanor.

'My lady, the chief inspector—'

'Is not here.'

'Indeed. But were he—'

She sighed. 'Okay, Clifford, I promised to change my middle name to Prudence for this interview. And not just because everyone giggles at Lettice, the one I was given.'

Clifford raised an eyebrow. She nudged his elbow.

'Look, you and Uncle Byron risked your life for Queen and Country. And then King and Country.'

'That was entirely different.'

'Why? Because you were in the army?'

He shook his head. 'No. Because we were both *men*. I am sorry, my lady, I agree with every aspect of the modern lady's attempts at equality, *except* as regards to placing themselves in dangerous situations or professions.'

'I know, Clifford,' she said softly. 'Which is why I am such a trial to you. No one appreciates your dedicated concern, nor your unwavering gallantry, more than me. But we've been asked to help and Hugh's hands are tied at this point.'

He nodded resignedly.

'Ready then?'

He stepped out of the car and opened her door. 'Always, my lady.'

Treacher was waiting for her in an elaborate black velvet wingback chair. He rose slowly, with a chivalrous nod, one hand on his monocle. She greeted him with a cheery wave.

'Good day, Fingers. Thank you for agreeing to see me again. That really is an exceptionally fine basil-green suit you have on today by the way.'

He held his hands out like an impresario taking his final curtain call. 'I prefer to think of it as shamrock-green, since it reminds me of home.' His Irish inflection seemed to strengthen with his last few words. 'However, most kind, Lady Swift and' – he eyed Clifford coolly – 'whoever you actually are.'

Eleanor waved her hand. 'A great many people. And all of them absolutely invaluable. Unfortunately, there is one person I've discovered recently that he isn't, which is why I'm here.'

Treacher ran a well-groomed forefinger along his jaw. 'And why would that be of any interest to me? I prefer straight-talking to double meanings, by the way.'

'Me too. But isn't that the trouble with all of us who have even a whiff of Irish descent. We're masters of turning a simple sentence into a confusing riddle.'

He laughed. Far from the menacing sound she'd expected, it was as musical as running water. However, his smile faded quickly. 'I hope your next words aren't going to bring out the worst in me.'

'I'm willing to take the risk.' She held her hands out. 'Because I genuinely need your help.'

'As a rule, people like me don't help people like you. We rarely have much in common.'

She shrugged. 'Well, I'm not really one for rules, as Clifford will vouch.' Her butler rolled his eyes, much to Treacher's amusement. 'But last time,' she continued, 'you were positively on your knees begging me to come join your wonderful organisation.'

He laughed again. 'On my knees. In my fine threads? The sun will never rise on the day that happens!' He looked her over. 'Although, now I know a little more about you...'

'You mean you've done your homework and found out that I really am who I said I was?'

'Maybe. I've been digging on you, of course. But I meant you're even queerer a lady than I took you for to begin with.'

She held up a finger. 'I don't do Vaudeville, though. Terrible singing voice.'

He gestured to a chair next to his. 'Take a seat. I doubt I'm interested in whatever you've come to ask, but I am enjoying the entertainment you provide.'

Taking a moment to make herself comfortable in the other wingback chair, she gathered her wits.

'Do you have a sliding scale of charges?'

'A what?'

'You know, a few pounds for a mild beating up to, probably, double figures for a more serious beating along with a black eye that actually promises permanent disfigurement?'

'No. But why do you ask?'

'Because my man's one failing' – she gestured at Clifford again – 'is that he always goes too far.'

Treacher's eyes narrowed as they darted to Clifford. 'How do you mean, too far?'

'Well, if I need someone roughed up, he goes in like an escaped lunatic. Instead of teaching them a lesson, he ends up making sure they'll never learn anything ever again.'

Slowly, Treacher removed his monocle, pulled a square of soft cream cloth from his pocket and rubbed it over the lens, all the while staring at her intently.

'I'm *Fingers Treacher*, Lady Swift. My reputation is known far and wide. Are you seriously trying to threaten *me*?'

'No. Someone else.'

'Like who?'

'Let's just say, for example, a disgraceful reprobate had challenged my honour. How much would you charge to send one of your chaps round to make sure he would never contemplate so much as nodding to a girl again?'

'Nothing.'

'Ah! I knew you were the chivalrous sort.'

Treacher leaned forward. 'Nothing, because my boys are not for hire.'

'What a shame. I've seen their handiwork. It's really impressive.'

'I doubt that. But go on, entertain me some more. Where do you think you've seen it?'

'On Bartholomew Darnley's face. Well, the huge screaming purple swelling that stopped him seeing out of one eye among other things.'

'Never heard of him.'

'Barty Darnley. I think you have. He had a habit he couldn't control. And now he's dead.'

She sensed that behind her Clifford had stiffened, ready to intervene if necessary.

Treacher leaned back in his chair, his eyes flicking lazily to her butler and then back to her.

'I take it you think something is up with the way this bloke choked. So, tell me straight, why come to me? Again?'

She pointed a finger at him. 'I believe Darnley owed you money. And likely a great deal.'

'And why would you think that?'

'Because he was Taylor-Howard's poorer relative. One whom everyone taunted as being his cousin's "puppy" because he aped everything his cousin did. Including trying to make a name for himself on the horses and gambling tables. And your tables are the finest there are, aren't they?' She had no idea, but it never hurt to massage a man's ego.

'You're right there. And lots of toffs like the classy ambience I've got going on.'

'If not the terms of non-payment.'

'Right again. But,' he said, leaning forward, 'this dead Darnley bloke wasn't one of them.' Something in his sharp green-blue eyes made her believe him.

She rose and walked round to the back of her chair, leaning her arms over the top. 'So, now I am confused because Darnley did everything on his cousin's tailcoats. Which is why when I heard that you'd threatened... sorry, your boys had threatened, Lord Taylor-Howard, I naturally concluded he had received the same courtesy.'

'That wasn't my boys,' Treacher said darkly. 'Young Taylor-Howard got to hear it from me. Direct.'

'That's what I heard as well.'

He started, but relaxed again immediately. 'Really? You are well, if sometimes misinformed.'

'Thank you. Anyway, my source told me you threatened Lord Taylor-Howard not with a beating, but with his life.'

'So?'

'So then why did you say last time I was here that killing your clientele was not your style? Something about it being bad for business?'

'Because it's true. But they're too terrified to know that.'

She stood up straight. 'As you've been very honest with me, I'll return the favour. I fear you'll have the police, both civil and royal, knocking on your door very soon.'

He shrugged. 'I can handle them. Why would they bother though, unless someone was out to make trouble for me?'

'Well, don't look at me. I really like my kneecaps.' Behind the chair, she lifted her skirt slightly and turned each leg. In her peripheral vision, she saw Clifford shake his head in horror. 'They're not too unsightly and they do allow me to bend my legs just enough to outrun trouble.'

Treacher laughed. 'I'm unconvinced. But even though your uncle disrupted parts of my operations on occasions, he never shopped one of my boys, so I'll tell you something.'

Clifford immediately stepped to her side, but she flapped a halting hand.

'Don't play with me, Fingers.' Her voice came out more rushed than she'd wanted. She'd found out six months after inheriting her uncle's estate, that he had in fact been murdered. Together with Clifford, she'd caught the hired killer responsible, but had never discovered who was behind the order to murder her uncle. All the killer would tell her was that it was the head of a crime organisation her uncle had angered. *Maybe it was Fingers, Ellie?*

Treacher obviously read her thoughts.

'Calm down, it wasn't me. I liked him. He was an odd sort of toff with unexpected methods. Bit like you.'

Her mouth was dry. She cleared her throat. 'Do you know who paid the person to kill my uncle or not?'

He shook his head. 'No. And if I did, I wouldn't tell you. But I genuinely don't. Though it wasn't any of the local bosses.'

'How do you know that then?'

'Because at one time or another, they've all asked me the same question. And no one knows who it was.'

'Okay.' She took several deep breaths. 'Thank you.'

'You believe me?'

'On that score, yes. I think you're a man of honour in your own way.'

'Good. Then I'll level with you about the other matter too. I can handle the police, but to be straight, that Sir Percival can be a right pain. Now listen, I won't repeat myself. I didn't murder Darnley because he didn't owe me a penny. And I didn't murder Taylor-Howard because, as I mentioned before, he told me he'd have the money to pay me in full soon. And, yes, I believed him. Even though he owed me a lot more than usual, he'd always paid up – eventually.'

She thought about what he'd said. Then she nodded. 'I believe you, Fingers. About Darnley and Lord Taylor-Howard. But where was Lord Taylor-Howard going to get that kind of money from, do you suppose?'

'I'm not big on supposing. So I had his tailored trousers grow a tail.'

She glanced at Clifford.

'Had the gentleman followed, my lady.'

'Ah! To anywhere or anyone you recognised?'

'Oh, yes. Another one who should be on the stage for entertainment value. You two would get on like a couple of terraced houses on fire. In fact, you did.'

She frowned. 'You've been tailing my tailored behind too?'

Out of the corner of her eye, she saw Clifford shake his head again.

'Only until I was happy with who you are. Enjoy the tea, did you?' Treacher grinned at her confusion. 'I didn't picture you as one of them lawn bowls crowd. Too dull and genteel for you.'

'Sergei Orlov,' she said slowly.

He nodded. 'Taylor-Howard would always cosy up with that particular card just before he coughed up my money. So maybe he had something to do with Taylor-Howard's insistence that he would soon be flush?'

Oh dear, Ellie, it looks like Sir Percival could be right about

Xander being a spy and passing on secrets to the Russians! Uncovering the reason for Xander's death might also uncover a royal scandal. And one that the royal family might not recover from!

23

Further along the bank of the River Thames, the crowds had dwindled, leaving only a bevy of Henley's resident swans hissing with irritation at having been ousted by the regatta from their usual nesting spots. Gladstone eyed them warily from a safe distance, growling quietly.

Eleanor turned back towards the marquees in the near distance.

'Dash it, Clifford! We've covered the whole thing and drawn a total blank.' A rower in a smart blazer and straw boater creaked past with a great deal of oar flailing and weed flinging. 'And not so much as a sniff of Sergei Orlov. I have to admit I was wrong about finding him here.'

Clifford coughed. 'Not your happy place, I know.'

'Let's just leave. We'll have to look elsewhere.'

Clifford held up a firm hand to a swan whose bright-orange bill was nibbling the hem of his jacket. 'Sir, you are supposed to dine on small fish, frogs and worms, not the lining of my attire.' He tugged his jacket out of the bird's way and turned to Eleanor. 'Shall we, my lady?'

'Shall we what?'

'Talk to Mr Orlov.'

'What! Orlov is here?' She looked around. 'Now I'm all the more irritated that you saw him first since I still can't spot him.'

'Naturally,' the smart blazer called from further up the bank. 'Because I am a master of my art.'

Despite herself, Eleanor smiled. 'Indeed, you are.'

The simple change of hair colour to light brown, along with a new side-parting and a pair of thick black spectacles rendered him almost unrecognisable from the man she'd met previously. She pointed to the boat he was tying to a ring on the bank.

'You are, however, not a master of rowing. I thought you said you rowed back in Russia?'

He looked genuinely annoyed. 'Lady Swift, I was only acting at being a bad rower to see if you'd notice me.' He straightened up and thumped one fist across his chest. 'Back home, I have rowed for my beloved country!'

'Lucky Russia. And good evening, Mr Orlov.'

'Good evening to you, Lady Swift.' He bowed. 'I was beginning to think I might need to dance a jig in front of you before you would see me.'

'But we hadn't arranged to meet.' She glanced at Clifford. 'So why would you think—'

'You are looking for me in connection with the tragic death of one Mr Darnley, are you not? How do I know? Because, like you, my dear,' – he tapped the side of his nose – 'I have an insatiable appetite for sniffing out the suspicious.' He gestured along the riverbank, away from the last of the regatta crowds. 'Shall we promenade and parley?'

She wrinkled her nose. 'I'd rather walk and talk. We might actually get somewhere then.'

Orlov laughed and turned to Clifford. 'Come, friend, stroll alongside us with your four-legged companion. You are here for more than just keeping this lady in one impetuous piece.' He looked Eleanor over appreciatively. 'Although, such fearlessness would be of great value working for your government. And mine.'

She waved dismissively. 'Stick to talking about Darnley, Mr Orlov. My secondment to Sir Percival's little club is purely temporary. And I am heartily looking forward to it being over.'

'I'm sure. But I may disappoint you. I only knew Mr Darnley by sight and by rather pitiful reputation.'

'And why would that be?'

'Because I had no reason for anything further. He merely scampered around on his cousin's heels. Wherever Taylor-Howard went, Mr Darnley was guaranteed to make an appearance soon enough. Invited or otherwise.'

'Then you must have seen him often?'

Orlov nodded.

'So I assume his plan was to take over Lord Taylor-Howard's mantle. To be the big attraction. Mind, the last person to see him evidently wasn't any more the fan than you were.'

'My dear, how could I have been a fan of Mr Darnley or not? We were not acquainted, as I said.'

'Perhaps.' She scrutinised his face. 'Where were you when he died?'

He tutted. 'Come now, how could I possibly say since I don't know when he died?'

It's no use, Ellie. He's an expert. He's probably been trained to lie. And lie convincingly. You're not going to catch him out that easily. 'Hmm. Friday evening around seven, I believe.'

'Ah, then I have an alibi. Though not one you can check, as I was with several of my superiors who would deny even knowing me. Naturally.'

'Naturally.' She rolled her eyes.

They paused as Clifford whipped his penknife from his pocket. In one swift movement, he bent and deftly cut off a length of frayed boating rope tangled around a swan's legs.

Receiving a sharp hiss and a jab of its bill by way of thanks, he shook his head. 'You're most welcome!'

Orlov nodded at the piece of rope which Clifford was tying into a neat set of knots. 'Some creatures you simply cannot help. I believe Mr Darnley had that very much in common with his cousin.'

'Like some of the poor choices they made over who they owed money to? Men like Mr Treacher?'

'Precisely. Like Mr Treacher.'

'Well, funnily enough, Mr Treacher told me only a short hour ago that Lord Taylor-Howard would soon be able to pay his debt back because he had a financial arrangement with you.'

He laughed. 'Like a thruppeny bit lemonade stall? Lady Swift, even that would have been beyond the limit of any money dealings I would have entered into with Taylor-Howard.'

She folded her arms and waited. He copied her stance.

'I love this interrogation technique. Mind if I steal it for my own?'

'Feel free. I've got all night.'

At this, Gladstone let out a long huff and flopped onto Clifford's shoes.

'As have I,' Orlov said. 'But not for standing still beside this exquisite river. I would rather be skimming her surface, straining at my oars. So I shall play ball.'

The bulldog jumped up at the 'b' word, but he sunk down again as Clifford patted his head. 'Later, Master Gladstone.'

Eleanor wrinkled her nose. 'I doubt that's the real reason, is it, Mr Orlov? As I'm beginning to find out, no one wants the royal police, especially not led by Sir Percival, on one's back.'

Orlov bowed. 'I admit that may be a factor as well.' He took off his spectacles and stared at her intently. 'Taylor-Howard did come to me a few times with an offer of insider royal gossip, which I refused. But the urgency of his deal increased, making me believe he owed money to some undesirable types who had tired of his excuses. Mr Treacher in the main, I'm sure, since his lackeys started trailing him to each of our meetings. Unlike me, subtlety is not their strength.'

'No, I think theirs is menace.'

'So crude a tactic, my dear. So unnecessary.'

'Surely you must need to resort to such things on occasion in your line of work, Mr Orlov?'

He jerked his head at Clifford. 'Don't we all, Lady Swift. Morality can be so fluid depending on one's situation, as we both know. But I repeat what I said last time. Any secrets Taylor-Howard might have offered me would have been so old or fabricated I did not deal with him. Which means' – he held his hands out – 'I had no reason to kill him. Or his cousin.'

'And how did he take your repeated refusals? Because he must have become increasingly desperate after Treacher himself threatened him. In fact, I would have thought he might have switched tack and maybe tried to... blackmail you.'

'Not at all. In fact, the last time I refused, he said he didn't care as he would soon have a new source of income.'

That wretched source of income, Ellie! If we could only find out who Xander believed was going to pay him enough money to get him out of debt, we'd have his murder solved.

'Did he say from where or whom?' she said without much hope.

'No. And I didn't ask him because if I wanted to know, I would simply have found out for myself. But I didn't.'

Eleanor tried another tack. 'Do you have a cyanide capsule?'

Orlov frowned. 'Whatever for?'

'In case you're caught, of course.'

He spread his hands. 'I see those wonderful spy novels have romanticised your view of my work.'

'There's nothing romantic about death by cyanide.'

'True, there are prettier ways to leave this earth. People really need to be more careful with such substances. However, as you so delightfully asked, if I was ever caught, the most painful outcome would likely be a curt letter. Or a suited minion at my door asking politely if I wouldn't mind awfully popping along to the British Embassy.'

'Who would then imprison you?'

'Tsk, tsk, dear lady. You should have more faith in your government's wonderful English public school manners. I would be treated to a sharp slap of the wrist, or at most, sent home if I'd been really naughty.'

'Like killing a minor royal level of naughty?'

He paused. 'Now for that level of naughty, there might be a little more than a slap on the wrist!'

Before Clifford could open the door for Eleanor back at Henley Hall, the sound of Mrs Butters' voice floated out to them.

'Might as well go out the front as you're in the hallway. Thank you for coming.' Eleanor's housekeeper stopped short on seeing her on the doorstep. 'Oh my stars, so sorry, m'lady. I didn't realise you was there.' She turned back to the blue-over-alled man, holding a small black tool bag. 'You'll have to go out the way you came in, the servants' entrance round—'

Eleanor held up her hand. 'Really, Mrs Butters, as he's already practically out the door, it's fine if he continues.'

The man touched the peak of his flat cap. 'Thank you kindly, miss.'

As Mrs Butters took Eleanor's coat, she nodded in the direction of the man now getting into the blue van Eleanor had noticed on her arrival.

'He's from the telephone company, m'lady.'

'Good! What was his diagnosis?' Clifford said.

Mrs Butters frowned. 'I think he said it was the...' – she

scrunched up her face – 'the... the diaphragms! That was it. Old as the hills they were. Needed replacing.'

'Well, no time like the present to enjoy the new improvement. I'll telephone Hugh.' Eleanor went over and picked up the handset. 'Oh, that was quick. Operator. Oxford 769 please.' A moment later, she was connected to the police station. 'Oh, hello. I'd like to speak to— What the?' she gasped as Clifford snatched the phone from her hand and held it to his ear.

'We'll call back later, thank you,' he said before placing the handset back on its cradle.

'Humble apologies, my lady,' he whispered. 'To the village. Swiftly.'

'What do you mean you think the telephone is tapped!' she said as they drove back up the drive.

'My lady, Mrs Butters said that the telephone man told her he had replaced the diaphragms because they were old. They were, however, changed only a few months before you arrived at the Hall.'

Eleanor shook her head in confusion. 'Then why replace them?'

'I believe, my lady, that the gentleman professing to be a telephone engineer was no such thing. I believe he may have installed listening equipment. I heard a series of clicks on the line. The technology to do so has been around for a little while. And depending on the sensitivity of the equipment installed, it might be that our conversations can be overheard even with the handset on its cradle.'

Eleanor stared at her butler in disbelief. 'The dashed cheek of it! I mean, who would dare to do such a thing!'

'Who indeed, my lady.'

She was still fuming when she stepped out of the Rolls outside Little Buckford's Police Station.

. . .

'Always a pleasure, m'lady. Mr Clifford.' Constable Fry's uniformed presence filled the front step of what was actually just a small, detached bungalow. He shook his heavy head. 'Long as you're not here on account of another dead body, likes before. Beg pardon for saying, mind.'

She patted her jacket down. 'No dead bodies on me today, Constable Fry, don't worry. I merely wish to use your telephone, since the one at Henley Hall is... causing problems.'

'Of course. Come on in.'

He motioned her into his front room, which also doubled as the office of the police station. It contained two shelves with neat stacks of files, a plain wooden table in use as a desk, and the de rigueur black telephone. 'Mrs Fry is out with our three young rascals but I can probably rustle up a cuppa that's almost fitting for a lady.'

'That's most kind, Constable, but I'm fine thank you.'

'Perhaps, instead, Constable Fry, you could tell me about this interesting article on your wall?' Clifford led him over to the one picture on the wall, a framed local newspaper clipping of Constable Fry's triplets in knitted police outfits for a charity fundraiser. While he kept the policeman busy, Eleanor picked up the telephone.

A few moments later she was connected to Oxford Police Station and then Seldon's extension.

'Oh, Hugh, finally, I've got through to you.' She cupped the mouthpiece to hush her words.

'Eleanor! What's happened?'

She smiled at the concern in his voice. 'Nothing. I'm at the police station in Little Buckford.'

A groan came down the line. 'That can't be good.'

'Now hold on! I'm only here because' – she glanced over her shoulder – 'your lot have tapped the telephone at the Hall.'

'What? Are you certain?'

'Very. Well, Clifford is.'

'Ah! In that case, I won't argue. But I'm sure it wasn't us. I'll double-check, of course, but how did you find out?'

Four hushed and frustrated exchanges later, Eleanor had passed on the salient details.

'That doesn't sound like our chaps,' Seldon said matter-of-factly. 'It must be Sir Percival.'

'But why? He ordered me onto his wretched team. Why would he—'

'Because he trusts no one. I doubt if he trusts the king!'

Eleanor felt herself flushing. 'Wait until I see that pompous oaf! I'll—'

'Oh, for Pete's sake. Please put Clifford on so I can make sure he restrains you from screaming off to do battle with the head of the royal police. Anyway, it might just be to our advantage.'

Eleanor's brow furrowed. 'How come?'

'For two reasons. Firstly, if Sir Percival thinks he is listening in without you knowing—'

'We can mislead him! Of course! Although, Hugh, let's remember, we are all on the same side.'

'Naturally, Eleanor. I only meant that it might make our end of the job – actually catching the murderer – a little simpler, ironically.'

She nodded. 'Okay, I can see that. And the second reason?'

'If we can't speak on the phone, it means you and I will have to meet up more often.' The line went quiet for a moment. 'How's that for a silver lining?'

24

'Ugh, Gladstone!' Eleanor gasped. 'What have you been swimming in?'

'That'd be the run-off pond, m'lady,' a disembodied voice answered from the other side of the topiary hedge that led through to the kitchen garden. Her gardener's thinning head of hair and weather-sculpted face poked through one of the perfect arches making her jump.

'Beg pardon. Thought as you knew I was watching Master Gladstone.'

She pointed to her bulldog who was happily unconcerned by the sprays of thick brown ooze flying off him as he shook himself.

'Morning, Joseph. No need to apologise, but why were you watching Gladstone swim about in the murky whichever pond you just said it was?'

'The run-off one, m'lady. It collects all the excess water, especially from the rose garden after mulching time.' At her blank look, he added. ''Tis when I gives them the treat of a good manure feast in springtime.'

'Lucky roses. Well, thankfully that explains why he isn't

offending the nostrils as well as the eyes. Why let him swim in it though?'

Joseph's watery eyes crinkled as he beamed down at the bulldog.

'Normally I wouldn't, but Master Gladstone dived in when I lost one of my special thick gloves that you was so kind as to buy me at Christmas last. He knows how they save me from the thorns.' With difficulty he wrested the leather glove from the reluctant bulldog.

'Oh gracious, but then you'll need another pair. Well, I'll take our hero back to the house and see about getting him scrubbed off then.'

'If you're really sure, m'lady? Mr Clifford should be back from town very soon.' At her nod, he disappeared back below the hole in the hedge, shaking his head.

A short distance away from the back step of the kitchen, she spied an old tin bath. 'Ah, perfect.' Leaving the mucky bulldog with a handful of his favourite liver treats, she jogged to the back door. But as she reached for the handle, the sound of voices floating out pulled her up short.

'You'll be in all kinds of hot water if Mr Clifford sees all them, Trotters!' That had to be Mrs Butters, her housekeeper, remonstrating with her cook.

''Taint my fault, Butters, if that ever so nice policeman needs a bit o' meat on his bones. Nor if they ain't the longest, finest bones we girls have had sight of in a very long time.'

Infectious giggling rang out to Eleanor, making her smile. The idea of them enjoying Seldon's visits almost as much as she did still tickled her. However, not wanting to eavesdrop, she knocked on the door and bent to unlace her boots.

'Oh my stars, 'tis you, m'lady.' Mrs Butters beamed. She patted Eleanor's arm as she gestured her inside. 'The lady of the house has no need of knocking on any of her own doors.'

'Not even if she doesn't want to catch her staff up to mischief?'

Both women glanced at each other and blushed.

'I'm only teasing.'

The cook and housekeeper relaxed.

'Cup of tea, m'lady?'

'Thank you, Mrs Butters, but I need to deal with Gladstone.'

'Oh lawks, what has Mr Wilful done now?'

'Suffice to say, he needs a great deal of mud scrubbed from his portly frame.'

Mrs Butters clapped her hands over her mouth. 'But that's no job for the lady of the house! Whatever would Mr Clifford say?'

'Absolutely nothing,' Eleanor whispered. 'Because he isn't here. And since all of you are busy kindly preparing for my visitor, I imagine, I shall quietly enjoy getting my hands dirty for once.'

Her cook and housekeeper shared an uncertain look. 'If you absolutely insist, m'lady.'

Five minutes later, Eleanor advanced on Gladstone dressed in an old pair of blue overalls she'd spotted hanging in the boot room.

'Mrs Trotman's special apple and rhubarb doggie shampoo should do, Gladstone old chum. We'll have you back to decent in a jiffy.'

Despite his protestations and overeager splashing, only ten minutes later Gladstone tumbled out of the bath, his short coat clean and sleek once again. She gave him a good rubdown with a towel and then released him. He careered around the lawn, periodically rolling on his back and growling to himself. Then his ears pricked up and, with a single excited woof, he shot off around the side of the house.

'What now, boy?' She sprinted after him. 'Gladstone?' But as she swung round the last corner, she jerked to a stop. 'Hugh!' The sight of the ever smart-suited chief inspector pressed up against the side of his car with a damp bulldog scrabbling up his suit trousers made her wince. 'Sorry!'

'I know I'm early, for which I apologise,' he called as she hurried over to grab Gladstone. 'But now I'm tempted to make an ungentlemanly habit of it.'

'Why? Not so you can have the early joy of an enthusiastic and damp bulldog?'

'No.' He gestured over her soggy boilersuit. 'So I can get another fascinating peek into the real world of Lady Swift.' His deep laugh rumbled in her ears. 'Dare I even ask how you browbeat Clifford into letting you do whatever unladylike manner of thing you've been up to?'

'That's easy. He doesn't know.'

Under the dappled shade cast by the impressive run of horse chestnut trees, Clifford was ineffectually remonstrating with a now mostly dry Gladstone. The lure of three wicker hampers, perfectly aligned along the edge of a large blue-and-green tartan picnic rug, was proving too much for the greedy bulldog.

'Chief Inspector,' Clifford said. 'Please forgive my not being free to meet you at the door on this occasion. We felt it best to be far from any chance of the telephone-tapping equipment being able to intercept any conversation. I hope you were met... ahem, appropriately?'

Eleanor watched in amusement as Seldon shrugged, seemingly oblivious to what her butler was actually asking. 'Yes, fine, thanks. But as they are always so busy, please do tell the ladies that I really don't need all four of them to greet me to make up for your absence, Clifford.'

He scooped up the tennis ball Gladstone had dropped on his shoes. 'Go... Fetch!'

Eleanor nudged Clifford over to the first hamper and pretended to engage him in a frightfully important conversation about the contents. Instead, in a low voice, she said, 'I know the rules have to be upheld, Clifford, but the ladies were just having a little fun with Hugh being here. After all, how often are they going to have the treat of a dashing chief inspector striding through Henley Hall?'

'That is for you to tell me, my lady. But hopefully, a great deal more regularly.'

Shaking her head at her butler's cheeky reply, she grabbed two sumptuous green velvet cushions from the largest of the hampers and bounced down cross-legged onto one. Seldon waited until she was settled, pinched his trousers up and then folded his long legs under him as he dropped onto the other.

Clifford gave a quiet cough and put back the fold-out wooden chairs he had pulled from the last hamper. From the next, he began pulling out a selection of covered dishes. Seldon reached inside his jacket pocket for his notebook.

'I thought I was here to talk about our individual progress on the two wretched murders, not devour more of your delicious pantry offerings.'

Eleanor folded her arms. 'Let me guess what you ate when you finally got home last night... Or likely early this morning. A couple of slices of toast, and a sliver of cheese?'

'Close. One and a bit slices. No cheese. Oh, and a slightly suspect apple.'

'Enough said. Hence the picnic.' She tilted her head. 'How does one end up with only a bit of a slice of bread, anyway?'

Seldon was scanning his notes. 'Hmm?'

'Are you ever going to get better at looking after yourself, Hugh?'

He looked up. 'Are you?'

'I don't need to. I looked after myself for years. Now, being a spoiled princess, I've got Clifford and the wonderful ladies to do that for me. For which I am, and always will be, beyond grateful.'

Clifford set down in front of them the first two of the myriad platters he had uncovered.

'Well, princess,' Seldon said, 'would it be rude to ask if we can eat and talk at the same time? I have the delight of a desk groaning with paperwork waiting for me after this.'

She nodded, struggling to choose among the amazing finger sandwich selection on offer. 'First though, how did it go with your superior, Hugh?' She plumped for an egg and cress, a roast chicken and a smoked salmon with dill relish, adding a few miniature herb sausages to balance the plate out. Then she turned to the ham and egg pie platter. 'He didn't rip you too much to shreds, I hope?'

On the rug, Gladstone slithered on his stomach closer to the pie until he caught sight of Clifford's stern look and shuffled back onto the grass with a huff.

Having placed a couple of chicken sandwiches on his plate, Seldon hesitated, then added a couple of Stilton pastry straws.

'First things first.' He waved a sandwich. 'This is so good. And sincerely appreciated.' He tucked his feet up tighter. 'And thank you too, for asking, but the name "Sir Percival" is fast becoming a swear word with my superior. He's heartily sick of the royal police throwing their weight around. He went on for most of our meeting about people like Sir Percival behaving as if the blasted war was still on. Then he ended it by telling me to do whatever it takes to get the heck on with my job of investigating Bartholomew Darnley's murder.' He lowered his voice. 'As well as Lord Taylor-Howard's, no matter what Sir Percival says. Just to do it extremely quietly, of course, so neither he nor Whitehall finds out.'

'And if they do?'

He shrugged. 'Then he'll deny all knowledge and I'm on my own.'

'Great! Well, I can help make sure that doesn't happen by quietly continuing the investigation at my end, Hugh.'

'Quietly? Lady Swift doing anything quietly?' He put his sandwich down and pointed at her. '*That* Lady Swift?'

'Hilarious. I've been making very discreet inquiries, actually. As quiet as the proverbial church mouse, in fact. Haven't I, Clifford?'

Clifford continued to unpack one of the hampers. 'Ahem. Forgive me, my lady, I must have been looking the other way at that particular moment.'

'You terror! You commended me earlier on how well I'd done.'

'Come on then,' Seldon said, his amusement evident. 'Enlighten me, do.'

She gave a mock huff and shoved her notebook under her cushion. 'You first.'

He ran a hand through his curls which Eleanor had been enjoying watching quiver in the light summer evening breeze. 'It's not much, I'm frustrated to admit. Mostly a raft of unreliable alibis for the time of Mr Darnley's death. Again, Clifford, no offence, but I checked with the two staff you asked previously. The one at Lady Montfort's and the other at Sir Roderick's. They both just confirmed their employers' alibis. I wasn't entirely convinced, I'm afraid.'

'A shame, Chief Inspector. My apologies for the wild goose chase.'

Seldon shook his head. 'Don't apologise. Their statements move Lady Montfort and Rumbold further up my suspect list, actually. Especially because the statements were—'

'Identical?' Eleanor said.

Seldon nodded. 'Perfectly so.'

'Hugh, you said you checked "a raft" of alibis?'

'Yes. All hopelessly inconclusive.' He turned to the last page in his notebook. 'Mr Treacher, or Fingers, as you disconcertingly refer to him, was next. But his alibi was only backed up by his completely untrustworthy associates.'

'Where did they all say he was?'

'In his club. All night.'

'Of course. And we know he wouldn't have personally got his fingers dirty, anyway. He'd have used a lackey, so he probably *was* at the club all night. But, Hugh, we do have an alibi for Sergei Orlov. He told us less than two hours ago he was with his bosses.'

'Who will all deny even knowing him, as he mentioned, my lady,' Clifford said.

Eleanor's salmon sandwich lost its allure. 'Drat! I'd forgotten that!'

'A glass of ginger beer, Chief Inspector?' Clifford said.

Seldon looked at it suspiciously, his hand hovering. 'Is this another of Mrs Trotman's lethal concoctions? Like the ones we all regretted enjoying so many of on New Year's Eve?'

'Indeed. Although this one was not borne of her secret distiller, so it is quite suitable for a gentleman on duty.'

As they sipped the refreshing amber liquid, Seldon sighed. 'Time is getting away from us. Which means the murderer is too. Anything else from your interviews, you two? What we really need is a breakthrough.'

Clifford put down the plate of cherry and almond pastry turnovers he'd picked up and reached into his jacket pocket, pulling out a neatly folded handkerchief.

'Actually, Chief Inspector, I may have just the thing.'

25

'Mr Clifford! My dear old rascal.'

'Squints, how are you?'

On the doorstep of a tiny, thatched cottage, Eleanor shared a surprised look with Seldon as a pair of disembodied arms in elbow-length leather gloves reached out and clasped her butler's shoulders.

'Mr Clifford, you grow more distinguished with every year that passes between your all too rare visits.'

'Then I can only surmise, you are long overdue another eye test, Squints.'

'Same Mr Clifford as always! Come in, come in, my friend.'

The gloves were followed out of the door by a shock of grey hair attached to the smallest man Eleanor had ever seen. He barely came up to her shoulder. Swamped by a leather apron, he had a wire contraption on his head that sported several pairs of spectacles. Which was confusing, since he was already wearing a pair that covered most of the top half of his face.

Clifford stepped to one side and held out his hand. 'Forgive my not having sent word ahead, but I have brought important company.'

'No. No. Don't tell me.' The man switched his spectacles for another set and stepped forward, hand outstretched. 'Dear lady, you absolutely have to be Lord Henley's niece.'

'I am.' She shook his hand. 'How did you guess?'

'My lady,' Clifford said, 'this is Mr Aubrey Frampton.'

The diminutive man laughed. 'Or "Squints" to my friends. Which, along with this old reprobate here,' – he pointed to Clifford – 'I was humbled to number your uncle, Lord Henley, among. Until his tragic parting, of course. My condolences.' At Lord Henley's name, Gladstone let out a soft whine and pressed himself against her leg.

'Thank you. It's an absolute treat to meet you, Mr Frampton.' Eleanor wanted to call him by his nickname, but worried she might laugh if she did.

'And this is Chief Inspector Seldon,' Clifford said. As the men shook hands, Clifford clapped their host on the back. 'Squints, we need to call on your inimitable expertise.'

'Thank heaven.' Their new companion ushered them into the house. 'Because the ghosts have been acting quite out of character!'

Trusting her butler's judgement, she bit her tongue and shrugged at Seldon's quizzical look as they followed Frampton inside. He led them through the sort of disorganised chaos only a bachelor could create to a sitting room, which opened onto a huge glass conservatory.

'Oh my!' she breathed. 'That is—'

'Amazing,' Seldon said.

The conservatory appeared to be filled with every conceivable kind of butterfly.

'Oh, not just butterflies.' Frampton waved his hands, seeming to read their thoughts. 'No. No. Moths as well. In fact, close to every intricately winged beauty known to man.'

Clifford stepped up behind Eleanor and Seldon and murmured, 'To allay your unspoken concerns regarding the lucidity of our host,' – he pointed to a cloud of silvery forms spiralling upwards in a strong shaft of sunlight – 'those are ghost moths.'

Frampton obviously picked up Clifford's last few words. 'Indeed they are. And they are worrying me no end. They should not be doing that so early in the year. Most perplexing!'

'Ah!' Eleanor tried to sound as if she were knowledgeable about the seasonal habits of obscure moths. She turned to find their host hurrying on out the door and into the garden. As she followed, she called, 'Might I ask what area your expertise lies in, Mr Frampton? Apart from moths, of course.'

'Only if you make an old man very happy by joining him for tea?'

'Deal. So you are an expert in...?'

By now they had crossed the conservatory and emerged onto a surprisingly well-tended lawn, bisected by a stone path leading to a workshop. Squints gestured to the building. 'This is my laboratory. I am, my dear, a life-long student of glass.'

Behind Eleanor and Seldon, Clifford whispered, 'Do not be fooled by appearances. Mr Frampton is in fact an exceptional expert, being a long-venerated fellow of The Royal Society. We are most fortunate to be able to call upon his superlative scientific knowledge.'

Seldon lowered his voice. 'Am I the only one who has no clue why we are here?'

'I'm as in the dark as you are,' Eleanor said. 'Even though I trust you implicitly, Clifford, my curiosity has entirely eaten me up to the point I'm now ready to boil your head.'

'Too kind, my lady.'

Clifford retrieved the handkerchief he had pulled out before they left.

'The pieces of Lord Taylor-Howard's champagne flute we stole,' she said without thinking.

'Stole?' Seldon scrunched his eyes shut. 'Eleanor, tell me

you haven't resorted to misappropriating items from a crime scene without telling the head of the investigation!'

She threw her hands out. 'Well, Hugh, since the head of that investigation is Sir Percival, what would you have done?'

'Not stolen those pieces. I might, however, have "borrowed" them briefly, which is what I'm sure you meant?'

She laughed. 'Not a chance. My scallywag butler and I swiped them so we could at least crow that we are more observant and thorough than Sir Percival. Anyway, he basically told us that he would dismiss anything we discovered as his men had already thoroughly searched the marquee.'

Seldon shook his head. 'But what do you think this Frampton chap can do for us then, Clifford? If the flute is Lord Taylor-Howard's and the poison has been confirmed, what else can we learn?'

Clifford spread his hands. 'With your permission, sir, I shall leave that to our expert.'

'But why is glass his obsession?' Eleanor said.

'Because it gave me my life.' Frampton bustled over. 'I was born almost blind. Until I was nine, I stumbled everywhere with two walking sticks, as the entire world was a hazy blur that swam in and out constantly. Nothing but shadows and fog. Then, thanks to my father's unfailing endeavours to scrape together every penny he could and a chance meeting with a benevolent and talented optometrist, everything changed.' He patted the series of spectacles on his head. 'Five different pairs of passionately crafted circles of glass opened the door for me on this breathtakingly glorious world we live in. And, at the age of nine, they let me see my parents' faces for the first time.'

Inside the workshop, Frampton busied himself at a large bench, observed by Clifford and Seldon. Eleanor, feeling restless, wandered around, marvelling that it seemed there was nothing this charming little man couldn't fabricate out of his beloved substance. She was running her fingers over sheets of coloured glass, tracing the patterns of tiny bubbles, when she looked up to see Seldon staring at her.

'Sorry, this is taking a while, Hugh. I know your hideous mountain of paperwork is calling you.'

'Don't apologise. Clifford usually comes up trumps.'

'I know. I just hope Frampton can do the same. Although, like you said, what can there be left to find out from two bits of champagne flute?' She wrinkled her nose. 'It might end up being a waste of your time.'

Seldon ran his eyes over her face. 'I still wouldn't have missed it, Eleanor.'

'Aha!'

They both spun round to see a very excited Frampton clapping Clifford on the back. 'As you suspected.'

'My lady. Chief Inspector,' Clifford called them to the workbench.

'What have you discovered?' She hurried over, Seldon beside her.

Frampton pointed to one of the glass fragments under the microscope.

'That this is not what you think.'

Eleanor frowned. 'So, you're saying it wasn't part of the base of Lord Taylor-Howard's champagne flute as we thought? But... but something else?'

He nodded. 'Something fiendishly secretive.' He took the long-nosed pincers Clifford held out to him and picked up the piece of glass from the microscope's polished plate. 'This little beauty is part of a powerful lens.'

Eleanor gasped. 'Like a spectacle lens? Or a monocle? Treacher wears a monocle.'

Seldon nodded. 'I know. Rather affected, I'd say.'

'My lady.' Clifford gestured to their host, who was shaking his head.

'Sorry, do continue.'

Frampton smiled. 'Not a piece of eyewear, dear lady. No. No. This is a section of a remarkably impressive miniature camera lens.'

Seldon slapped his notebook on the workbench and began making a series of notes. 'Good work, Clifford. And you, Mr Frampton. I am extremely grateful.'

'But what size would a camera have to be to have a lens that small? And why?' Eleanor said.

'Good questions, my lady,' Clifford said. 'It would have to be the size of an ingenious but rare "spy camera". His lordship had one he used on... ahem, certain occasions.'

'I bet he did,' Seldon muttered. 'Which also answers your second question, Eleanor. To spy on something. Or someone. Mr Frampton, can you guess more about the size and type of the camera from the lens?'

'Perhaps better still, I might sketch it for you?'

A few minutes later, Eleanor took the small sheet of squared paper their host held out to her. 'Is that an approximation?'

Clifford gave a quiet cough. 'It will be precisely to scale, my lady.'

Seldon leaned over Eleanor's shoulder. 'That could have been concealed in many things.'

'Ah, but see how it is shaped, Chief Inspector.' Frampton waved his pencil over the picture. 'The elliptical edging means it was most likely set in something not round, square or oblong.'

Eleanor's brow furrowed. 'But what shape does that leave?'

'Something curved,' Clifford said slowly. 'Like the handle of a cane.'

Back in the Rolls, Eleanor could see that Seldon was as excited as she was.

'If Lord Taylor-Howard had a spy camera in his cane, Sir

Percival's theory of him selling secrets seems more and more likely. Now—'

'But hang on,' Eleanor said. 'What about the other piece of glass? Frampton said that was from the champagne flute.'

Seldon frowned. 'And? What am I missing?'

'And that the scratch was part of an engraving.'

'Again, and?'

Eleanor poked him in the ribs, evidently harder than intended, as he grunted. 'Oops, sorry. Clifford and I examined all the champagne flutes the officials drank from in the marquee.'

'They were still there?'

'Yes. Sir Percival said he wouldn't waste resources on having them tested as no one else was poisoned.'

'Fair point.'

'But don't you see? As none of them are engraved, it means Lord Taylor-Howard must have been given a special flute. Which is how the murderer knew which one to poison!'

'Brilliant!' Seldon said. 'If irritating, seeing as I'm supposed to be the detective.'

'You are. And the best there is,' she said softly.

'Thank you. Now, we need to find out who ordered that flute to be engraved.'

'Absolutely. But who do we ask?'

'The chief official who was on stage, my lady?'

'The portly fellow? Good shout, Clifford.'

Seldon stroked his chin. 'Excellent. And while I follow up on this spy camera, I think I'll also pay a visit to a certain young Lady Araminta Taylor-Howard.'

Eleanor frowned. 'What!? You never mentioned Xander had a sister before. Clifford, it seems we have another meeting to arrange.'

In the rear-view mirror, she saw her butler's eyes dart to Seldon.

Seldon shook his head. 'Oh, no, Eleanor. You are not going. I am.'

She locked eyes with him. 'I thought you trusted me, Hugh.'

'I do. But Sir Percival has told you who to interview, and she is not on the list. He will be suspicious at the least if he finds out you have interviewed her.'

'True. But he's also made clear he'll make sure you're sacked if he finds out you're investigating. So, what's it to be?'

26

Running the length of fifteen porticoed terraced entrances, the tall cream stone edifice of Regina Mews rose five grand floors to her sculpted roofline. This monolithic and unashamed testament to wealth was betrayed only on the last doorstep by the brass panel of bell pulls.

Beside her, Clifford arched a brow at Eleanor.

'Not quite what we were expecting, I know.' She tapped the nameplate beside number three of five. 'Given her royal connection, I wonder if she's embarrassed it's only an apartment, not quite the full prestigious address. There's no reason why she should be, but if you have any connection to the royal family, I'm sure keeping up appearances is essential.'

'Actually, she couldn't care less,' a female voice rose sharply up to them.

Oops, Ellie! Her brain went into panic mode as the young woman's heels clicked up the stone steps from the basement towards her. This was absolutely no footing to start out on. And since the fine-featured, dark-haired beauty now standing in front of her was the double of Lord Taylor-Howard, there was no doubting this was the sister she had come to interview. But as those lagoon-blue eyes glared back at her, she couldn't miss that the angry glint was tempered by sadness.

'I'm so sorry,' Eleanor said genuinely. 'I really didn't mean to be insulting.' Eleanor pointed to the ribbon-wrapped cake box Clifford was holding, her calling card placed neatly under the bow. 'I was just hoping to offer my condolences, accompanied by fine Parisian-style macaroons. With extra chocolate. I'm Lady Swift.'

The communal marble-floored entrance hall and stairwell with its gold-painted wall sconces and tasteful figurines made the inside of Lady Taylor-Howard's apartment seem even more overdue for a significant refurbishment. The sunlight filtering in through the faded voile drapes of the two floor-to-ceiling windows dominating the room highlighted that the polished oak boards were closer to worn than fashionably shabby. Paintings of hunting scenes in dark oils hung in faded frames while the Chesterfield's brown leather was as cracked as the matching armchairs'. To Eleanor, the decor seemed peculiarly masculine.

Lady Taylor-Howard obviously read her thoughts. She waved a hand around the room. 'Dear old father kitted it all out to be quite the spiffing pied-à-terre for the second son he never had.'

Her tone was more resigned than bitter. She dropped into an armchair and gestured for Eleanor to do the same.

'That can't be easy.' Eleanor sat and leaned back. 'Especially now, since your brother's passing. My sincerest of condolences.'

'Thank you. Really. I'm sorry if outside, I was a bit—'

'Sharp?' Eleanor smiled. 'Yes. But with excellent reason. I have the most traitorous tongue ever. It trips me up all the time.'

That brought a wan smile to her hostess' face. 'And yet somehow I also have the feeling it makes you delightful company. If one is in the mood. Which I confess I am. I thought I wanted to be alone, but it seems I was wrong.' Her eyes fell on the macaroon box. 'Oh, coffee, yes. Would you like a coffee Lady Swift?' She paused as Clifford took a respectful step forward.

'Perhaps I might be permitted to assist as your maid is obviously absent, Lady Taylor-Howard?'

'Lovely. It's along through there.' She indicated through an archway to the left with an airy wave of her hand.

'Do call me Araminta,' Lady Taylor-Howard said as Clifford disappeared into the kitchen with the macaroons. 'I haven't the puff for any formality today.'

'Nor I. It's Eleanor.'

Lady Taylor-Howard's eyes misted over. 'Xander used to call me Minty.'

'I always wanted a brother,' Eleanor said. 'And a sister too, but mostly a big brother to chase about through the woods, build stick forts and sail with. It sounded such fun. Especially after I lost my parents.'

Lady Taylor-Howard leaned forward. 'Does it get easier quickly? Losing someone, I mean.'

'I think that depends,' Eleanor said carefully. 'You haven't lost anyone before Xander then?'

'A few stuffy aunts and uncles when I was tiny. And we lost relatives during the war. And after due to the influenza, of course. But none close. We Taylor-Howards seemed to receive a divine pardon from all that. But Xander wasn't that kind of brother, anyway. Not like the one you just described. Not that I would have done any of those things you described either, though.' She looked Eleanor over with a puzzled frown. 'But Xander never mentioned you. I mean, I know he had a lot of... female friends, but you've popped up out of nowhere.'

'It's a terrible habit, I admit.' Eleanor caught Clifford's eye as he returned with a tray of coffee and the macaroons artfully arranged on a china cake stand. He gestured discreetly to the silver-framed photograph she hadn't noticed on the side table at her elbow. She pointed to it.

'Might this be one memory you can draw some comfort from, Araminta? You look so similar there, it's wonderful. And not just because you're in matching pirate costumes.'

'Oh.' Lady Taylor-Howard glanced at the photograph. 'That was a long time ago. Xander stopped being my party partner as soon as he could shake me off for real girls.' Again, she looked Eleanor over.

'It's alright, Araminta, you've no need to tread carefully. But thank you. I know all about his reputation for love affairs. I wasn't one of them. Nor did I want to be.'

Her hostess accepted her cup from Clifford and chose a macaroon. 'Well, you must be one of the few women in England who wasn't and didn't.'

Eleanor was in a quandary. She didn't want to lie and pretend Xander and she had been good friends. They had barely been acquaintances. On the other hand, she had a double-murderer to catch.

'It's just as well, then. That we were never really acquainted like that, I mean. I probably would only have led him even further astray.'

Lady Taylor-Howard shook her head. 'No. That could never have happened. Xander was the master of courting trouble. I think you had a lucky escape. Stupid boy. So much for being the sensible big brother.' She bit into her macaroon and then finished the second half before reaching automatically for another. Clifford topped up her coffee.

Eleanor took a sip of hers. 'He must have been even naughtier than I realised. Were you able to help him though, Araminta? Did he listen to you?'

Lady Taylor-Howard waved her macaroon. 'Of course not! He was the invincible Xander! Or so he believed. Besides, look around you, how could I possibly have helped him with his ever-mounting debts. He got the son's allowance.'

'And you get the smaller daughter's, perhaps?'

'Vastly smaller. Like my so-called apartment here. And like my standing with Father.' Lady Taylor-Howard shrugged. 'Not that it matters much. I'll be married off to someone rich enough for my father's and His Majesty's liking when they deign to get around to it.' She stared into her coffee. 'That's the ridiculous thing about it all. Boys have all the pressure to make their name and their fortune. Or at least preserve the one they've already got. But what happens when they can't? Some of them just aren't built that way. Like Xander. He was clever, funny and creative. And yet all he ever seemed to succeed at was getting caught up in all the wrong things. I would have helped him if I could have, although he never would have let me.'

'Too proud?'

'Too stubborn. And more and more of late, too secretive to really open up about what was going on with him.'

'Did you worry about who he might have owed money to?'

'I worried about everything he did. Especially after he let slip he'd been threatened. Of course, he then did his usual thing of laughing it off.' She imitated her brother's voice. '"No one's going to mess with a royal, Minty! Relax!"' Araminta shuffled forward to the edge of her seat. 'You think he was in even more trouble than I know, don't you?'

Remember, Ellie, she doesn't know Xander was murdered. And you can't tell her.

'Genuinely, I... I don't know. But I think he might have been. And'– Eleanor scrambled for her words – 'for some inexplicable reason, I feel I owe it to him to find out.' She looked up into those big blue eyes, holding her gaze. 'Do you mind?'

Lady Taylor-Howard surprised her by laughing. 'Even though I have no real idea who you are or why you're here, for some inexplicable reason no, I don't.'

'I was told that he was coming into some money just before he died. Enough, perhaps, to pay off his debts?'

Lady Taylor-Howard took another bite of a macaroon and a sip of coffee. 'I don't know where he was getting the money from, if he was. Like all the family his age, he was living off credit only a few days after he got his allowance each month, as he lived so extravagantly. And gambled like a fool.'

'He never hinted at any financial schemes or new acquaintances to you?'

'No. The only way Xander could ever have paid off his considerable debts is if he inherited Uncle Gerald's money and estate. He's my late mother's brother, you see, so he is the nearest surviving male relative to inherit from. Although Xander always said that the old codger, as he'd nicknamed him, would outlive him.' She took another macaroon. 'And he was right.'

'Again, I'm so sorry,' Eleanor said. 'What about other members of the family? Any cousins or other royals in line that Xander was... close to? Maybe he might have tried to get them to help him quietly with his debts?'

Araminta rolled her eyes. 'Much to His Majesty's immense irritation and a fluke of bad luck for the eminent lineage, the majority of our cousins are female. So the only thing my darling brother would have been trying to do was get them into bed. And not quietly!'

Outside, before she reached the Rolls, a familiar finger wave from across the street drew Eleanor's attention.

'Yoo hoo.'

'Tipsy!' Eleanor waved back.

The traffic slowed to a stop as Lady Fitzroy sashayed across. 'Fancy meeting you here, sweetie. You never mentioned you know Araminta.'

'I don't. Didn't until now. I just came to offer my condolences.'

'Oh, you are the sweetest.' Tipsy slipped her arm through Eleanor's. 'But that's why I'm here too. We could have come together though, what a shame.' Her dark eyes widened with glee. 'Ooh, but what about cocktails in an hour? I know this fabulous place. Say you will.'

Eleanor smiled at her friend's pleading look. 'I can't, Tipsy. I have things to do.'

'I hope you mean getting to know some eligible boys!' She fluffed Eleanor's curls with a painted nail and pouted. 'Why don't you let me help you make the most of what you've got, sweetie?'

Eleanor laughed. 'Goodbye, Tipsy. It was good to bump into you. See you soon.'

'That had better be a promise, sweetie,' Tipsy called over her shoulder. 'I refuse to give up on you, you know.'

Clifford held open the passenger door to the Rolls. 'My hearty commendations, my lady.'

'What for? Grilling a grieving sister while deceiving her I was friends with her brother? And for deceiving Tipsy? Again? Not my finest hour. And now, to add to my shame, Araminta has filled me with a terrible thought. One so dreadful it necessitates a swift drive home to a generous brandy with my favourite impeccably suited voice of reason to help me process it.'

'Of course.' He closed her door, before taking the driver's seat and easing the Rolls into motion. 'Might I request, though, that you share your thoughts, so I am mentally prepared as it were?'

'Only if you roll down your window so I can't hear how hard you tut at the images swirling round my mind.'

With an amused quirk of his lips, he did as she bid.

'Good. Because Araminta has left me wondering if our

naughty minor royal might have been misusing his position of family chaperone.'

'In what way, my lady?'

'By using his royal connections – and charms – to gain the trust of his cousins' titled and rich lady friends in order to swindle those friends out of their allowances or even inheritance! How's that for a royal scandal?'

27

A few minutes later, Eleanor was aware of the Rolls slowing down. The country lane ahead was empty save for a battered Model T Ford parked at an angle by the side of the road.

She frowned. 'What is it, Clifford?'

Her butler's eyes scanned the surrounding beech woods.

'I am unsure, my lady. But I have a feeling—'

'Agh!' She clutched her chest as a tweed-suited man with a shock of white hair appeared at her side window.

Clifford brought the Rolls to a stop. The man rapped on the glass with the handle of a riding crop.

'Orlov!'

She went to open her door, but Clifford put a restraining gloved hand on her arm.

'Forgive me, my lady. Disarmingly charming and entertaining he may be, but he is still a murder suspect.'

She nodded and waited for Clifford to come round, then stepped out beside him.

'Good afternoon, dear lady.' Orlov bowed. 'We meet again.'

She folded her arms. 'Since I've no idea why you have waved me down in the middle of nowhere – or how you knew I would be coming this way – spare me the routine. What do you want?'

'Ah, a great many things, for what doesn't Orlov want.' He stroked his chin. Beside her, Clifford's hand strayed towards the inside of his jacket. 'Relax, friend,' Orlov said. 'If I had wanted to harm Lady Swift, we would now be somewhere far more fitting for such an elegant and titled maiden to come to a sticky end.'

'State your business, Mr Orlov.' Clifford's tone was steely. 'While you still can.'

'Oh, he is good,' Orlov whispered to Eleanor. 'Really, you are quite the pair.' To Clifford, he said, 'I would have thought my business obvious, friend. I need Lady Swift's help.'

At their confused looks, he held out his hands.

'It is simple. Thanks to you, instead of my usual relaxed arrangements with your British Intelligence fellows about my whereabouts, I now have every stout-booted Jonathon with a badge crowding my shadow.'

'Jonathon?'

'As in "Johnny", my lady,' Clifford said.

'Ah, I see. So, Mr Orlov, do I take it the police are following you?'

He snorted. 'Not just the police, dear lady. All manner of nosey official types who have less discretion than an elephant carrying a full brass band. It has gone far beyond my telephone being tapped.'

'Sir Percival tapped your phone?'

'Of course.' He shrugged. 'Even his own staff are under constant scrutiny. Why? Because he daren't trust anyone. And how could he? It is his unenviable job to keep your royal family safe. And scandal free. Good luck to him, I say.' He grimaced. 'But I see you do not quite understand why I am here. It is purely that you are working for Sir Percival and then seeking me out all too often. Which means none of my regular contacts will come within sight of me.'

'Why ever not?'

'Because they fear any words they share with me might somehow end up tickling the ears of Sir Percival.'

She sighed in vexation. 'Then, Mr Orlov, save us both time and just tell him everything you know about Lord Taylor-Howard and Bartholomew Darnley! Then we needn't meet ever again.'

'It is impossible to do so! Because not only my contacts, but also my bosses, would prefer I keep well away from the likes of him.'

Eleanor nodded, thinking that was a pretty sound way to go.

Orlov looked pleadingly at her. 'Dear lady. What will it take for you to clear me of anything to do with these unfortunate deaths, so I am no longer of interest to Sir Percival and his impressive nose?'

'Oh, just the truth. Which you could have told me at our first meeting.'

'True. And I did. At least to a degree.'

'So what exactly did you lie about?'

'Nothing. My business is not about lying. It is about squirreling away secrets and then avoiding being caught with them. Which is why Lord Taylor-Howard was a lapse of judgement on my part.'

'So, he *did* sell you state secrets!'

'Secrets, yes. Ones of state, no.'

She studied his face, searching for signs of whether he was telling the truth, but it was an impossible task. She shook her head. 'I don't understand, but I'm listening.'

He looked over his shoulder. 'May I enter your magnificent Rolls Royce? Even trees have ears.' He held his arms out to Clifford. 'You are welcome to check me for a weapon first, friend.'

In the car, Clifford slid into the back seat beside Orlov,

having blocked the man's way with an arm across the door until Eleanor was seated in the front.

'Enough theatre, Mr Orlov,' he said firmly.

He nodded. 'As I am the guest that comes cap in the hand, I shall rush to the point as you ask.' He looked at Eleanor. 'Dear lady, Lord Taylor-Howard and I had an agreement, but it is not as you suspect. And not as Sir Percival fears.'

'Nothing that would cause a scandal, then?'

'Only if sating the appetite of my fellow Russians for scandalous news is so.'

'Well, of course it is! So much for not lying. You said only a moment ago that Lord Taylor-Howard didn't sell you state secrets.'

'He didn't.'

Eleanor glanced at Clifford, who arched a bewildered brow in reply.

Orlov laughed. 'Dear lady, what do you imagine the majority of ordinary people in Russia are doing right now?'

'I've no idea,' she said, thinking she should have a better grasp on international affairs.

He leaned forward, but then dropped back apologetically as Clifford pressed a hand to his chest. 'Dreaming. Just like here.'

'Dreaming?'

'Yes. Dreams of the secret life of the aristocracy. The elegance. The money. The glamour!'

'So... Lord Taylor-Howard used his royal connection to...?'

'To pass on insider secrets about the elite of English society! Especially royal society, of course. Who was where, with who, doing what. But, most importantly, scandalous affairs of the royal heart. And wardrobe. Every fashion triumph – and disaster. Isn't it wonderful? Fashion and gossip uniting our two magnificent countries!'

Eleanor took a moment to process what he'd said. 'But why would you pay him for English society gossip?'

'Because I got triple what I paid him for it from the Moscow magazines I passed it on to. Even though he made up a proportion of it, I'm sure, the Moscovites devoured every illicit morsel they could get.' He shrugged. 'It wasn't my place to find out what was true and what he had painted with a gilded brush. He was my golden goose, after all.'

'And you really think we'll believe that?' Eleanor said.

'I do. Because of these.' He held his hands up to Clifford and gestured to his inside jacket pocket. From there, Clifford pulled out a slim sheaf of papers and a folded, glossy-covered magazine. Orlov motioned for him to give the notes to Eleanor. 'Those handwritten papers are Taylor-Howard's last report to me, of which I sent copies on to my editor in Moscow. Translated into my mother tongue, naturally. I'm sure a lady of your bold intelligence will easily find a way to check it is his handwriting. Meanwhile, your man here can improve his mind by translating enough of the magazine to see that the contents are exactly what is on those sheets. With a journalist's enthusiastic embellishments, of course.'

As she scanned the first page, Clifford flicked to the article Orlov indicated. After a few moments, they looked questioningly at each other.

'My lady, my humble strides through Tolstoy's masterpieces in Russian do not permit me a full translation by any means. However, this article does seem to be gossip about the royal family – mostly minor royals – and their clothes. And, ahem, as Mr Orlov stated, affairs of the heart. Imagined or otherwise.'

Eleanor frowned. 'Compared to stealing our national secrets, this' – she waved the magazine – 'is hardly likely to get you into that much trouble, is it, Orlov?'

He shrugged. 'Perhaps. Perhaps not.'

She sighed in exasperation. 'So why didn't you tell us the truth the first time we met?'

He held out his hands. 'Because, dear lady, it will certainly spell the end of my credibility as a spy! Besides, I am paid by certain people who would not take kindly to news that I am, or was, getting extra rum with my pickles.' He looked at Clifford for help. 'This English expression I do not understand.'

Clifford shuddered. 'That is because someone has had fun at your expense, Mr Orlov. Rum and pickles should never be taken together. It would be sacrilege.'

Eleanor bit back a smile. 'What you're saying though, Orlov, is that you would get a nasty slap on the wrist from your bosses if they knew about this.' She tapped the papers.

'Absolutely. It would result in a most unpleasant meeting with...' – Orlov swallowed hard – 'the Committee. Not a pretty picture. They know as well as I do that Russians are as obsessed with the English royal family as the rest of the world. After all, our now expelled royal family was entwined with yours. However, they do not want this... unhealthy interest officially acknowledged or encouraged in any way.'

'I see.' She thought for a moment. 'Did Lord Taylor-Howard give you photographs along with his notes?'

Orlov's brow creased. 'He did not. But he was going to before he died.'

'And did you furnish him with a miniature spy camera?'

Orlov whistled softly. 'I think Sir Percival may have under-estimated you. I did indeed. The articles are worth double with pictures, however poor.' He glanced at his watch and then up and down the road. 'I fear I must go.' He reached for the door handle. 'You will find that I have told only the truth. And in doing so, I look forward to being erased from Sir Percival's watch list.' He slipped out of the car, but then popped his head back in through the window. 'By the way. Now that Lord Taylor-Howard is no longer with us, I have an opening, dear lady. With your connections and guile you could easily become Moscow's next secret source of all things scandalous and fashionable!'

At the word 'fashionable', Clifford hastily turned away, apparently to cover up a fit of coughing. Eleanor eyed him with amusement.

'Thank you for the offer, Mr Orlov, but it seems my butler, for one, believes I would not be quite as suitable a candidate as you might think.'

Orlov shrugged. 'Do ponder on it, won't you? For the moment, toodle-pip as you English love to say.'

As Orlov drove away, Clifford stepped out of the back of the Rolls and into the driver's seat. Eleanor stared after the receding car.

'Well, Clifford. What do you think?'

'I think not, my lady.'

She fixed him with a steely glare. 'I meant, did you believe he was telling the truth! Not whether I should take him up on his offer. Now just get us back to Henley Hall before I change my mind and I do decide to become the next royal gossipmonger! I need to update Hugh.'

28

'Ready. Steady!' Eleanor waved the tennis ball at Gladstone, who was spinning in lopsided circles on the lawn. 'Fetch!' She turned and threw it as hard as she could.

'Nice throw!' a deep voice called from the other side of the lawn. She looked up and bit her lip at the unexpected sight of the ever smart-suited Seldon dropping his briefcase and leaping to deftly grab the ball.

She clapped. 'Nice catch!'

Gladstone lumbered over as fast as he could, ball forgotten. On reaching Seldon, he hurled himself up on his back legs to offer a licky welcome. Seldon fought off the kisses as best he could, while quickly throwing the ball again.

'Fetch, old friend!' The bulldog woofed and set off in stiff-legged pursuit. Seldon jogged over to Eleanor. 'We so need to work on his greeting.'

She smiled. 'Do we? Since when did Gladstone become our joint problem?' His cheeks flushed so much she immediately felt bad. 'Well, let's at least discuss more pressing matters first. We'll have to start without Clifford, though.'

His face clouded. 'Clifford's always here. What's happened?'

'Nothing. He's just running some errands in the Rolls.'

'So you are here alone with the ladies?'

'Not exactly.' She hoped he wouldn't ask any more questions, since she didn't want to go into the details about Silas, her game-keeper, as Clifford referred to him. It had taken months before she realised Silas was, in fact, a security guard with no qualms about doing whatever was necessary to keep the occupants of Henley Hall safe. That he was so elusive she still hadn't ever set eyes on him had ceased to seem odd. But explaining any of that felt a step too far right now. She shrugged. 'Anyway, what would be the problem if I was? Clifford needs to escape me sometimes, poor chap.' She motioned for them to move into the house.

'I don't doubt that,' Seldon said sincerely.

'You rotter! Shall we head inside?'

In the snug, she opted for her favourite chaise longue. Having wrestled Gladstone for space, she waved Seldon into the two-seater leather Chesterfield on the other side of the oval onyx-topped coffee table.

As he sat down, he frowned. 'Clifford's sure?'

She nodded. 'Absolutely. Whatever contraptions Sir Percival has secreted into the telephones are his only means of listening in. There isn't even one in here. And they can't pick up what we're saying if the handset is on its cradle either. Relax.' The set of his shoulders, however, told her he was anything but. 'Hugh, you know how irritatingly thorough Clifford is. He's checked everywhere.'

'I'm sure. And he's also incredibly knowledgeable about a great many things. But Sir Percival has access to the latest of everything. No disrespect, but Clifford has been out of whatever slightly questionable game he supported your late uncle in for too long to be completely up to speed.'

'Ah! Well, you see, he has help. There's a member of staff here at Henley Hall who you haven't met. And neither have I, if I'm honest. But between him and Clifford, you can rest assured anything we do or say here will not reach Sir Percival's eager beaver ears.'

There was a knock at the door.

'Coffee, m'lady.' Mrs Butters came in, balancing a tray with a tall silver pot and another of hot water. Polly followed, bearing two cups and saucers. Lizzie came behind, with a milk jug and a sugar bowl. Bringing up the rear, Mrs Trotman bore a cake stand of delicious smelling golden brown sweet pastries. With each of their burdens set down, the women stood in line and curtsied. Then they lingered, trying not to stare at Seldon. Eleanor couldn't stifle her amusement.

'Can we bring anything else?' Mrs Butters said.

'Anything at all?' Polly and Lizzie chorused.

'I'd say we're fine.' Seldon gave them all a genuine winning smile, oblivious to the effect this had on the four of them. 'Highly spoiled, I appear to be again, thank you.'

Eleanor hid a smile. 'Clifford isn't back yet then, I gather, ladies?'

'Not yet, m'lady,' Mrs Trotman said.

'But he's been gone ages,' Mrs Butters said. 'Should have been back afore now.'

Mrs Trotters nudged her friend. 'Probably getting the Rolls sorted in town. He said it needed something or other doing to it.'

'Then we can manage quite well, ladies! Thank you.'

'So,' Eleanor said, once they were alone. 'We know from the delightful Mr Frampton, our glass expert, that Xander's champagne flute was engraved, unlike the others used by the officials on the stage. I've already got it on my list to talk to that portly official chap next.'

Seldon poured them both coffee. 'No need, actually. Beat you to it. I bumped into the fellow at the regatta. He told me it's long been tradition to have a royal guest award the prizes at the regatta, if one was available. They've had a new flute engraved to mark the occasion for years now.'

'Are the flutes kept then and displayed somewhere?'

'No. Why?'

'Because surely that means then that the murderer must be familiar with the tradition? Neither you, I, or Clifford knew that one flute was engraved. So, I bet none of the crowd knew either.'

'Excellent thinking.' He made a quick note. 'So, the killer probably attended the regatta every year or was actually an official there. Keep going.'

'Well.' She smoothed her own notebook open on her lap. 'I really wanted Clifford here to talk about the spy camera we realised Xander had, after Mr Frampton confirmed that curved piece of glass was from a camera lens. Even if he's a bit out of touch, Clifford knows a hundred per cent more than I do about such things.'

'Will he be a lot longer, do you think?'

She glanced up at the clock on the mantelpiece. 'Gracious, he's been absolutely ages now. So much for Mister Meticulous Schedule. I'll have hours of fun teasing him about us having to pour our own coffee!'

'Poor fellow. You don't think maybe he's dragging his heels because he's run out of puff for squabbling with you?'

'No chance! He loves it.'

'Peculiarly, I think you might be right. Tell me what you can and then we'll backtrack when he gets here.'

'Well, Orlov told us something very interesting. He was the Russian spy chap I met the other day. And again yesterday when he waylaid the Rolls on our way home.'

'Waylaid! Eleanor, do you see now why I worry about your safety?'

'Don't fret. Clifford was the perfect Jack Russell – or is it Fox Terrier? – and had Orlov pinned in the back seat with ease.'

Seldon put his face in his hands. 'Don't tell me more things I cannot hear, please.'

'Look, eat some more pastries. Try the gooseberry and blackcurrant, they're delicious.'

'I have. And they are. Now, back to this Orlov character?'

'Yes, he gave me these. Hold on.' She wriggled her legs out from underneath Gladstone's bulky form to perch beside Seldon. She showed him the handwritten notes and the glossy Russian magazine while explaining the story of the gossip Lord Taylor-Howard had supposedly been selling.

He stared at her quizzically. 'People will really pay to read about this?'

'Don't ask me. As Clifford delighted in pointing out when he declared I would be doing the Muscovites a disservice if I took up Orlov's offer, I'm not noted as the queen of hot gossip. Or fashion.'

He ran a quick eye over her clothes. 'You don't say?'

She gave a mock huff. 'How lucky that Clifford isn't here for you to gang up with, Hugh. Although, it appears you are quite capable of treading on a lady's sensibilities on your own.'

'Not true. And not possible. Since the lady is adamant, she doesn't have any.' He smiled. 'When it suits her, that is. Anyway, back to work. I'm busy.'

'As am I. Now, can you find a way to check if that is Xander's handwriting? While Clifford wrestles with the intricacies of the Russian text in the magazine, that is.'

'Absolutely.' He looked up from his notes. 'Clifford speaks Russian?'

'Only marginally, according to him. He can read more though.'

'Mmm. It seems unlikely then that this Orlov fellow would make that up as it's an easy bluff to expose.'

'That's what we thought. But he's a slippery fish for sure. Although he would hardly kill Xander if he was making money out of him, would he?'

'I can't answer that as it would be pure supposition.'

'See! That's how different we are. I spend every murder investigation dining on supposition and conjecture.'

'I'd prefer to dine on these pear and walnut pastries, personally.' He bit into one. 'Amazing!'

She nodded, taking one for herself. 'Orlov said he'd been paying Xander for his fashion and gossip tattle for a while. But it didn't sound like he paid a huge amount.'

'Not enough to be paying off big debtors?'

'Definitely not the impression I got. But Orlov said he'd get double for any with photographs. So maybe that was what Xander was hoping would pay enough?'

'Could be.' He made a few quick notes.

She cleared her throat. 'There's also a possibly indelicate matter that came to light about Xander while I was speaking to his sister.' Feeling unusually embarrassed, she filled him in as delicately as she could on her theory that Lord Taylor-Howard might have been using his connections to gain the trust of his royal cousins' titled and rich lady friends in order to swindle them out of their allowances or inheritance.

Seldon whistled. 'I'm amazed you were decorous enough to spare me embarrassment by not blurting out something hopelessly improper for once.'

She flapped an airy hand. 'Watch it. I think you look better with a little colour in your cheeks and I know just how to make that happen.'

'Right, yes.' He stared back down at his notebook. 'Back to the spy camera. Did he ask Orlov for it, or did Orlov offer it to him?'

'He asked Orlov for it.'

'So maybe he wanted the camera for another purpose, not just to take pictures to pass on to Orlov?'

'Maybe to blackmail one of his lovers, you mean? But honestly, despite having suggested it, I'm now having a hard time believing Xander would have stooped so low.'

'Maybe. But it would also explain his unexpected new source of income if it wasn't going to be from selling photographs to Mr Orlov.'

'I know. Blackmail can be a pretty lucrative business.'

'And a deadly one.'

She took another pastry. 'But if Xander was killed because he was blackmailing a lover – or lovers – why would they then kill Barty? I know he apparently aped everything Xander did, but surely not to the point of blackmailing the same person?'

Seldon groaned. 'This is one of the most confusing cases I've worked on. The whole illicit liaisons and cuckolded spouses' element could just be a red herring.'

'Maybe, but...'

'But what?'

'Oh nothing. It's just a feeling. It's so poorly formed, I'm not even sure what it's trying to tell me. I mean—' She broke off at a familiar knock at the door. 'Clifford! Come in! We were wondering where you'd got to... Oh gracious!' They both leaped up from the settee. 'What on earth happened to you?'

29

'Please forgive my shameful appearance, my lady, Chief Inspector,' Clifford said. 'But as I am so disgracefully late, I merely wished to let you know I have returned. I will now go and make myself presentable and return shortly. If you will excuse me.'

He turned to go.

'Clifford. Wait!'

Eleanor looked him over in horror. Her butler's normally immaculate white gloves were streaked with dirt, while his jacket was similarly grubby and had several long tears in the sleeves. His suit trousers and ever-shiny shoes were caked in mud, and an angry swollen red gash along his right-hand jaw made his face appear lopsided. He gave his customary bow from the shoulders but winced as he did so. 'As you wish, my lady.'

'Are you hurt? Where have you been? What happened? Why... oh gracious. Clifford!' She felt hot tears prick her eyes.

Her butler's lips quirked. 'I am fine, my lady. However, perhaps I might be permitted to change whilst you sort the order of your questions?'

Seldon stepped to Eleanor's side. 'Someone set upon you, didn't they, Clifford?'

'More so her ladyship's Rolls Royce, Chief Inspector. That has fared far worse than I.' He turned to Eleanor. 'For which I am most sincerely and humbly apologetic.'

'I don't care about the car, you daft thing!'

Seldon opened his notebook and pen at the ready. 'This blasted case is escalating far too quickly for my liking. Can you bear to give me the salient points before you go and get cleaned up, Clifford? I need to get my men onto this immediately.'

'If you prefer, Chief Inspector.' He gathered his thoughts for the moment. 'I was returning along Short Inch Lane.' He looked at Eleanor. 'That is the road the Atwoods' farm is on. It's the only dwelling in that area.'

'Ah! I know now. I helped Mrs Atwood round up her piglets from the lane once.'

'Quite.' He turned back to Seldon. 'Despite its name, Chief Inspector, it is, in fact, a seven-mile stretch connecting the edge of Little Buckford, our village, with the outer reaches of Chipstone. Chipstone is where I had been engaged in completing a few overdue errands. Anyway, only a mile and a half out from the town, a vehicle shot out from behind the tithe barn, forcing me to swerve into the ditch.'

'Was it that wretched Orlov chap again?' Seldon said. 'Waylaying you yesterday and now upping the stakes? Eleanor, how can I get you to heed my cautions about your cavalier attitude—' He broke off as Clifford shook his head.

'Neither the two men who dragged me from the car, nor the driver of the ambushing vehicle, were in any way familiar to me.' His brows flinched. 'Neither did the whole scenario have any sense of Mr Orlov's notably singular approach that her ladyship and I have experienced to date. The men "roughed me over" as I believe the expression is. They then punctured the car's tyres before speeding off, leaving me to walk back to the village, since the Atwoods were not at home. Mr Wilkes, the milkman, happened past me at the bottom of Henley Hall's hill and kindly dropped me back here.'

Eleanor pointed to the cut on his jaw. 'We need to get some ice on that and probably a fair few other parts you are pretending don't hurt.'

Clifford flexed his fists. 'I am delighted at least to report that the two thugs each received a significant crack to the jaw themselves.'

'Good for you!'

Seldon looked up from taking notes. 'Was that before or after they told you what it was all about? Assuming they did?'

Anger flashed across her butler's face. 'After, sir. But perhaps I might finish the story in private with you?'

'Of course.'

Eleanor stepped between them. 'Of course not! Whatever it is, Clifford, you'll have to tell me sooner or later and I shall only be consumed with worry until you do. Someone clearly threatened you.'

Clifford swallowed hard. 'No, my lady, they threatened *you.*'

'Blast it!' Seldon muttered. 'Thank God you weren't in the car, Eleanor.'

'I don't see why! If I had been, I would have fought the animals off too!'

Clifford rolled his eyes. 'Precisely!'

The two men shared a look.

Seldon sighed. 'What did they say, Clifford?'

'Regrettably, to quote verbatim, "Tell your mistress to stop poking her nose into things that have nothing to do with her. Next time the Rolls will end up at the bottom of the river..."' His hand strayed to his tangled tie.

'With me in it?' she finished for him.

Clifford nodded, his face etched with concern. 'Perhaps a restorative might be required? With your permission, my lady?'

'Oh gracious, of course. I am sorry, Clifford. There you are in dire need of sewing parts of your anatomy back together and I'm being a brat. Huge apologies. Do go.'

Clifford returned some minutes later looking miraculously restored to his usual impeccable self, save for the still angry mark along his jaw and a certain stiffness in his gait. On the silver tray he carried, there was a decanter of warmed brandy and three glasses.

'Good show, Clifford! Finally, you're going to relent and have a more than well-deserved snifter in my presence without my having to badger you into it.'

He bowed. 'Only in the name of saving time, my lady.'

With the brandy having worked its nerve-soothing charm a minute later, Seldon finished grilling Clifford on a description of the men who had jumped him. 'Excellent observations. Hopefully, they should help us catch these ruffians.' He rose and gestured towards the door. 'Can I use your telephone, Eleanor? I need to call my office.'

'You don't need to ask, silly. But actually, you can't because Sir Percival's chaps will probably be listening in, of course.'

'We haven't got time to worry about that,' Seldon said firmly.

Out in the hallway, he picked up the telephone handset as Eleanor slid onto the upholstered settee and pulled her knees up to her chin. Clifford stood his usual respectful distance to her side, his hands behind his back.

'Ah, Brooks, just the chap,' Seldon said into the mouthpiece. 'I need your help. Please note these descriptions down carefully and start a search for them immediately would you? They are wanted in connection with an attack on a motorist along Short Inch lane.' He glanced at Clifford, who nodded. 'It's between Chipstone and Little Buckford.' After he'd given the descriptions of the men and car, he frowned. 'What?' He paused, listening intently. Eleanor wondered if he could look any more handsome. She had just decided he couldn't possibly when he let out a long sigh. 'Really, Brooks? And it has to be now? Alright, yes, I'll hold.'

Eleanor tapped his arm. 'What is it?' she mouthed.

Seldon covered the mouthpiece and whispered, 'My superior wants a word urgently.'

'Oh, dear!' She pulled a face as she glanced at Clifford, who arched a brow in reply.

'Yes, sir,' Seldon said a second later. 'I know, but there's been a complication. One with you too, sir? Yes, I understand you need to be quick but what is it? Sir Percival has done what? Officially taken over jurisdiction of the Bartholomew Darnley case?' He took a deep breath and closed his eyes as the muffled voice continued. 'Yes, sir. Yes, I hear you. Goodbye.'

'Oh, Hugh!' Eleanor said once he had replaced the handset. 'I am sorry.'

He shrugged. 'Sir Percival strikes again. He's at our Oxford headquarters right now. My boss is on his way downstairs to hand over all the evidence we have so far on Bartholomew Darnley's murder.'

'And let me guess. Your boss has no choice but to play ball?'

'Of course. And that means no more investigating Lord Taylor-Howard's murder either. It's one thing to let me do it on the quiet, but quite another to go against the head of the royal police openly, Eleanor. No one can do that.'

'I know, but—'

The telephone rang. Clifford stepped over. 'Little Buckford 342... Lady Swift? Yes, sir. One moment, please.'

'I'll let you speak to whoever it is in private,' Seldon whispered, his deep voice making her tingle. He went to leave, but as she took the handset, Clifford mimed a large, hooked nose, and she spun round, clicking her fingers at Seldon. In three long strides, he was back beside her.

'Hello, Sir Percival.' She held the handset so he could hear too and beckoned Clifford in closer.

'Lady Swift, I am in Oxford,' Sir Percival barked.

'How pleasant. A bit of shopping? Spot of lunch? It's very pretty.'

A muttered 'Infernal creatures!' was just audible. She stuck her tongue out at the handset. Sir Percival's voice came back on louder. 'I've just heard what happened to your man. On the road. In your car.'

'You have?' She shot Seldon a look, but he shrugged. 'Well, he's fine enough, thank you. But nice of you to check.'

A loud snort came down the line. 'I am not wasting my time telephoning to enquire after your butler's welfare, Lady Swift! He can look after himself, I am well aware of that. I have called about you.'

'Then please cut to the chase, Sir Percival. I have a full afternoon ahead of me.'

'Not any more. I accept now that involving you in the investigation of Lord Taylor-Howard's murder was not my finest decision.'

'What do you mean exactly?'

'That your services are no longer required. In any capacity.'

'Now wait a moment—'

'Lady Swift, if I put a man, soldier or not, in the firing line in order to protect King and Country, I do it with a clear conscience. But when a woman is threatened! Well, that is a different matter.'

Eleanor hesitated, her feelings confused. 'Sir Percival, I appreciate your solicitude. However, I knew the risks involved when I—'

'Lady Swift, as the head of the royal police, I am ordering you to stand down. End of discussion. Unless this country is in a state of war, I will not, repeat, will not, put a woman in danger. Good day.'

The line went dead.

'Well, of all the dashed cheek!' Eleanor dropped the receiver on its cradle. 'That man—'

'Has finally redeemed himself,' Seldon said.

She opened her mouth, but then closed it. She passionately believed in equality for women, but at the same time, she found Sir Percival's chivalrous attitude towards her unexpected. And, she had to admit to herself, strangely endearing.

Seldon shrugged. 'Well, that's that.'

She stared at him, open-mouthed. *If he really thinks, Ellie, that you're going to just walk away from getting justice for—* She closed her eyes, trying to work out how to avoid another argument. When she opened them, she caught sight of Clifford's expression in the hall mirror.

'Clifford, what are you so pleased about?'

His amused expression was quickly replaced with his usual deadpan one.

'I really couldn't say, my lady.'

'Yes, you bally well can! Because if, like Hugh, you're pleased I've been banned by Sir Percival from investigating any further, you are in for a very long night with an extremely grumpy mistress!'

'I think not, my lady.' He glanced at Seldon and then quickly away.

'Dash it, you two. What is this now?' She scanned Seldon's face and gasped. 'You were just ribbing me! You're not going to abide by your boss' command, any more than you are going to Sir Percival's, are you?'

Seldon laughed. 'No. Absolutely not. Because as Clifford has worked out, I finally understand how you think. At least a little. You are not going to stand down despite Sir Percival's extremely clear dictum to you. And thus, neither will I.'

Her jaw fell open. 'But you'll be in all manner of trouble, Hugh. Why would you—?'

'Because at the end of the day, justice is more important than my job. And you will be marginally safer if I stay on the investigation.'

Her heart skipped. 'Hugh, I never meant for you to put your job at risk, but I do think we owe it to Xander and Barty to bring their killer to the proper authorities. And then how justice falls is out of our hands.'

Clifford caught sight of Mrs Butters hovering in the background and strode over to her.

Seldon watched him and then turned back to Eleanor. 'Agreed. However, it's going to take the combined creativity of all three of us to do so as we are up against a cunning double-murderer. And also now Sir Percival, his entire team, and mine, including my boss. All of whom will throw us either in jail or the Tower for obstructing justice and disobeying orders at the very least.'

Eleanor nodded. 'It would seem, therefore, we need to achieve this marvellous feat in complete secrecy. We are, officially, on our own.'

'Actually, my lady,' Clifford said, having returned. 'It seems we are not on our own. We have company.'

30

Eleanor and Seldon shared a look. 'I'm not expecting anyone, Clifford. Unless you've made me an appointment I've forgotten about, that is?'

'I doubt, my lady, that the persons in question have made an appointment. Silas has reported two men are watching the main gates. He is currently scouring the perimeter for any more. If you will excuse me, I will go and assist him now.'

Seldon strode to the window and looked out.

'Eleanor, you should at least wait in that room we were having coffee in. It has the least number of windows and I can keep a good look out.' He spun her round by the elbow and gently propelled her towards the door. 'Seeing as I doubt you'll agree to hiding out in the safety of the cellar.'

Appreciating his concern, she let him lead her back to the snug. Once there, she paced the room instead of taking the seat he gestured to.

'I do hope Clifford and Silas are alright.'

'We most certainly are, my lady,' Clifford's measured tone came from the doorway. 'However, Silas has spotted two further men prowling the east perimeter as well as cars with drivers.'

'Blast it, I want to get you out of here, Eleanor.' Seldon ran a hand through his dark hair. 'But if we leave, they'll follow. And likely' – he shook his head as he stepped nearer to her – 'carry out their threat against you, even if they see me with you. Whoever they are, I'm sure they've done their homework on who I am, so will know I'm also working on the investigation.'

'Which means you are no safer than I am, Hugh. If they've been paid by the murderer, they aren't going to hesitate to attack a policeman.'

'Right. Options. We could call Sir Percival, but as we are officially nothing to do with him now—'

'Why would he care? And you'd almost certainly lose your job. What about your chaps, Hugh? Can't they help us?'

'Not without my boss knowing we are still working on the case. Which means Sir Percival will almost certainly find out again. And then it's the Tower! Clifford, thoughts?'

'We need to decamp.' His brow creased. 'I am trying to consider the safest place.'

Eleanor clicked her fingers. 'Oh, I know! That hideout. You remember. When we were hiding Lancelot from the police...' She bit her lip, avoiding Seldon's eye.

He was staring at her in disbelief. 'The *fugitive*. The one who had escaped from his jail cell? *That* Lancelot? Lancelot Fenwick-Langham?'

The person in question had been Eleanor's boyfriend at the time. Wrongfully accused of murder, she'd hidden him while she helped prove his innocence. Seldon had headed the manhunt.

She made an apologetic face. 'Hugh, that was then. Things are different now, you know that. Look how much better I'm getting. Now I get to hide a chief inspector from the bad guys instead of a fugitive from justice. And anyway, you let him escape, remember?'

He groaned. 'Have I told you, you are completely impossible?'

'Yes. But keep it up and one day it might filter through.' She turned to her butler. 'What do you say, Clifford?'

'An excellent suggestion, my lady.'

Seldon looked doubtful. 'But wherever this secret hideout is, Eleanor, we haven't got your Rolls at our disposal. We'll have to take my Crossley.'

Clifford cleared his throat. 'If I might be so bold, Chief Inspector. Your Crossley is a fine automobile, but hardly one that will outrun those outside.'

'He's right, Hugh. Uncle Byron kept several fast cars. We just tend to use the Rolls because it was his favourite. And I like riding along imagining he's still with us.'

'Alright. These other vehicles are in good running order then, Clifford?'

Her butler looked almost offended. 'Perfectly. I see to them personally.'

'Of course you do. Silly question. But these men will follow us, no matter which car we take.'

'Not to worry, Chief Inspector. Silas will deal with that.'

Eleanor nodded. 'And Clifford can outwit a couple of thick-headed thugs. Especially as they've already shown him their hand earlier today.'

Clifford's brow creased. 'Assuming, my lady, they are the same gentlemen with backup, as it were.'

Seldon snapped his fingers. 'You know, they might not be associated with the two who attacked you at all, Clifford. They might be Sir Percival's men sent to keep an eye on us. He's wily enough to guess that we're probably not just going to drop the case because he says so. And he has the manpower.'

'Well, whoever they are,' Eleanor said, 'we need to lose them.'

Seldon's brows knitted together. 'And fast. This entire business is getting out of hand, as I said before. I don't like it one bit.'

'Ready?' Clifford whispered a few minutes later.

Eleanor nodded from her position, crouched down in the rear seat. Next to her, doing the same, with his long legs bent awkwardly, Seldon hissed, 'Absolutely. But what about the ladies? If your Silas chap is caught up helping us, they're rather vulnerable.'

She smiled. 'Don't fret. They are currently having a wonderful tea and cake party safely locked in the surprisingly comfy cellar with Gladstone.'

Clifford nodded. 'And with Joseph guarding them. Shotgun at the ready. However, I do not believe they are in any danger since it is her ladyship these men are after, whoever they are working for.'

Seldon grunted. 'Then drive like the wind, man!'

As Clifford spun the three litre Bentley out of Henley Hall's gates, Eleanor saw two shadowy figures jump into a black saloon car. Clifford's eyes flicked to the rear-view mirror. 'Ah! There they are. We just need to let the other catch up.' As he spoke, a second car appeared behind the first. 'Right, Brace!'

Clifford swung the car violently right down a narrow strip of tarmac, the back of the car fishtailing out sideways.

Despite hanging on to the passenger seat in front, Eleanor slid into Seldon.

'Sorry, Hugh.' She shuffled back over to her side and pointed to a high stone wall flashing by the window. 'That runs along the rear of Henley Hall.'

Clifford nodded. 'And this next corner is where at least one of these two sets of blaggards takes their leave.' He jerked the car left, mounting the grass bank. A moment later, the sound of four explosions and then metal hitting stone rang out.

Seldon glanced out of the back window.

'Ha! That's the leading car's tyres punctured. And it crashed right into the wall. Good show, Clifford! What was that?'

'A simple trap which can be laid across the road consisting of four inch nails on a metal base. Adapted by Silas from the "caltrop" or spiked snare used by the likes of Darius the Third against Alexander the Great.'

'Thank you for the history lesson.' Seldon glanced behind again. 'But the driver of the other car was quick to react. He's followed you along the bank. How do we shake him off?'

'By relying on local knowledge they do not have, Chief Inspector. Apologies, however, our ride is about to become even less comfortable.'

He slammed a foot on the accelerator and launched the car off the end of the grass bank and back onto the tarmac. Seldon offered Eleanor a hand to grip on to as they lurched in every conceivable direction. Linking his fingers with hers, he pulled her closer, wedging her against his shoulder with his forearm. 'So you don't whack your head against the side of the car,' he muttered.

'Thank you,' she managed as her heart pounded even harder at his touch.

Five minutes later, the remaining car was still behind them.

'You should have lost them by now, Clifford. These men must be professionals.'

'That's it!' He thumped the wheel. 'The two men who ambushed me earlier acted like typical hired thugs. Unimaginative mercenaries carrying out instructions. Except for the way they punctured the tyres on the Rolls. That was performed with slick and precise expertise.'

Eleanor winced as she cracked her head against Seldon's jaw with the force of the car's next spin. He rubbed her temple gently.

'And they are doing too good a job of keeping up with you, Clifford. Believe me, Hugh, I've seen him outrun hoodlums in cars before and it's never taken this long.'

Seldon's brows met. 'So, what are you saying, Clifford?'

'I believe these men are exceptionally highly trained. Ex-military, perhaps. Does Mr Treacher employ such personnel?'

'Not to my knowledge. His men are usually the thick-headed kind. All busy fists and no finesse.'

Clifford raised his voice over the squealing of the tyres as they spun around another sharp corner at high speed. 'The thought does strike that a foreign government might employ such.'

'Like a Russian one!' Eleanor said.

Seldon gritted his teeth. 'Blast that Orlov. I told you, Eleanor...' He shook his head and tightened his fingers against hers. 'Not now, I know.'

She nodded. 'But they could just as easily be Sir Percival's men, as you suggested earlier. If they are, then at least they aren't a physical threat, unlike the men who attacked Clifford.'

'We still need to lose them, Eleanor.'

Clifford risked taking one hand from the wheel to get their attention. 'Forgive my offering a contrary opinion, but if they *are* Sir Percival's men, we need to lose them because they *are* still a threat. From my experience with his lordship, that man is quite prepared to go to significant lengths to carry out his job.'

Eleanor's eyes widened in disbelief. 'Even to the point of harming us?'

'Not quite perhaps. But certainly as far as disabling this car, as he may have ordered the Rolls to be.'

Seldon grunted. 'And as I said, I'd think he'd go so far as locking us in the Tower to protect the king and royal family's standing.'

The car skidded to the right, halting conversation as she was thrown even harder against Seldon's side. He swapped hands, intertwining his fingers with hers again and using his free arm to hold her tighter.

'One minute, though. What about Sir Roderick Rumbold? Or Lady Montfort's husband? Do either of them have the ability to hire ex-military?'

'Good thinking,' Seldon said. 'Sir Roderick and Lord Montfort both have the connections and money.'

Eleanor's brow furrowed. 'Hmm, I'm doubting my own suggestion now. It seems rather extreme for a jilted lover. Or a cuckolded husband.'

Seldon shook his head. 'I would agree except for the fact that the person responsible for the demise of Lord Taylor-Howard and Mr Darnley is liable for the deaths of two members of the royal family.'

'But Xander was eighteenth in line and Barty, well, he must have been fortieth or more?'

'Eleanor, however far down the line of succession the two of them were, they had royal blood. The murderer must know if he's caught, he's for the drop!'

'So maybe they *would* go out on a limb and hire whoever they needed to keep their secret safe, seeing as the stakes are so high?'

Clifford swung the Bentley up onto the top of what looked like an abandoned bridge. 'Please prepare for a harsh landing. We are about to finally lose these irritating leeches...' He paused as the engine seemed to fade in the suspended silence of the car leaving the end of the concrete. Eleanor's stomach rose up to meet her thumping heart.

The car landed hard, throwing them together, cracking heads. Seldon shook his. 'You alright, Eleanor?'

She nodded, wincing. 'I'll live. Amazing driving, Clifford.' She peered over her shoulder and waited. After a minute, she turned back around. 'And you've finally lost them!'

Clifford checked the rear-view mirror. 'Excellent. Now it's

time to employ his lordship's vanishing trick and lose them permanently.'

The three of them sat in the dark, catching their breath. Seldon finally spoke. 'Did you just drive us through that solid earth bank, Clifford? I confess I closed my eyes.'

Eleanor laughed. 'Yes, he did. Except there's actually an entrance to this tunnel hidden behind the vegetation covering the bank.'

Clifford turned the car's headlights on. Seldon looked around.

'We're going to hide out in this tunnel?'

She slapped his hand. 'Of course not. It must almost be time for tea.'

31

Eleanor looked around. The low, black-timbered ceiling of the secluded cottage gave the room an oppressive atmosphere, especially with the shutters down. *It's like everything is closing in on you, Ellie.* She shook the thought from her mind. The only light came from two oil lamps Clifford had just lit, the smoke hanging in the air. *They obviously haven't been used since you were last here over a year, no, almost two years ago.* At least it masked the smell of damp plaster. The rest of the room was how she remembered it, too. A simple wooden table and a couple of hard chairs. Elsewhere in the tiny cottage, she knew there was a bedroom and minimal washing facilities, but that was about it.

Despite being July, the room was cold. From a wicker basket, Clifford produced a pair of cable knit jumpers. He shook them and passed one each to Eleanor and Seldon.

'I do apologise for the state of the clothing. Also, for the suggestion that we do not venture outdoors and that we keep our voices down.' His eyes flitted to Eleanor and away. Before she could say anything, he continued, 'I, however, have to make one brief foray myself. Please excuse me.'

As he closed the front door silently behind him, Eleanor

turned her attention back to the jumper he'd given her. Her nose wrinkled as she sniffed it. It smelt musty, but she gratefully pulled it over her head. Seldon draped his around his shoulders and tied the arms like a scarf.

She laughed quietly. 'Very Henley Regatta, daarling!'

At the words, a shadow passed over his face. 'The regatta. It all comes down to that wretched regatta. I wish I'd never been given the duty now. And that you hadn't been dragged there by that equally wretched woman.' Eleanor opened her mouth to reply, but then thought better of it. This wasn't the moment to defend her friend. Seldon sighed. 'Sorry. Look, I know you... we've been in tricky situations before. But this time, well...' He rubbed his face. 'Anyway, whoever it is, we've only shaken them off temporarily. The minute we leave here in the Bentley, they'll spot us. Silas only managed to disable one car with those spikes. Whoever sent these men seems to have plenty of money and resources. I reckon they'll soon have a replacement car or two out scouring the roads for us.'

A cough made them spin around. Eleanor's hand flew to her chest.

'Clifford! You almost gave me a heart attack. I didn't even hear you come back in.'

'I'm sorry, my lady. I have in fact locked the door now.'

'Fine. So why did you cough?'

'I wished to respectfully point out the chief inspector's error.'

'Which is?'

'Believing we will be spotted when we leave here in the Bentley.'

Seldon looked at him quizzically. 'I know you're used to it, Clifford, but there really aren't that many Bentleys like that around here. It's quite striking.'

He nodded. 'Indeed it is, Chief Inspector. But its most striking feature at the moment is its prominent oil leak. Caused,

I fear, by the rather vigorous way I was driving. I just went to check on it.'

Eleanor grimaced. 'Ah! So we won't be spotted in the Bentley because we won't be leaving in it?'

'Precisely, my lady. It requires a garage or workshop to repair. And even if the facilities were available here to render a repair, it would be far too noisy.'

Eleanor opened her mouth to reply, but paused for the second time.

Seldon's laugh surprised her.

She put her finger to her lips again. 'What exactly is so funny, Hugh? A minute ago you were telling me the bad guys are closing in and our backs are against the wall.'

He shook his head, still smiling. 'They are,' he said quietly. 'And it is. More so now. We're not going to get very far on foot, are we? And even if we made it back to Henley Hall, we can't ask for help. The phones are tapped and we've no one to ring, anyway. It's just, I've never seen you fail to have a ready reply.'

She tried to hide her smile. 'I'd quit while you're ahead.'

Clifford stepped forward.

'Yes?'

'I agree there is no point in trying to return to Henley Hall, but there are few buildings in this area. The enemy is obviously well trained and well equipped. I do not think it will take them more than a few hours to find us after first light.'

Eleanor slapped the table, remembering to do so quietly at the last minute.

'Then let's do the only thing we can.'

Half-an-hour later, her brain hurt. Working out the puzzle of who was responsible for the two deaths and, rather pressingly, who the men hunting them were working for, was proving damn tricky. And that was with all three of their minds concentrating on the problem.

During a pause in their collective efforts, Clifford busied himself by unpacking the small hamper he'd brought in from the Bentley when they'd first arrived. As he did so, Eleanor and Seldon agreed reluctantly to start again from the beginning in the hope that whatever they'd missed would jump out at them.

Eleanor smoothed out the centre pages of her notebook so hard the spine cracked. She didn't miss Clifford's shudder out of the corner of her eye. Seldon leaned over and pointed to her notes.

'What on earth? Have you given the genteel pastime of pressing flowers a unique Lady Swift twist by pressing spiders instead?'

'Hilarious.' She tapped her pen on his page, spraying it with a few dots of ink. 'Oops, accident, sorry! However, over-neatness says just as much about a person, you know?'

He shook his head. 'No. I don't. Anyway, please tell us again what brilliant insights you worked out. Starting this time with Lady Montfort.'

'Well, something has been bothering me about her liaison with Sir Roderick.'

'Which is?'

'Not easy to put as delicately as I'm supposed to, dash it! Clifford, help.'

Her butler stepped over with two small glasses of deep amber sherry. 'Perhaps, my lady, you wish to hint at the notable difference in appearance between Sir Roderick and the considerably younger Lord Taylor-Howard?'

'Nicely expressed. And, yes, that is precisely what I noted. No disrespect, but Sir Roderick must have quite the compensating personality hiding under his burgeoning waistline and bulldog jowls. Not that we found it, did we, Clifford?'

'I couldn't say, my lady, as you interrupted Sir Roderick's

round of golf in front of his fellow players. Such behaviour would incense even the most good-natured of gentlemen.'

'Seriously though. Think about it. Doesn't it strike you as odd that a woman who can snare pretty much any man she fancies, would slide out from under Xander's sheets, straight into Sir Roderick's?'

Clifford hurriedly returned to unpacking the hamper. Seldon ineffectually buried his head in his notebook.

'And there goes Lady Swift's last ounce of decorum. Again,' he muttered without looking up. But the curve of his lips suggested he was more amused than embarrassed. 'So what are you suggesting? That she might have only formed an alliance with Sir Roderick in order to kill Lord Taylor-Howard as revenge for abandoning her?'

'It's possible. Sir Roderick would have been the perfect ally because I definitely got the feeling, despite what he said, that he hated Xander for seducing his wife.'

Clifford set down two plates. 'Might the animosity of one have fanned the flames of anger in the other?'

'Good point,' Seldon said, making another note. He looked up. 'How the heck did you find time to organise this before we rushed off in the car?'

Clifford eyes twinkled. He cupped his hand over his mouth and whispered, 'You might quickly discover, Chief Inspector, that her ladyship is usually at her most sharp-witted whilst... ahem, eating.'

Eleanor tutted. 'I can hear you. And that's a malicious rumour, nothing more.'

'Nevertheless, Chief Inspector, I asked Mrs Butters to put together an emergency hamper of whatever food was available on the spot. It is not up to one's usual standards, but hopefully will do in the circumstances.'

Seldon cast his eye over a selection of cheese wedges, ham slices, chunks of bread and sausage rolls.

'I'm sure it will do just fine, Clifford.'

Having loaded her plate, Eleanor picked up her pen and tapped the open page of her notebook. 'What do we think, then? Lady Montfort and Sir Roderick egged each other on to dispatch Xander?' She bit into her sausage roll. 'Oh, another thought has just struck.'

Clifford cupped his hand over his mouth again. 'You see what I mean, Chief Inspector? One bite and the ideas just come flooding in.'

Eleanor put down her sausage roll and fixed her butler with a withering look. 'We are here to solve a murder case. Not to advance your strange theories about the correlation between my eating and coming up with brilliant ideas. Of which, by the way, I've just thought of another.'

Seldon's pen hovered over the next clear line of his notebook. 'Go on. Not with the squabbling, with the idea.'

Once again, she restrained herself. 'I'll deal with both of you later. For the moment, think about it. Since poor Barty's murder reduced our suspects for Xander's murder to four, Lady Montfort and Sir Roderick are the only two who had no financial stakes in Xander staying alive.'

Seldon nodded. 'Well pointed out. He was a source of income to the other two. Orlov because he was apparently making money out of his gossip and fashion secrets and Treacher because he was making money out of him with interest. When Lord Taylor-Howard paid up, of course.'

'And I believed Treacher when he said he'd thought Xander would have the money to pay off his debt soon.'

Seldon looked down at his notes and grunted. 'This is all well and good, but it's hardly a solid case against Lady Montfort and Sir Roderick, is it? We must be missing something.'

Clifford cleared his throat.

'What have you got?' Eleanor said hopefully.

'Only that the suspects have been thoroughly interrogated

twice by yourself, my lady. And the chief inspector has also investigated them in his usual thorough manner with all the resources available to him. Given this, do you feel at all confident that you could list the suspects in probable order of guilt? Or, perhaps, eliminate one or more? My lady? Chief Inspector?'

Eleanor and Seldon looked at each other before shaking their heads.

Clifford clicked his fingers. 'Precisely. Which means?'

Seldon stared at him, then Eleanor. Finally, he slapped his notebook. 'Blast it, I'm sure he'll prove himself right in a second as usual, but is he always this mysterious first?'

Eleanor started to laugh, but immediately clapped her hand over her mouth as Seldon put a finger to his lips. She lowered her voice again. 'Always.'

Seldon held up a hand. 'Well, come on, Clifford. If we're struggling to prioritise our suspect list, what's the answer?'

'That we have the wrong list.'

32

For a moment, there was silence in the room as Eleanor and Seldon digested Clifford's unexpected suggestion. Seldon looked down at his notes and then back up at Clifford. He opened his mouth to speak, only for Eleanor to flap a furious hand at him. He stared at her enquiringly.

Then he heard it, too.

Clifford swiftly extinguished both oil lamps. The room was plunged into darkness.

In the blanket of blackness that enfolded her, Eleanor strained her ears. There it was again! The sound of a car coasting along the road. She stayed stock still in the dark, knowing not to speak until her butler did. She heard someone move – Clifford, she was sure – and then a small beam of moonlight shot across the room. A peephole in one of the shutters, she guessed. After a moment, the sound of the car's engine picked up and then faded in the distance.

It was a full minute before Clifford relit the lamps. They returned to their discussion in a sombre mood.

Seldon rose and paced the small space, his brow furrowed. 'Are you seriously suggesting that Sir Percival with all the men and money at his disposal – not to mention the intelligence he's privy to – has come up with a dud list of suspects?'

Clifford spread his hands. 'It is an unlikely scenario, Chief Inspector, I grant. However, given the evidence—'

Eleanor waved him down. 'I don't think it really matters that much. We're trapped like rats in a rapidly shrinking hole and we've got nowhere near uncovering our killer using the list Sir Percival gave me. So I suggest we start again with a new list as you suggested and see if we have more luck.'

Seldon stopped pacing and dropped back into his seat. 'Okay.' He regarded his notes. 'Sir Percival gave you the name of Sir Roderick because he was, it seems, a cuckolded husband. Cuckolded by Lord Taylor-Howard.'

Eleanor nodded. 'And we know there must be more cuckolded husbands since Sir Roderick, Lady Montfort, Fingers and even Xander's own sister told me about his penchant for liaisons with married ladies.'

Seldon groaned. 'Any suggestions that narrow the field?'

'Perhaps, Chief Inspector,' Clifford said. 'Sir Roderick himself gave us the clue we need. If you remember, my lady, he suggested we look for, "a more possessive and jealous man" than himself.'

'He did, you're right. Almost as if he might have had a few names in mind. And Fingers said something very similar too.'

Seldon sighed. 'Okay, it seems there are certainly more cuckolded husbands who might have wanted Lord Taylor-Howard dead. What about jilted lov— partners?'

Eleanor smiled to herself. *He couldn't bring himself to say the word 'lover' in front of you, Ellie. He really is the ultimate gentleman.*

'Actually, I think you're onto something there, Hugh. Lady Montfort said the last unmarried girl he threw over made a terrible scene. And disgraced herself by saying the most unbecoming things about him.'

Seldon jotted down a second note. 'Possibly another jilted partner.' He looked up. 'If we are going to be logical about this—'

Clifford raised an eyebrow. 'What other way could we possibly approach it, Chief Inspector?'

Seldon slid his eyes round to Eleanor. 'The Lady Swift approach?'

They both shuddered. Eleanor gave them another contemptuous look, half in jest. 'While you're enjoying yourselves at my expense, a murderer is running around free and we're a step nearer to getting carted off to the Tower! Or worse!'

The minute she said it, she regretted it. She avoided Seldon's eyes and kept hers on her notebook. 'So, what would be the logical approach?'

Seldon cleared his throat. 'To work out if Lord Taylor Howard was selling secrets to a spy other than Orlov. Or if he owed money to another crime boss other than Treacher.'

He threw his head back and stared at the ceiling.

She sighed. 'I know what you're thinking, Hugh. And I agree. How can we possibly find any of this out?' She rubbed her forehead. 'But continuing on with Clifford's reasoning, perhaps Sir Percival's list *was* a dud. Not in terms of suspects, but perhaps in terms of *motive*?'

Seldon grimaced. 'I'm impressed by the thinking, Eleanor, but do you have anything to go on?'

'Actually, yes. When we spoke to poor old Barty for instance, he said we had the wrong man. He would inherit almost nothing from Xander. However, he did say something along the lines that we should look for someone who stands to gain more than him.'

'A "great deal more", if you will forgive the correction, my lady.' Clifford regarded the floor, tapping one hand against the palm of the other.

'That means he's deep in thought,' Eleanor whispered to Seldon. 'Wait a sec.'

After a moment, Clifford looked up. 'It is a long shot, I admit, my lady. And needs us to focus on Lord Taylor-Howard's *own* motives, not that of his murderer for a minute.'

Seldon grunted. 'Out with it, Clifford. As you yourself reminded us, we don't have all night!'

He bowed. 'My apologies. Lady Araminta Taylor-Howard mentioned their uncle Gerald had named her brother, Lord Taylor-Howard, as his sole heir.'

Eleanor's eyes flashed. 'I see where you're going! You think maybe Xander planned to murder his uncle Gerald in order to inherit his fortune?'

'Indeed, my lady. And pay off his gambling debts before he lost his kneecaps, or worse, as we have said. Even though Mr Treacher stated he never kills those who owe him money, he was also honest enough to admit that people like Lord Taylor-Howard don't know that.'

Seldon tapped the table with his pen. 'A very interesting, if far-fetched, twist in the investigation at this late juncture. Well done. But this,' – he glanced at his notes – 'Uncle Gerald. Is his money and estate substantial?'

Eleanor nodded. 'Certainly, to Xander's mind. It was a rather macabre running joke he apparently shared with Araminta, his sister, that inheriting his uncle's money was the only way he would ever be debt free.'

Seldon's pen flew across his notebook. Suddenly, he looked up. 'I can't believe I'm about to ask you this, Eleanor. But, going on gut feeling, do you think Lord Taylor-Howard would have planned to kill his uncle himself? Or, would he have run the risk of using a hired killer?'

'Hired killer, definitely. Honestly, Hugh, I believe Xander was a good-time chap who lost his way. Badly. I make no excuses at all for anything he may have been involved in, but I doubt he would have killed his uncle himself. But why did you ask? And how is this relevant to his own murder?'

Seldon nodded slowly to himself. 'Because I deal with them in my job. Hired killers, that is. If Lord Taylor-Howard was foolish enough to seek out such a person, that person would have known immediately that Lord Taylor-Howard was completely out of his depth. It would be a simple matter for the killer to double-cross him. Take the money and then kill Lord Taylor-Howard as the easier target and because he would have been the only one who knew about the deal.'

Eleanor whistled softly. 'So he simply took Xander's payment and then poisoned Xander, so there was no trace. It's a wild theory, but we do need to think laterally if we're going to get anywhere. Although, none of that explains why the killer should then murder poor old Barty?'

For a moment, no one spoke. Then Clifford broke the silence. 'As I am, in a way, responsible for this current impasse by suggesting Sir Percival's suspect list was, as you put it, Chief Inspector, "dud", perhaps I might rescue the situation? I suggest instead, we concentrate on the, admittedly few, solid clues we have already.'

Seldon slapped the table, making Eleanor jump. 'Sorry! I forgot,' he whispered. 'But that's something I can get my teeth into.' He turned to the beginning of his notes on the case. 'Right, if it's okay with you two, I'll just run through my' – his eyes flitted to Eleanor – '*ordered* notes and you stop me if anything strikes you? Such as the name of the killer, for instance?'

Eleanor hid a smile. 'Don't think you got away with that. But as time is running out, off you go.'

Seldon took a moment to check his notes and then cleared his throat.

'Right. Lord Taylor-Howard was murdered at Henley Royal Regatta. He was poisoned with potassium cyanide, which was dropped into his champagne flute before he came on stage to award the prizes. The poison is easy to come by without raising suspicion. Given the dose – estimated from the traces found in the champagne flute and the speed with which Lord Taylor-Howard died after exhibiting the first symptoms – it is believed that the poison was introduced no more than fifteen minutes before he collapsed. Possibly less.'

He looked up. Eleanor and Clifford both nodded.

'Excellent *ordered* note taking, Chief Inspector,' Eleanor said.

He cleared his throat without looking at her. 'Right. Continuing. There was only one entrance, so the murderer must have entered the tent in full view of everyone. They must have also been allowed into the rear of the tent. But as security wasn't particularly tight – there was no reason why it should have been – that would include officials and ' – he coughed – 'members of the public of a certain rank or standing.'

Eleanor hid a smile. 'You mean "toffs". And you don't have to be so defensive. I'm sure on your part you did everything you were supposed to in order to protect Xander. After all, he wasn't a defenceless woman!' Her brow creased, and she lapsed into thought.

Seldon nodded. 'Exactly. I think. Anyway, at the crime scene, two pieces of glass were found. One showed Lord Taylor-Howard drunk out of an engraved flute, which is how the murderer knew which flute to poison. Which also tells us the killer was a regular visitor to the regatta or had insider information. Now, the other piece of glass—'

'Is utterly irrelevant.'

This time Seldon tried to hide a smile. 'Is this the Lady Swift approach to crime solving? Because fun though it is, we agreed to let me continue unless we had a question. Or, of course, came up with the name of the kill—' His words froze on his lips, his eyes wide. For a moment, he just stared at her. Then he slowly shook his head in disbelief. 'You know, don't you?'

33

Her own words were still ringing round her head as she walked along the imposing Georgian crescent up to the central entrance, with Clifford a few respectful paces behind. She took what should have been a calming breath. But now, on the formidable front step, staring at the bell pull below the brass plaque, those words weren't working as well as she hoped in quelling her nerves.

'Chaps,' she had said confidently half an hour before, 'I will be fine. We've got a foolproof system for me to signal if anything goes wrong. Plus, Hugh, you've admitted you can't show your face. If you appear, it will be a complete tip-off. And, Clifford, you're far better placed as my backup as originally planned.'

That they had finally agreed showed their trust in her. But that Seldon had pulled her into his side so he could whisper that he would never forgive himself if anything happened to her, had made her breath catch.

She stared back up at the brass plaque and swallowed her nerves. *Focus, Ellie.*

. . .

The inside was as grandiose as the outside. She was led through a dizzying maze of oak panelled corridors with lofty ceilings. Only the plethora of earnest grey suits and absence of anything personal stopped this feeling like an actual royal apartment.

Her haughty escort paused at a set of imposing doors and indicated she should wait. Clifford had been dispatched to the securely fenced grounds until her return. On either side were chairs for visitors, but she chose to stand tapping her foot, more from nerves than impatience.

After what, even she had to admit, was no more than a few minutes, her escort returned and ushered her into the room. Three voile-curtained sash windows threw long fingers of weak light across the wide stretch of polished wood floor between her and Sir Percival, who sat behind a vast mahogany desk.

He rose as she came in.

'What is the meaning of this, Lady Swift! How did you get here?'

She smiled at his surprise. 'By car, of course, Sir Percival. So lucky to find you in.'

So those men were sent by him, Ellie. Otherwise, why would he ask how I got here? In fact, she had to admit, it had been courtesy of her butler's meticulous planning. He had arranged before they left for Silas to wait until the Bentley had drawn the enemy away from Henley Hall, and then to sneak a backup car to the cottage and hide it in the tunnel. 'Just in case, my lady, we have to abandon the Bentley,' he had told her, adding he hadn't mentioned it until the car arrived in case there was a hitch.

Pretending to admire the decor, she looked around the room, making a note of the exits. The three windows gave out on to the enclosed gardens and pathways as she'd hoped. She nodded imperceptibly to Clifford, who sat on a bench, enjoying the sunshine, ostensibly merely waiting for his mistress. Satisfied, she turned to Sir Percival, who strode away from his desk to stand in front of her.

'Lady Swift.' Hands behind his back, he peered down at her with the disdain of a man having discovered a cockroach in his coq au vin. 'Perhaps I didn't make myself clear during my last telephone call to you?'

She smiled sweetly. 'Well, do you know, I think you did.'

He stared at her impassively, but in the flicker that flashed across his eyes, she spotted an element of confusion.

'Then, since you have not come to admire my private office, please enlighten me as to the purpose of your presence?'

'Oh, delighted to.' She wandered back over towards the first of the windows and pointed at the garden while giving Clifford the agreed signal that she was fine. 'This is quite an upgrade on your field ops tent at the regatta.'

She could see his confusion at her being there was rapidly spiralling into exasperation.

'Lady Swift. Despite your assurance a moment ago, for an intelligent woman, you seem to have entirely missed the thrust of my telephone message!'

'Not so. I simply realised you had only given me *half* the message.' She held up a hand as he snapped his mouth open to reply. 'Just as I had completed only half of my duty to you. Silly me, how could I do as you commanded and stand down from my investigations before I'd given you the report on my latest findings?'

Sir Percival hesitated. 'Whatever they are, I have no interest in them.'

'Actually. You do.' She stepped forward, staring him in the eye. 'Because, you see, I know who murdered Lord Taylor-Howard. And Mr Bartholomew Darnley.'

To her admiration, he didn't flinch. He held her gaze for a moment and then turned and walked slowly back to his desk. He sat down and steepled his fingers.

'Okay, Lady Swift. Let's hear what you think you know. But be warned. If I believe you have been investigating this matter after I expressly told you to stand down, I will have you arrested and imprisoned. You have five minutes. Go ahead.'

She dropped her amiable smile. 'I shall take as long as I wish, seeing as you wasted so much of my time.'

He waved a dismissive hand. 'That is not a habit I indulge in.'

'Then I should be honoured that you made an exception in my case. Only I'm not. Because I must point out before I tell you my findings, the entire investigation you sent me off on was a wild goose chase. But without the merest whiff of goose ever existing.'

Sir Percival frowned. 'Blaming others for one's failings is a rather unbecoming trait for a young woman.'

'Really? Well, there was no way to succeed in identifying the murderer from the suspect list you had me chasing my tail over because none of them were guilty. And you knew that all too well. Just like you knew the clues you dangled were false, too. Like your ruse about poor Darnley. He never owed money to Treacher.'

'Lady Swift, please get a grip on your runaway imagination! Why on earth would I have done such inconceivable things? I am the head of the royal police.' His tone remained the same, but his eyes darkened. 'Do you understand what that means?'

'I do. It means you knew there would have to be an investigation after Lord Taylor-Howard's death, even if it had looked like he'd died of natural causes. However far removed from immediate succession to the throne he was, it is policy that all royal deaths are investigated, isn't it?'

Sir Percival leaned forward, his dark eyes fixed on hers. 'If you have a point to make, kindly make it.'

'Willingly. Where was I? Oh yes, it was easy for you to wield your eminent title and claim jurisdiction to ensure the civil police were prevented from investigating Lord Taylor-Howard's death. Especially as you knew what a strong track record Chief Inspector Seldon had for solving murders. But your own men are the elite of the elite. How else could we all sleep happily knowing that our king and country are safe? So, you had to do the unthinkable. Pretend there was a crack in the supposedly impenetrable hull of the very ship you captain. I should have realised long before that was the act of a desperate man. That must have really hurt. Especially when you had to tell His Majesty the King and then me that there was a mole in the royal police. But I see now that your hands were tied. You couldn't risk any of your men investigating because they were too likely to discover the truth. And you couldn't let that happen. Only that was your error. You not only let it happen, you guaranteed it by engaging someone outside of your organisation.'

'The only person I engaged was you!'

'I know. Bad choice, as it turns out. But I can see why you did. You thought I had no chance of solving the actual murder, especially as you misled me from the outset. And on paper, I must have been an easy sell to His Majesty. Lots of women worked undercover in intelligence during the war, and no one suspected them. We women have an uncanny way of appearing like hopeless wretched creatures whilst disarming our targets, you know.'

'I am not seeing that in any regard at this moment, Lady Swift.'

'Then be a good chap and concentrate harder.' She hurried on. 'You were also able to easily convince His Majesty because of my involvement in previous murders.' She wrinkled her nose. 'Can you believe, someone once suggested I attract dead bodies like spinsters attract stray cats?'

Sir Percival rose. 'Lady Swift, I have heard enough to make me believe, even though what you have told me is nonsense, that you are still investigating this affair. I am not known for my patience—'

She shook her head. 'Neither am I. Which was your final and fatal error. You used up the last of my patience when you set those animals on a man who I regard as your superior in every way. So what are you going to do now? Rough me up like you had them rough up my butler?'

Sir Percival took another step forward, his face thunder.

Eleanor stepped up to meet him, forcing him to stop. 'Of course not. We both know that. You would never do that to a woman. Your natural instinct is to protect the frailer sex. Which is how I came to realise who murdered Lord Taylor-Howard and Darnley. And why. However, there is one thing I simply don't understand. Why didn't you just take me off the case when you realised I was smarter than you thought? Why go through all that charade of attacking my butler and wrecking my car?'

He walked slowly over to the window, his back to her. *Blast, Ellie. Let's hope he hasn't spotted Clifford.* He said nothing for a moment and then nodded. Without turning around, he spoke.

'Because it would have looked too suspicious. I needed a genuine reason to remove you from the case.' He turned to her. 'I would have liked to have given your butler a crack on the jaw myself but,' – he waved his hand around the room – 'like all senior officials these days, I am mostly desk-bound. Also, not that I care if you believe me, but I meant it when I said I will not put a woman in danger unless this country is in a state of war.'

She slid back over to the window as he returned to his desk. 'But I do believe you, Sir Percival. Which is the real reason I am here. You see, that misguided act of gallantry made me realise precisely why both men were killed.'

He slapped his desk, making her jump. 'Are you actually accusing *me* of murdering Lord Taylor-Howard and his cousin!'

'Actually... no. I am not. You didn't murder anyone.'

He threw his hands up. 'Then what *are* you saying, woman!'

She sighed. 'You see, Sir Percival, I finally realised that you are not only obsessed with protecting the king, but you are also obsessed with protecting a woman.' She raised her voice. 'The woman who murdered two members of the royal family and is right now listening in to this conversation.' She pointed to the door at the far side of the room. 'In there, I believe.'

34

The silence seemed to stretch forever. Sir Percival's icy stare never strayed from her face. *He's a cool customer, Ellie. Let's hope you haven't underestimated him.*

Finally, the door was flung open.

'Hello, Tipsy.'

The young girl flounced in, giving her signature finger wave.

'Hello, Eleanor. A peculiar joke, even for you, sweetie.' She flicked her glossy mane over the shoulder of her baby-blue silk jacket as she perched on the edge of a chair. 'But that's what I keep telling you about living the hermit life in Henley Hall. You need to get out more.'

'I tried that,' Eleanor said. 'With you. Only you dragged me to a ringside seat so I could witness a man being murdered.'

Tipsy's dark eyes flashed behind the slow bat of her lashes. 'Darling, it's hardly my fault that your Hugh let us sneak up to the front of the stage. I told you he isn't at all the right ticket for you.' She spun around, her long tresses fanning out in an arc, before she smoothed them back into place. 'Delectable desserts like me don't get mixed up in unseemly things like murder, silly.

Honestly, Eleanor, you have been my most tricky protégée ever. I'm not sure we've made any progress at all.'

'Maybe that's because you didn't heed the most important lesson of all. The one you missed from your evidently not so comprehensive list.'

'Oh, you've been studying. Go on.'

Eleanor struggled to keep her voice from betraying the genuine sorrow behind her words. 'Don't befriend a girl who has solved murders before if you want to kill a man in front of her and get away with it.'

Sir Percival had remained impassive throughout this conversation. Now, however, he opened his top drawer and took out a revolver. Placing it on his desk in front of him, he leaned back in his chair, his face still impassive. Tipsy didn't even glance at it.

'Sweetie! Are you being serious?'

Eleanor glanced at the revolver out of the corner of her eye. *That was a lot sooner than expected, Ellie!* 'Absolutely. I've never found murder a laughing matter.'

Tipsy's high-pitched giggle sounded forced to Eleanor's ears. 'I'm the girl who wants to bag a royal, remember? Think about it. I'm hardly likely to go round boffing them off.' She whirled her hand in the air. 'Or whatever the expression is.'

'For killing someone? I'd say you know exactly what the expression is. Just as you know how deadly potassium cyanide is. And exactly how to gain access to the rear of the stage at the regatta. And later, how to use your feminine wiles to have Barty let you slide up the back staircase to his apartment, thinking you had come to sample his "strawberry ice cream."'

Tipsy's eyes narrowed. 'Sounds rather like the pot calling the kettle black if you know the layout of his place so well.' She leaned forward, waving a perfectly painted nail. 'Here's another important tip. Jealousy is terrible for the early onset of wrinkles.' Sliding off the arm of the chair, she pulled an exaggerated pout. 'Poor Eleanor. You keep pretending to like Hugh, even though you really liked Barty. Only he wasn't into you, was he?'

'It's no use. Your act doesn't wash with me any more. But to answer your question, unlike you, I've never pretended. I do like Hugh. A lot, actually. And I liked Barty. But mostly I liked that he was alive. And just for the record, he wasn't my number one fan after Clifford and I interrogated him while he was still reeling from being beaten up by Sir Percival's men.' She turned to him, trying to ignore the gun. 'I assume somehow he became suspicious of Tipsy and you sent the boys around to silence him. Why Tipsy then poisoned him, I can't imagine.'

Sir Percival shook his head. 'Neither can I.'

Eleanor blinked in surprise. Not just because he had admitted Tipsy murdered Darnley, and by default, Lord Taylor-Howard, but because of the genuine sadness in his tone.

Sir Percival continued. 'He was hanging around Lord Taylor-Howard's coattails when he saw Tipsy slip something into one of the champagne flutes. Of course, once Lord Taylor-Howard collapsed on stage, he put two and two together. He confronted Tipsy, but she persuaded him it was a joke gone terribly wrong and she was going to go to the police herself. Of course, she didn't. She came straight to me and I sent some of my more personally loyal men to show him the folly of going to the police himself.' He looked at Tipsy, shaking his head again wearily. 'I told you I had it sorted. Why did you have to go and—'

Tipsy's eyes flashed. 'You know why! He would never have kept quiet! He was a liar! Just like Xander!'

A vein pulsed in Sir Percival's neck. He turned to Eleanor. 'Maybe I killed Lord Taylor-Howard and Darnley myself. Neither of them conducted themselves in any way worthy of a royal connection. And you know how fiercely dear I hold the reputation of our royal family.'

She shook her head sadly. 'You're just trying to protect

Tipsy again. Just like you were when you persuaded the king that the only way to be sure no scandal would be leaked, was to use an outsider, not one of the civil or royal police.' She shrugged. 'Ironically, you only engaged my services to protect Tipsy because you believed I was bound to fail. But back to the point. You couldn't have murdered Lord Taylor-Howard. Sure, you had the means, the motive and the opportunity, but you were far too noticeable.' She wrinkled her nose. 'I'd hate to be in your shoes. Every time you appear, everyone snaps to on their best behaviour. They watch you like a hawk, ready to jump at your slightest instruction. You could never have slipped the poison into Xander's drink without being noticed. Besides, the old adage has proved correct, just as Treacher said. Poison really is a woman's weapon. Isn't it, Tipsy?'

Sir Percival dragged his eyes from Eleanor and looked at Tipsy, who stamped her foot. 'Why would I have killed Xander, Eleanor? Tell me that!'

'Because, like you said, he was a liar. He got tired of you, just like so many other girls.' She gestured over Tipsy's beautiful face and feminine curves. 'And you believe you are so much more than all the other girls. Which is why you said the most unbecoming things about him. With great vitriol, in fact. Made a complete fool of yourself according to Lady Montfort.'

Tipsy was shaking with anger. 'Shut up! SHUT! UP!'

'I've a piece of advice for you, Tipsy. Acting out of revenge brings something far worse than wrinkles. You thought you'd been so clever, opting to poison Xander at the regatta. All those crowds to give you cover. No chance anyone would be suspicious that you were in the marquee. You were, as someone put it, just another toff wanting to be seen with a member of the royal family. Only you didn't want to be seen with him, did you?'

She glanced out of the window. Somehow, she managed not to gasp. *Where's Clifford gone, Ellie?*

Sir Percival followed her gaze. 'Looking for your butler? He's just keeping a couple of my chaps company.' She spun around. He picked up the revolver. 'Your policeman friend will be joining him soon.' *He's knows about Hugh as well, Ellie!* Her eyes swept the room. He laughed curtly. 'My office is sound-proof for classified meetings. You wouldn't hear a small bomb going off in here from outside, let alone a gun. And ingeniously, the doors are locked by a single button under my desk here.' The sound of the doors locking simultaneously made her jump. He held the gun pointed lazily at her. 'Now, you were saying?'

Think, Ellie? Or at least, keep talking. She swallowed hard, her throat dry.

'It was all there, all along. I... I just missed it.' She addressed Tipsy. 'When I first met Xander, you pushed me into him and then disappeared so he wouldn't know you were there. And you didn't watch a single race and yet were desperate to beat the crowds to the marquee to see the prizes awarded. In reality, that was so you could murder Xander. You dropped the poison into his champagne flute when you slipped off on the pretext of having spotted a friend of your aunt's. You're shorter than me. You'd never have been able to see your aunt or anyone else in that crowd. You also proudly declared you could easily get us into the champagne reception Xander would attend. And again, you inadvertently let slip that you've attended the regatta regularly by noting that "each year the rowers have got dishier". So you certainly knew the tradition of the royal guest drinking from a specially engraved flute.'

Tipsy let out a wail. 'Tell her to stop!'

Sir Percival waved the revolver.

'That's enough, Lady Swift!'

Whatever you do, keep talking, Ellie. 'No. No, it isn't. Because I'm still confused about one key element. Why did you cover for her, Sir Percival? You had so much to lose?'

Sir Percival said nothing, but the look in his eye told Eleanor everything.

'Ah! As I thought. Well, if Xander could court older women, I guess it's very modern of Tipsy to court older men.'

Sir Percival's face contorted with rage. 'How dare you suggest such a thing!' For a moment, she thought he was actually going to fire.

'Oh gracious!' Eleanor's jaw fell slack. 'Tipsy... Tipsy's your daughter!'

35

She stared between the two of them.

All the fight seemed to drain out of Sir Percival. He collapsed behind his desk, the revolver pointing away from her. *That's a start, Ellie. You have to keep going. Maybe Clifford will reappear.* It was a forlorn hope, but it was all she had.

'How? I mean—'

'Her mother was the daughter of my field marshall.' Sir Percival's voice was distant. 'I was just starting to make my way up the ranks at the time. I loved her. Would have married her, but of course her family wouldn't countenance it. When... when they realised she was... with child, they married her off to Lord Fitzroy immediately and when the baby arrived said it was...'

'A premature birth?' Eleanor said gently.

He nodded. 'I watched her grow up from afar. Her mother died when she was young and her father had no interest in her.' He sighed heavily. 'She tried her whole childhood to gain his love. He didn't deserve her.'

Eleanor turned to Tipsy. 'But when did you find out Sir Percival was your real father?'

She laughed. 'Not until after Xander died, silly.'

Sir Percival groaned. 'Lord Taylor-Howard was always high on my surveillance list because of his questionable antics. So I knew he had' – he clenched his fists – 'taken advantage of Tiffany and then discarded her. I wanted to wring his wretched neck myself. But, of course, I couldn't do anything. After he collapsed on stage, I saw Tiffany's face and I knew. I knew it was her.'

What's the chance of you reaching his pistol before he aims and fires, Ellie? She knew the answer. None. *But maybe a chance will present itself. Don't lose hope.*

'So you sought her out and told her who you really were?'

Tipsy smiled through the tears now running down her cheeks. 'He did. And he promised to cover for me. That's what *real* fathers do.' Suddenly she switched moods again. 'We had it all sorted out! All planned! And you've ruined it!' She burst into more tears and threw herself on Sir Percival, blocking his view of Eleanor.

Now, Ellie! She ran towards him. He pushed Tipsy out of his line of sight. But Eleanor had already launched herself at his desk. Her momentum propelled her forward, hand outstretched.

Only the revolver was no longer there.

Standing by the side of the desk, Sir Percival regarded her impassively, revolver trained on her.

'Not bad for a woman, Lady Swift. Not bad at all.'

Picking herself up with a wince, she brushed herself down to gain time she didn't have. *Nothing broken, just a few bruises, Ellie.*

Sir Percival felt under the desk and the doors unlocked. He swiftly pointed the gun at Eleanor's heart again to make sure she stayed where she was. 'Tiffany, my darling, leave now. I'll meet you where we planned.'

Tipsy frowned. 'But I want—'

'Go! Now!' His tone brooked no refusal. With a pout, Tipsy swaggered out of the door. Quickly, he locked the doors again. Eleanor swallowed hard. He raised the revolver.

'I'm sorry, Lady Swift, but it's time—'

'You're right, Sir Percival. It is time. Time to do the right thing.'

His finger tightened on the trigger.

'Time to do what *real* fathers do. Those who *truly* love their daughters.'

His finger loosened. 'Really? What exactly *do* they do, Lady Swift?'

Match point, Ellie. Lose this and there's no coming back.

'They protect them.' He went to reply but she hurried on. 'And not only from others. Sometimes a father that truly loves his daughter knows what she really needs is to be protected... from herself. And what she might do.'

'And what might Tipsy do?'

She willed her eyes to remain fixed on his, not on the gun still trained at her heart.

'Kill again.'

Sir Percival's left eye twitched. 'And why would you think that?'

Eleanor swallowed hard. *Last chance, Ellie.* 'Because I met her when I left Lady Taylor-Howard's apartments. I—'

He brought his fist down on the desk with a crash. 'She promised me she wouldn't go near the woman!' His face was ashen.

Eleanor had no time to congratulate herself on her hunch, she had to keep him talking.

'Why, Sir Percival? Is that because you were afraid yourself that she'd kill again?' His silence was answer enough. She nodded. 'I assume she had the same thought as me after I visited Darnley. He wouldn't confide in me, so who might he confide in about his cousin's death? Lady Taylor-Howard, perhaps?

Maybe she let something slip that Tipsy misinterpreted? Or maybe Darnley *did* confide in her? Either way, you know in your heart of hearts no matter what Tipsy says, it's only a matter of time before Lady Taylor-Howard suffers the same fate as Darnley.'

Eleanor held her breath. Sir Percival seemed frozen. Only the ticking of the mantlepiece clock told her time hadn't actually stopped moving. Eventually, he turned and walked back to his desk as if sleepwalking. He sat slowly and laid the revolver on the desk. Putting his face in his hands, he breathed in deeply. After a moment, he exhaled and looked up.

'So, Lady Swift, how does this end?'

36

The Rolls swung gracefully around the central fountain of Henley Hall's horseshoe driveway and came to a halt by the front steps. For a full minute, no one spoke. The companionable silence felt like a soft wool blanket around Eleanor's shoulders after the funeral they had just attended. Perhaps for Hugh and Clifford as well, she mused as she looked at each of them sitting in their smart black suits. Not that they would ever articulate such a thought, of course. She caught Clifford's eye in the rear-view mirror. He nodded.

'A most fitting joint service, my lady. My sincere gratitude for arranging that I might attend at the back of the chapel. For Mr Darnley,' he ended softly.

'In truth, I'm the one who's grateful,' said Eleanor. 'Having you both there made it so much easier to bear. May it help us all lay some ghosts to rest over poor Xander and Barty's early passing.' She sighed. 'And at the end of the day, we did it. The three of us. Just as we promised each other we would. We found out who was responsible for their murders.'

Seldon nodded. 'We did, Eleanor. Although I'm horrified

that the plan went so badly wrong and you ended up in danger. Again.'

'But I'm still here.'

Seldon opened his mouth as if to argue, but then closed it again. 'But are you going to be alright? Really? I mean Tipsy was your friend.'

'Fine.' Clifford's hand appeared discreetly round the back of his seat, offering her a pristine handkerchief, which she took gratefully. 'After all, she killed Xander out of pure revenge. And Darnley just to save her own skin. She probably deserved to ha —' She couldn't bring herself to say it. 'Instead she's ended up in a psychiatric sanatorium.'

Seldon nodded. 'I think it was inevitable the palace wouldn't allow her to go on trial. The gutter press would have had a field day. "Young woman seduced by royal and then thrown over loses her mind and turns to murder for revenge." The scandal and muckraking would have gone on for months. If not years.'

'I concur, Chief Inspector,' Clifford said. 'Agreeing for her to reside in a sanitorium away from public view was the royal family's only real option.'

'And she'll likely end her days there.' She sighed. 'Sir Percival understood that when we came to an arrangement back in his office.' She patted Seldon's hand. 'It's alright, Hugh. I was never really in that much danger.'

She avoided looking at Clifford, who knew the true story. Sir Percival had been seconds from pulling the trigger. But Eleanor had gambled everything on her belief that he was actually honourable. A product of his age – and army upbringing – yes. But still a good man.

'He just did what any father would have done. Protect his daughter, no matter what.' She looked between the two men. 'Could either of you truly say you would have acted any differently?' They both shook their heads.

'For my part, I have forgiven Sir Percival for his actions relating to myself,' Clifford said. 'Once I realised that he never intended to carry out his threat against you, that is, my lady.'

She nodded. 'And that he never intended to kill anyone. Just scare them enough to keep them from discovering the truth. Or blabbing about it if they already knew, in the case of Barty. Again, it was terribly wrong to have him roughed up, but he never planned to harm him beyond that. In fact, it was his shock at Tipsy poisoning Barty that made him finally realise that day in his office that he couldn't go on letting her walk around free. It was just a matter of time before she killed again. Which is why he finally agreed to our deal. He'd confess and take as much blame as he could if I guaranteed his daughter wouldn't...' Again, she couldn't bring herself to say the word. 'Anyway, once I left' *–best leave out the part about almost getting shot again, Ellie –* 'I went immediately to see the king's counsellors. Sir Percival had rung ahead, so they saw me straight away. The truth is, I didn't need to persuade them. They all agreed she could never stand trial, anyway.'

Seldon grunted. 'And despite Sir Percival's part in all this, he won't stand trial either. He's such a public figure, awkward questions would have been asked.'

Clifford nodded. 'Indeed. The story the palace has put out about Sir Percival's ill health was, again, their only real option. The veracity of which has been helped by his present pallor and demeanour.'

Seldon rolled his eyes. 'And all he gets for trying to pervert the course of justice is a cushy posting to somewhere far overseas that has, according to the palace, "fewer responsibilities".'

Eleanor shook her head. 'His real punishment is knowing that he will in all likelihood never see his daughter or country again. He's as likely to be allowed to return to England as Tipsy is to be let out of that sanitorium.' She ran her hand over the black lace of her skirt. 'Well, I say we move away from this sombre subject. And on that note, definitely no more funerals for a good long while.'

'Hear, hear!'

'Amen, my lady.'

In her bedroom, out of her funeral clothes, she felt brighter if no less disappointed that Seldon had needed to dash off. *It was true what Tipsy said, Ellie. He is married to his job.* But even though, in some ways, their relationship of late seemed to have gone backwards, she consoled herself that in other ways it had moved forward.

With her robe pulled round her, she opened her wardrobe and looked along the exquisite things she'd chosen at Madame Vermeer's gown shop. None of them were her quite yet. *But in time, Ellie, you can change. No more Miss Havisham. On some days, at least.*

As she descended the stairs, Mrs Butters came bustling up the hall.

'M'lady, 'tis all cleared up in the snug now if you fancied a quiet afternoon fighting Master Gladstone for space on the Chesterfield. Little monster had only up and raided Mr Clifford's office and hidden the entire collection around the room.'

Eleanor laughed. 'Clifford's office as in the boot room? And the entire collection being every shoe and slipper in Henley Hall?'

'They'll be the ones, m'lady. Normally he buries them in the garden, so I suppose I shouldn't complain.'

Mrs Trotman appeared from the kitchen, wiping her hands on her apron. 'Mr Clifford said as it was alright to ask you directly, m'lady?'

'Naturally. But ask me what?'

'If as you'd mind a different sort of dinner tonight. On account of young Lizzie.'

'Oh gracious, is she alright?'

Her cook's face lit with a motherly smile. 'She's just a little homesick for Scotland since you was so kind as to bring her back as a second maid after we'd holidayed up there.'

Eleanor nodded. 'Of course. Whatever you're planning will be lovely.'

'Actually, m'lady, 'twill be a recipe Lizzie's grandma used to make when Lizzie was a nipper. Naturally, I'll make sure it's fit for an English lady's table.'

'I'm sure it will be anyway, Mrs Trotman.'

They all looked up as Lizzie and Polly went past, chattering excitedly with armfuls of laundry. The two young girls both dipped a curtsy to Eleanor as they passed.

'Right then, Trotters.' Her housekeeper rolled her sleeves up. 'You and I have a date with Victor.'

'Victor, the vacuum cleaner? Oh no, is he broken again?'

Mrs Trotman chuckled. 'Just a bit... tongue-tied, my lady. After he sucked up something unmentionable.'

Eleanor shook her head. 'Too unmentionable, I'm guessing, for you to confess to Clifford so *he* can fix it?'

Mrs Trotman failed to hide her amusement. 'Yes, m'lady. 'Tis a pair of Butters' underfrillies!'

As her staff left to do battle with the new-fangled vacuum cleaner, Eleanor laid her head back against the front door. She closed her eyes, letting the comfort of home wash over her.

'My lady.' Clifford's measured tone cut into her thoughts. 'Perhaps a little to the right if you would?'

'Hmm?'

He pointed a gloved finger at the section of door behind her. 'The postman is trying to avail himself of the letterbox.'

'Sorry!'

Clifford collected the mail, and after sorting it, handed her two letters.

She opened the first and gasped. 'I bet even you can't guess who this is from? I'll give you a clue. It's thanking me for getting Sir Percival off his back. With the promise I can call on him for help in exchange.'

Clifford's brow furrowed. 'I did not notice a Russian stamp, which precludes Mr Orlov as he has returned to his beloved motherland for the honour of representing her in the sport of rowing once more. Therefore I assume it is from—'

'Fingers Treacher. Yes, well done, clever clogs! That's trounced his protestations that his sort and mine don't mix, huh?'

'Yes, my lady.' Clifford sighed. 'But would that it hadn't, since it appears you have made more progress in mastering the rules of organised crime than polite society.' His eyes roved over the portrait of her uncle. 'However, his lordship would be as proud as I am of your following so adroitly in his unorthodox footsteps in that regard.'

She swallowed the lump in her throat and took the long cool glass of elderflower cordial he held out on a silver tray. Suddenly feeling at a loss as to what do with herself, she headed out into the garden to try to let the breeze blow through her jumbled thoughts.

Twenty minutes later, despite the heat of the early afternoon sun, her glass was still full beside her on the stone edging of the ornamental pond. She trailed her hand distractedly in the water and spoke to her reflection. *Well, Ellie, who knows what might gallop over your—*

The words died on her lips as a blurry reflection of Seldon appeared beside her own. She peered closer at the water then spun round, staring up in shock at his summer flannels and pebble-grey jumper.

'Hugh! What are you doing here?'

'Surprise!' His hand strayed awkwardly through his curls. 'A nice one, hopefully?'

'Why wouldn't it be, silly? Especially to see you out of your work suit. For the first time ever, actually. But I thought you were frightfully busy elsewhere?'

He shrugged. 'I realised that I am always frightfully busy elsewhere.' He looked sheepish. 'So, I badgered my boss for the afternoon off. I thought, perhaps, we could go for a walk and—'

'Master Gladstone! NO!' Joseph's panic-stricken voice came from the nearby rose garden. A moment later her bulldog shot through the arch with her gardener following as fast as his elderly legs would let him. On seeing Eleanor he waved wildly.

''Tis the run-off again, m'lady! Only much worse than afore!'

She glanced in horror at Gladstone, now making a determined beeline for them. He was covered in thick brown sludge, only his excited eyes showing through.

'Hugh!' She darted a look at the ornamental pond they were standing on the edge of. 'We should probably—'

'Kiss?' He grabbed her hand and spun her into an embrace as, with a triumphant woof, Gladstone launched himself at them.

A LETTER FROM VERITY

Dear reader,

I want to say a huge thank you for choosing to read *A Royal Murder*. If you did enjoy it, and want to keep up to date with all my latest releases, just sign up at the following link. Your email address will never be shared and you can unsubscribe at any time.

www.bookouture.com/verity-bright

I hope you loved *A Royal Murder* and, if you did, I would be very grateful if you could write a review. I'd love to hear what you think, and it makes such a difference helping new readers to discover one of my books for the first time.

I love hearing from my readers – you can get in touch on my Facebook page, through Twitter, Goodreads or my website.

Thanks,

Verity

www.veritybright.com

facebook.com/veritybrightauthor
twitter.com/BrightVerity

HISTORICAL NOTES

Henley Regatta

I've lived just down the road from Henley Regatta for some years. It's always very exciting to see all the preparations for the big event each year. The regatta was first held in 1839 and originally organised by the Mayor of Henley and included amusements and a fair, very different from the regatta Eleanor attended. Another big difference would have been the clothes, for the satirical magazine, *Punch*, recorded in 1923 that the men's fashions quite outshine the ladies!

Influenza

The Spanish flu killed around 228,000 people in the UK in 1918 (20-50 million worldwide). This made 1918 the first year ever where there were more recorded deaths than births. The pandemic continued until 1920 when it thankfully petered out, but 3 years later it would still have been fresh in Eleanor, and everyone else's, memory.

Line of Succession

Eighteenth in line to the throne sounds a lot nowadays, but given the turbulent times Eleanor lived in (WW1 and the Spanish Flu spring to mind), it was not inconceivable that, had he lived, Lord Taylor-Howard might have sat on the English throne. There are around 60 in line to the current British throne, so Lord Taylor-Howard would be considered quite royal indeed by modern standards.

Cyanide

You've read – or seen – it before. Whenever a cyanide poisoning occurs, the detective or sleuth leans over the victim and declares, 'Cyanide!' How do they know? Because of the smell of bitter almonds cyanide gives off. Only it doesn't. Not always. And not everyone can detect the smell even when it's present. A more consistent sign, which Seldon picks up on with Xander's death, is an unusually pink tinge to the victim's skin caused by oxygen staying in the bloodstream, rather than migrating into the body's cells.

Official Secrets Act (1911)

Sir Percival gets Eleanor to sign the Official Secrets Act, but it may not have been strictly necessary. He could simply have informed her that as she was now working for him, she was officially bound by it. In one of my former lives, I was actually bound by the Official Secrets Act even though I never saw a copy, and, like Eleanor, had no real idea what it said.

Women in the Intelligence Service

Despite the fact that people like Sir Percival thought women mostly vapid, illogical creatures, (he certainly underestimated Eleanor!), around 6,000 women worked for the British Intelligence Service from the beginning of the century to the end of WW1. Some women were even recruited as spies, although perhaps the most famous female spy of the era, Mata Hari, was Dutch.

The Tower

Built by William the Conqueror in 1078, the Tower of London has been used as many things: a palace, a menagerie, the royal mint, an armoury, a public records office and a tourist attraction. Of course, it's most famous use was as a prison. Luckily, Sir Percival never managed to carry out his threat of imprisoning Eleanor in the Tower and, in fact, it stopped being used as a prison in 1952 (two of the last inmates were the notorious Kray twins).

Canes

Canes have been popular with gentlemen for many years. At first, they were often a substitute for carrying a sword (a man wasn't a man without a weapon in his hands), but they soon came to represent status. By Victorian and Edwardian times a true gentleman would have a different cane for work, evenings and weekends.

Many canes contained concealed flasks, hidden weapons like swords, or had secret moving parts that performed different functions. For instance, some of the heads were in the shape of a bulldog who, at the press of a button, would open his mouth to hold your gloves. A word of warning: don't try that with a real bulldog like Gladstone – he's more likely to bury them. And, most fascinating of all, a few like Lord Taylor-Howard's, concealed miniature spy cameras!

Phone Tapping

Unfortunately, tapping telephones has been in existence almost as long as telephones themselves. The first telephone tapped was back in 1890 in the US. The UK was late to the party (although they've more than made up for it now), but by 1923 Sir Percival – and Seldon – would have had access to relatively sophisticated tapping equipment.

Telephones, Telegraphs and Radio

Sir Roderick was a man in tune with his times. In 1922 the BBC had first begun broadcasting and wireless radios were all the rage. The actual radio licence you paid to receive the BBC's broadcasts was rather complicated, being determined by the components of the actual wireless set. There was a further levy based on something to do with valves, but I've never understood quite how it worked.

ACKNOWLEDGEMENTS

Thanks to our editor, Kelsie, for her inspired editing and Lauren and her team for their thorough proofreading (and more). Thanks also to the rest of the Bookouture team for making *A Royal Murder* better in every way.

Milton Keynes UK
Ingram Content Group UK Ltd.
UKHW011319300424
441995UK00022B/154